I0647939

THE MAKER'S PROPHECY

Shadow of the Phoenix

Book II

J.B. Vosler

The New Atlantian Library

Habent Sua Fata Libelli

The New Atlantian Library

Manhanset House
Shelter Island Hts., New York 11965-0342

bricktower@aol.com • tech@absolutelyamazingebooks.com
• absolutelyamazingebooks.com

Library of Congress Cataloging-in-Publication Data
Vosler, J.B.
The maker's prophecy, shadow of the phoenix, book ii
p. cm.

1. FICTION / Thrillers / Pscychological. 2. FICTION / Romance / Suspense.
3. FICTION / Mystery & Detective / International Mystery & Crime
Fiction, I. Title.
ISBN: 978-1-7330119-0-7, Trade Paper

December 2022

THE MAKER'S PROPHECY

Shadow of the Phoenix

Book II

J.B. Vosler

" 'Tis the times' plague, when madmen lead the blind."

~ William Shakespeare

Prologue

It was darker than usual along the waterfront. Abid Mensah walked the length of the pier, his short legs moving slowly under the weight of his heavy nets. He reached the edge and looked out at the sea. It was midnight, and the quarter moon was his only light as he threw the nets into the water. He hiked his collar. It was colder than usual along the West African coast, but it hadn't stopped the shrimp. He could see them swarming beneath him and he grinned. It should be a good night.

He set his empty cooler on the dock and unfolded a plastic chair. He sat down, propped his feet on the cooler, and looked out at the Atlantic, a sea he knew well but hardly knew at all. She was like a woman ... dark, inviting ... and utterly terrifying. He shivered and pulled a cap from his coat.

He had lived his entire twenty-seven years on the west coast of Africa, but he was a newcomer to the town of Guinea-Bissau. His mother had died when he was a boy, and his father had died eight days ago, shot in the head by poachers. They had boarded his boat as he and his father were heading to shore. They had sliced his father's neck, and had then cut him into pieces, tossing him in the sea as if he were chum for the fish. Abid had dived into the water and clawed his way to shore, his chubby body not used to the exertion of such an effort. They had shot at him, but had missed. He bristled as he touched the knife in his jacket pocket. He would use it to open the nets once they were full ... *and to kill the poachers if they come for me.*

1

He rubbed his eyes and brushed strands of stringy black hair from his face. He had let it grow; it was nearly to his shoulders. He scratched his whiskered chin as he looked around the pier. He was alone. The other fishermen had gone home to their families. He had no family and he had no home. Not anymore.

After an hour or so, he leaned forward and tugged at the nets. Nothing. The shrimp were taking their time. It was going to be a long night. He sat back in his slatted chair and stretched his legs.

"You're fishing out here all alone?"

Abid looked over his shoulder, startled. A man was walking toward him about thirty feet away. He was white and not very tall, and he had the hint of a limp. He was wearing a suit and tie, and he carried a briefcase; he looked out of place on the dock.

Abid gripped the knife in his pocket as he stood and stared at the man.

"You won't need that," the voice was deep and even, "...I've come to talk." He kept walking toward him. "You speak English ... correct?"

Abid hesitated and then nodded.

"Good." The man grinned, his white teeth reflecting the moonlight. "My Portuguese is rusty."

"What you want to talk about?"

"An opportunity. The chance of a lifetime, Abid Mensah."

Abid narrowed his eyes. "How you know my name?"

The man laughed; Abid felt the hair on the back of his neck stand up. "I know a lot about you, Abid." He stopped only inches from where Abid was standing. "I make a point of learning all I can about the men who are important to me."

A sliver of moonlight shone on the man's face. Abid felt uneasy as he looked into eyes as dark as the sea. He reached for the knife.

The man sneered. "I said ... you don't need it." He cleared his throat. "But if you would feel better holding a knife to my throat, then, by all means, go ahead."

The two men stared at one another. They were about the same height, but the man in the suit was in far better shape. Abid gripped the knife tighter; he could feel sweat between his fingers. "Why me?"

"You know the sea, Abid," the man frowned, "...and you've lost your home, your family." He walked to the side of the pier and looked out at the ocean. "I can give you both."

Abid let go of the knife. His hands were shaking and he shoved them in the pockets of his pants. "I don't want new family."

The man turned and stared at him, his gray eyes piercing. "You will once I tell you about us." He moved closer. "I'm forming a militia, Abid ... an army of soldiers."

Abid frowned. "Why should I join?"

"Because your parents are gone and so is your home; you have nothing." He smiled, "And I have everything." He combed a hand through clipped brown hair. "I can give you money, a home in America. More important; I can give you a family."

Abid frowned. "How much money?"

The man laughed and Abid felt his legs go weak. "How is ten thousand to start, with twenty more when the job's done?"

Abid's eyes widened; he grabbed the back of the chair. "That ... that is a lot of money. What must I do?"

The man tugged on his lapels. "Deliver shirts for me, Abid. That's all."

"Where do I take your shirts?"

"To America."

Abid frowned. "It is a long way."

"Yes. That's why I'm willing to pay you so much."

Abid rubbed his chin. "When do I get my money?"

The man set the briefcase on the cooler and opened it. "How about now?"

Abid looked inside the case. It was filled with stacks of hundred-dollar bills. He began to salivate. He had never seen so much money. "Again ... why me?"

The man pulled out a stack of bills. "You are the beginning, Abid ... the flint that ignites the flame ... the opening volley of a long and fruitful war." He took a step closer and waved the money under Abid's nose. "You will change your name to Reuben," he handed him the cash, "...and you will be the first." He chuckled. "The first is always the best, don't you think?"

Abid thought he might faint. He could smell the money. It reminded him of the mold in the cellar outside his home in Senegal. He took it and rubbed it between his fingers, marveling at the feel of it. The man's words were insane...*but this money is real.* He stuffed it in his pocket and frowned. "I cross the sea to America with shirts to sell. I change my name to Reuben. Is that it?"

The man handed him another stack of bills, and Abid put it with the first.

"Yes. But not today ... and not tomorrow. In a few years, Abid. That is when it all begins." He cleared his throat. "In the meantime, I want you to find a boat and hire a crew. One other man; that's all." He handed him another stack of bills. "Maybe run the route a time or two. Get comfortable with the journey."

Abid nodded, clutching the money as sweat poured from his forehead.

The man stared at him, his steel-gray eyes almost black. "One final point. You must call me Jacob. I am now your father." He handed him two more stacks, and then closed the briefcase and tucked it under his arm. As he was about to walk away, he looked at Abid and grinned. "You are my son, Reuben ... a son of Jacob. Welcome to the family."

Week #1

Chapter 1
MIAMI BEACH, FLORIDA

Current Day – Monday, January 12th, 2004

Martin Henderson looked out at the sea, astounded by the beauty of the sun as it cleared the horizon and lit up the farthest reaches of the dark blue Atlantic. There were moments when he cherished it; the fact that he had survived the impossible. But then he would see his reflection, or feel the pain from his scars, and he would despise it; his life and all that had happened. And then, as if he had never been anyone other than who he was now, he would get on with it; he would plot and plan ... and endure.

He breathed in, the smell of saltwater heavy in the air as he cast weighted lines and watched them drop to the ocean floor. The bobbers floated, barely visible in the mist. He went to sweep back his long blonde hair, and then he remembered; it was gone. Five days ago, he had changed his identity to Sam Dawson, local fisherman. With little more than a haircut, a hat, and rimmed glasses, Phoenix had disappeared.

But the assassin had come through when he needed him. It was Phoenix who had exposed an attempt on Maddi's life six days ago in Jacksonville, and it was Phoenix who had then saved her ... *only to watch her walk away with Hank Clarkson.*

He sighed as he stretched his legs by the fire he had built in the sand. Hank Clarkson, his one-time friend, had become Maddi's eternal protector. Hank loved Maddi every bit as much as Henderson, and, ironically, the two men had worked together to save her. Hank didn't realize that, of course. He didn't know that it was Henderson who had contacted him just in time to get her out of that hotel. It didn't matter. Maddi was alive and Henderson knew he had Hank to thank for it.

The authorities were still at a loss as to who was behind the sarin gas attack at the hotel in downtown Jacksonville. But Henderson knew. He knew because he had seen him ... he had seen Simeon. Morningstar's favorite goon had run from the pier and jumped in a rowboat before anyone could get to him. It was Simeon who had been willing to poison a hotel full of people in order to eliminate just one. But who had sent him? *Edward Morningstar.*

Henderson narrowed his eyes. He hated Morningstar. The man had ruined his life. He had saved him from a hotel fire only to force him into a role he would never have chosen for himself. Henderson had killed many men, but only because Morningstar had threatened to harm a little girl ... to harm Lili ... if he didn't.

But, finally, about six weeks ago, Henderson had had enough. He had been about to carry out an assassination on Yemen leader Abdulkarim Al-Gharsi, when he had seen her. Sitting next to the leader was Maddi, the woman he had not stopped loving since their weekend together nearly four years ago. He had gone ahead with the hit, knowing that if he didn't, Lili would be in danger. But the instant he had pulled the trigger, it wasn't Al-Gharsi he saw; it was Maddi ... her horrified expression as her entire body was jolted from the impact of his bullet in the forehead of the man sitting next to her. It was that moment – when he grasped what he had done to the woman he loved – that he knew ... *I have to stop.*

Weeks before, in anticipation of just such a day, he had put together a plan to protect Lili. It included a safehouse in Riga, Latvia, with twenty-four-hour protection. But, before he had had a chance to put the plan into action, Morningstar had arranged for Lili to be kidnapped. Henderson had looked everywhere for her; he hadn't found her. That was when he decided – no matter what it took – he would end Morningstar.

But not until I find Lili. He guessed that Morningstar had left instructions for Lili to be killed should something happen to him. Morningstar had stated clearly in his online Bible that death wouldn't stop him. *"Even if it is I, myself who is killed, I will command my sons to follow the path I have set forth."*

Henderson didn't know the sons ... other than Simeon, whom he had known since the beginning. It was Simeon who had dragged him out of the burning hotel ballroom four years ago ... and it was Simeon who had tried to kill Maddi last week. Were there more sons out there? Morningstar saw himself as a born-again Jacob. Did that mean that – along with him and Simeon – there were ten other men just waiting to carry out Morningstar's plans?

He pulled in a hefty cod and tossed it in his cooler. *God, I hope not.*

He recast the line and sat back in his chair. Fishing calmed him; it helped him think. And there was a lot to think about. For starters, why had Morningstar tried to have Maddi killed in Jacksonville? Henderson felt confident that Morningstar didn't know about his and Maddi's relationship. If he had, he would've gone after her long ago. So why did he suddenly want her dead? Whatever the reason, Henderson's goal hadn't changed: *Stop him ... and his agenda.*

A first step would take place tomorrow night, when he sabotaged an arms shipment arranged by Morningstar through a weapons manufacturing company, Silverton, Inc. Posing as the owner of a freight company, Henderson had sent in a bid to transport the shipment. He had been granted the bid, which meant that he now knew the time and place for the transfer.

He also knew the destination: Yemen. The guns were intended to accelerate a war that Henderson himself was responsible for starting. His assassination of Al-Gharsi six weeks ago had ignited a resurgence of hate in the Middle East. He shook his head. *I did that.*

The shipment was set to leave from a Miami warehouse in two days, on Wednesday, the 14th. He had gotten to town five days ago and had checked into a hotel he had used in the past.

He knew the neighborhood; he liked the people. There was a diner down the street that served unbeatable ribs, a few old stores that sold curiosities and collectibles, and a Chinese pawn shop that had been there for nearly thirty years.

But, before he had allowed himself to start working on destroying the arms shipment, he had felt the need to offer Maddi an apology. It wasn't the normal thing for an assassin to do ... to offer an 'I'm sorry' for a hit ... but he needed her to know that killing her friend had never been his intent. And, though every one of the men he had killed had likely had someone who merited an apology, Maddi was the only one he was in love with.

He had spent the entire first day working on it, and, by sunset, had put together an acceptable message. Though it felt good to write it, he had never meant to send it ... he knew the Pandora's Box it would open if he revealed that Al-Gharsi had not been murdered by the Omani leader, as originally thought. But, the following day, as if driven by some higher power, he had suddenly *needed* to send it ... as if he would explode if he didn't tell her how grieved he was for what he had done to her friend.

So, he had sent it ... by email. No return address, no way to trace who had written it or where it had come from. It had been both exhilarating and terrifying. He hadn't so much as looked at Maddi for nearly four years; the thought that he had now *spoken* to her was jaw-dropping. And he wasn't sure what he expected. There was no way for her to reply. More importantly, there was no way for her to fix the mess he had made in the Middle East. *I guess I just needed her to know it hadn't been easy.*

But there was another reason he had reached out to her; he needed her help.

He pulled a folded newspaper from inside his jacket and spread it on his knee. It was from Providence, and he opened it to an article about a friend of his, Marco Solvino. The man was in a fight with the local government over his land. Battling Eminent Domain was a cause Maddi had championed many times, so, in spite of the fact that Henderson had reignited a war, and in spite of the fact that he had killed one of Maddi's friends, he had sent her a second email – about an hour ago – asking her to look into the case.

A cool breeze blew in off the ocean and he shivered. He put the newspaper in his pocket and scooted closer to the fire, warming his hands as he watched several determined souls jog down to the beach. He would need to leave soon. In spite of the glasses, the shorter hair, and the wide-brimmed hat, the scars on his face were impossible to hide. He couldn't risk being noticed.

He put out the fire, pulled back his reels, and set his catch in a creel. He would sell the fish in town, and then donate the cash to the local homeless shelter. He didn't need the money; he had plenty. Morningstar had paid him well over the years.

He packed his gear and threw it over his shoulder, welcoming the weight of it as it challenged every muscle and every healed fracture. Pain felt good. It reminded him of who he had been ... *the good man inside me who hurts when he's pushed.*

He walked to his pickup truck in the lot down the beach, careful to avoid the eyes of those along the way. He had grown tired of the stares; the quick look by a frightened child as she laid eyes on "the monster."

And he was a monster ... in every sense of the word. And not just on the outside. He was an assassin, and, though he would give anything to change it, there was a part of him that needed it. He felt a strange sort of comfort in being the Phoenix. In knowing that he had fallen so low that nothing mattered. His life was empty. He needed little more than food, water, and a place to sleep. To change would require that he care. Numbness would then turn to compassion, or – even worse – to kindness. And that would likely kill him.

So, he would hold on to Phoenix ... at least a little longer. He would need him; his skills, his temperament ... even his ice-cold heart. Morningstar had brought life to Phoenix ... Phoenix would bring death to Morningstar. *And I will start with the sons.*

Chapter 2

WASHINGTON, DC

Edward Morningstar stretched his arms and looked at the clock. *Seven a.m.* He sat up and rubbed his eyes. He pulled a half-smoked cigar to his lips, lit it and puffed, grinning as the smoke filled the hotel bedroom. He looked down at the woman lying next to him. She was asleep. Good. He wanted silence. Edi was a talker.

He got up and walked to the window. The sun had started to rise. He raised the window slightly, allowing cold air into the room. He pulled up a chair and sat there, staring out at the city, watching it come awake as he smoked his cigar.

After a few minutes, he turned on a lamp and reached for his Bible, locked securely in his briefcase. Unlike his online Bible, which charted details and directives, this Bible contained a blueprint ... of his future, and the future of all humanity. Depicted with red-inked changes to God's own words, it went beyond Genesis ... even beyond Revelation; Morningstar had written his own Revelation. He was the predictor of the future because he was in charge of that future ... he and God.

He set the Bible in his lap and opened it. It went automatically to Genesis, chapter 49, where Jacob was instructing his sons as he bid them a final farewell. It was there that Morningstar had interjected his truth. *He* was now Jacob; those sons were now his. He grabbed a red pen from the briefcase. He would read through their names and either cross them out or write in what was new. He smirked as he raised the pen in the air. *God thinks His words are timeless ... little does He know; I can change not only God's plan, but God's words, as well.*

The first entry, Reuben, needed no alteration. Morningstar smiled as he looked at the name. He had learned of Abid Mensa four years ago through an African envoy. *"There's a man from Senegal who lost all he had in a single night. He had already lost his mother, and was then forced to watch his father get murdered by poachers. He somehow made it to shore, but everything was gone."* The perfect ingredients: no home, no family, and the wherewithal to swim his fat ass to the shoreline after he saw his father killed by thieves. Yes, Abid was a good pick. Morningstar checked the date on his watch. *Monday, January 12ᵗʰ ... he should've reached America by now.*

He went to the second entry, shaking his head as he stared at the name. *Simeon.* His favorite mercenary had failed him. Tasked with killing Senator Cynthia Madison less than a week ago, he had botched it, forced to make his getaway in a tiny fishing boat off the coast of Florida. The failure to kill her would normally justify elimination, but Morningstar was fond of the skinny, cross-dressing ex-military man. *I'll give him one more chance.*

He moved on to the third name, Levi. Far more expensive than his other sons, Morningstar felt certain that Clint Molinaro's unique ties to Martin Henderson would make him worth the extra cost. After all, the former Marine had once been Henderson's right-hand man. *Instant trust.*

"And who is Martin Henderson, you say?" Morningstar had said it aloud, as if speaking at a seminar. "Why, he's only the most elegant of bachelors ... the most accomplished of the thirty-something high-enders to come out of Boston." He raised a finger and feigned a frown. "No ... wait; Martin Henderson was burned alive in a hotel fire." *Until I saved his ass and made him my hitman.*

He flinched and went on. The fourth and fifth entries, Judah and Dan, were highly capable, accomplished men who had set into stone their prospective identities, one as a well-respected politician, the other as a notorious assassin. Both of them were marking time, just waiting for Jacob to give them the word. *No changes needed.*

The next entry made him sneer. Son Number Six, Naphtali, had vanished. Though it had been only six days, the fact that he wasn't taking Morningstar's calls left little doubt as to what had happened. He was either dead or in the wind ... *which means he'll be dead soon.* Morningstar crossed through the name.

Gad was next. Morningstar had scooped up Marcus King from a DC jail, after a drug bust involving a couple of low-level Pentagon aides. The small, wiry black man had proven to be remarkably proficient, especially with a rifle. He was far too recognizable on the streets of DC, however, and was biding his time overseas.

The eighth son, Asher, had come to Morningstar as a disgraced CIA agent, accused of sharing secrets with the enemy. Morningstar had intervened in his court martial, inspired by the smug attitude of the small, stocky man. Though limited in intellect, Asher more than made up for it with nerves of steel. *Asher ... the brave one.*

Son Number Nine had been a grave disappointment. Curt Simpson, Issachar, had botched a mission, and had then gotten drunk and had run from a bar fight in Cleveland, Ohio. Morningstar had had him killed. That sort of weakness could never be allowed. There was no need to cross through his name; it had already been done.

He smiled at the next entry, Zebulun. Vladimir Karev was awaiting orders in Estonia, and, though Morningstar rarely saw him, he was convinced that his Russian son was the most loyal of them all. Disillusioned with his homeland, even more so with his life, Zebulun had sworn his allegiance to the cause. *"I will do whatever you ask, Jacob."* Morningstar grinned. *Nothing better than a devoted son.*

He moved to the last name on the page and frowned. *The same can't be said for my eleventh son.* He stared at the name: *Martin Henderson.* The man – Joseph –had defied him; he had left Jacob and his sons when they needed him most.

Known as Phoenix to the CIA, he had gone AWOL over a month ago, and had been missing ever since. Morningstar knew – sooner or letter – he would find him. The question was ... what would he do when he did. Would he kill him? *Could* he kill him?

He leaned back and sighed. *No.* Not only was he fond of Joseph, but his skills would be useful in the days ahead. Before his transformation to world-class assassin, Henderson had been a notable presence, both in DC and among the Boston elite. He knew that world better than most; it was an asset not to be taken lightly. He circled the name. *Yes, he's betrayed me, but I'll give him one more chance.*

That was it. Eleven sons – the twelfth had not yet been chosen. It had been God's command. *"Wait on the last one, Jacob. He will be your greatest blessing."*

Morningstar closed the Bible and locked it in his briefcase.

He stood and walked to the bed. Edi was still asleep, her long black hair teasing the edge of her cheek like a spider's web. Her lips, still red from the lipstick she had worn the night before, quivered with each breath, causing her dark Arab skin to crease and her closed eyes to flutter. The Saudi attaché was beautiful; there was no denying it. He had met her at a meeting six months ago, and had bedded her that same night. They got together when they could. She was in love with him; he saw her as a handy distraction. He chuckled. *And very well-connected.*

He checked the time. *7:20.* He had a meeting at 8:00. *There's time.* He slid under the sheets and put his hand on her breast. She turned to him and, without hesitation, spread her legs. As he climbed on top of her, he looked down at her and grinned. "Tell me, Edi, what's it like to make love to the future king of the world?"

She grinned as she reached her arms around him. "Like ... heaven ... on earth," she said.

He pulled her hands from his back, gripping them by the wrists as he pressed them to the bed. "That's ... right, baby. Edward Morningstar ... heaven on earth."

Chapter 3
WASHINGTON, DC

Cynthia Madison ran a hand through shoulder-length blonde hair as she stared at an email on her desk. She had gotten to work early for a meeting, and had then gone straight to the Senate chamber for a vote. This was the first chance she had had to sit at her desk. The email, in the same format as the first, had been addressed to her using the nickname few even knew: Maddi. She had received another one four days ago – also anonymous – from someone claiming responsibility for the murder of her friend, Al-Gharsi. Whoever it was had actually *apologized* for killing him. Maddi had been stunned ... and angry. Al-Gharsi's assassination had been blamed on the leader of neighboring Oman, who had then allegedly turned the gun on himself. The assassination/suicide had derailed a delicate peace between the two countries and had once again thrown the Middle East into turmoil. But, if the emailer was telling the truth, then the Omani leader had *not* killed Al-Gharsi, which meant that the peace process should never have been derailed. But to discover it now was too late ... bridges had been burned, treaties had been annulled. She frowned. Maybe that had been the intent; to disrupt the peace. If so, it meant that the emailer wasn't just a killer, but a conniving one, at that. The last thing he deserved was her forgiveness.

She had tried to send a reply, but it had been returned as undeliverable. It was probably for the best. She had just survived an attempt on her life. The fewer crackpots she let into her world, the better.

So, she had ignored it ... or thought she had. She knew she should hand it over to the authorities, but she couldn't bring herself to do it. She wasn't sure why. There was just something pathetic – and sincere – about it.

And now ... this. She stared at the email, reading it through for the fourth time. She pushed the intercom. "Phil, could you come in here please?"

Phil Jenkins stepped through the door, looking much as he had when she had plucked him from the Evansville Prosecutor's office eight years earlier, after she had won her state senate seat. He was short with a medium build, had thinning dark hair, and wore wire-framed glasses. His smile was warm, and his greenish-gray eyes sparkled when he grinned, which was most of the time. "Yes, Senator?"

"This e-mail about the Eminent Domain case in Providence ... it's intriguing."

"Yes Ma'am."

"When did Amy pull it from the site?"

"A few hours ago."

"Is there any way to determine who sent it?"

"No ... not yet, anyway. Amy said she almost deleted it, but then she recalled that you know someone in Providence, and thought you might be interested."

Maddi looked up. "*Knew* someone. I *knew* someone in Providence."

Phil frowned. "Yes, Senator. I'm sorry."

"Have Amy continue to try to trace it."

"Yes, Senator." He left the office. Maddi stared again at the e-mail.

The City of Providence v. Rocky's Restaurant. Could you look into this? After all, you've been there.

Maddi's heart was racing. She tossed the email in her top drawer, grabbed her briefcase, and walked out of the office. As she passed by Phil's desk she said, "I'll want to submit a brief concerning the case in Providence."

Phil nodded. "Yes, Senator. Should I have the attorneys take care of it?"

"Yes, have them refer to my prior arguments from the case in Vermont. And get me info on the restaurant owner. I think his name's Solvino. Marco Solvino."

"I'll take care of it, Senator."

"And put an article in the Providence paper. Reference the Solvino case, and then add something about Eminent Domain, and how it allows the government to steal America from its citizens."

Phil nodded. "Yes Senator."

Maddi walked out the door of the main office and headed for the exit. She gave a quick smile to her agent as he fell in beside her. "Are you up for some breakfast, Larry?" He nodded. As they walked down the hall, she forced herself to stay calm, but inside she was a wreck. Two emails had been sent to her – not as Senator Madison, not even as Cynthia – but as Maddi. Both of them were anonymous and remarkably personal. The first dealt with a murder that had turned her world upside down. The second dealt with a memory ... a memory that could still make her smile, though it haunted her nearly every day of her life. Who had sent those emails? Was it the same person? *Who actually knew I had been to Rocky's?* She trembled as she and Larry walked outside and slid in back of her waiting sedan. *Only one man ... and he died in a hotel fire four years ago.*

Chapter 4
COLUMBIA, SOUTH CAROLINA

*W*here are they all coming from? Doctor Amanda McKinney-Madison frowned as she brushed bangs from her forehead and walked into her office. The clinic was busy ... too busy. And most of the overflow appeared to be drug addicts. Downtown Columbia had its share, but never had she seen so many at one time.

She jotted notes on a chart and tossed it in a rack as she looked around, half-expecting to see the man who had been her companion for the past four years, Andrew Madison. But he wasn't there. He was at a medical conference in Charleston and wouldn't be back until Friday. She sighed. *I could sure use your help, Andrew.*

Amanda had met Andrew through his sister Maddi. Thanks to his remarkable sense of humor, and Amanda's uncanny urge to laugh at everything he said, they had hit it off immediately. Within weeks, he had moved to Columbia, and had applied for, and gotten the role of Medical Director. They had married three years later, and – except for the occasional medical conference – they had not been apart since.

But there was more keeping them apart than just a conference. They had been arguing ... about one thing in particular. Amanda wanted to start a family. And, though Andrew had wanted that when they married, he suddenly wanted nothing of the sort. *"I've changed my mind, Amanda ... I don't want to bring a child into this world."* Yesterday they had argued again, failing to resolve it by the time he left for the conference.

Amanda flinched as she thought of him storming out of the townhouse, tossing out a remark as he stood at the elevator. *"I can't do it, Amanda … I can't risk putting a child through it."* She had wanted to say *"Through what?"* but she already knew the answer.

Her eyes drifted to a handmade coffee cup sitting on his desk. Andrew had sculpted it for his mother when he was five, but had taken it back when things started to go wrong. *"Before she broke it, too,"* he had told Amanda. That was all he had been willing to say about a past that clearly haunted him.

She knew some of it, however. Maddi had told her, but she, too, had been cautious with the story … as if to tell it would shatter both of them all over again. Their father – a cop – had been killed on the job, and it had sent their mother into a spiral of alcoholism and bad choices. She had left them both, emotionally, anyway, at a time when they had needed her most. *No wonder he doesn't want to start a family.*

On Amanda's desk was a photo of her parents, who had died in a plane crash while she was away at college. From that moment forward, she had been alone … no brothers or sisters, no uncles or aunts … no one to hold her hand as she buried her parents alone. *And no wonder I do.*

She walked to a mirror and combed back her hair as she stared at the face in the glass. She looked terrible. Her normally bright eyes seemed empty and dull, and her chestnut-brown hair – one of her finer features according to Andrew – hung lifeless down her back. *Must be the flu.* She had been fighting something for the past week or two, and it was taking its toll. There were dark circles under her eyes and her face was pale. She shook her head and frowned. *You need to get over it, Amanda.*

She cleared her throat determinedly and walked out of the office to the next treatment room. She pulled the chart from the rack and saw a black sticker pasted on the front, denoting a history of IV drug use. She sighed. *Not another one.* There had been more than usual in the clinic that morning, and they all seemed to be suffering the same symptoms: fatigue, fever, chest pain. She had noticed tremors in a few of them, and one had had some bleeding from his gums.

She walked into the treatment room. A thin woman was lying on the table. It was hard to tell her age; she looked old and tired. It was obvious she hadn't bathed, and her clothes were ragged and a size too big. Amanda's heart went out to her as she glanced at the name on the chart. "So, Lucille, what brings you in today?"

The lady looked up at her and frowned. "Huh?"

Amanda walked closer, feeling waves of nausea as she caught a whiff of dirt and decay. She raised her voice. "What's troubling you?"

Lucille struggled to sit up. "I ... I don't feel right. I have an awful headache ... and I can't keep from shaking."

Amanda saw the tremor, and noticed that Lucille's cheeks were swollen. She listened to her heart and lungs. She helped her lay down, and then pushed gently on her abdomen, which produced a grimace and a groan. As Lucille opened her mouth, Amanda could see blood on her gums.

"We'll do lab work, and get a urine sample."

Lucille nodded and Amanda helped her down from the table. They walked to the front desk and Amanda wrote out the order. She handed it to Lucille, whose thin, cracked fingers took the paper and slid it in a pocket. Amanda smiled. "Take that to the lab next door. I'll see you back in a week, Lucille."

Her mind was still on Lucille as she trudged to the next treatment room. She grabbed the chart, again noting a black sticker, and walked into the room. "Hello..."she looked at the name, "...Robert, what can I help you with today?"

Robert was in worse shape than Lucille. He was lying on the table, unable to lift his head when Amanda entered the room. He was thin and dirty, sharing with Lucille the cloak of despair which seemed to cover those who lived on the streets. Amanda walked over and helped him sit up. "What's going on, Robert?"

He suddenly leaned over and vomited. Amanda held onto him so he wouldn't fall. When he finished, she helped him lay back down while she went to get someone to clean up the room. As she walked out, she suddenly felt like she was about to vomit herself. She ran by the front desk and informed them of the situation in the treatment room, and then made it to the bathroom just in time as she retched in the first stall. She walked to the sink, rinsed her mouth, and wiped strands of damp hair from her forehead. *I've got to get out of here.*

She went out to the reception area. "How many more patients this morning?"

The receptionist, Lisa, looked at the list. "Three."

Amanda hesitated. "I hate to do this ... see if Lorraine can finish with room two, and add the other three onto her schedule. Tell her I owe her one."

Lisa nodded, eyeing Amanda with concern. "Are you okay?"

"I'm fine. I'll be back after lunch."

Amanda went to her office, grabbed her coat and purse, and ran out to the car. She opened the door, climbed in, and leaned against the seat. She was rarely sick; it made her mad to think she had succumbed to whatever virus was circulating through the clinic. It also made her mad to think that she and Andrew were fighting about something that should be joyful.

She started the car and headed for home. She would take a bath and a quick nap, and would hopefully feel better. *Hurry home, Andrew, so we can make one another well.*

Chapter 5
MIAMI BEACH, FLORIDA

Henderson rubbed the back of his neck as he stared down at his computer. He had driven from the beach to the downtown market, where he had sold his fish for cash. He had walked the money to the shelter, and had returned to his hotel room, where he had been ever since. His first task had been to secure the weapon he would need to destroy the arms shipment intended for Yemen. A few quick clicks on an obscure website, followed by a phone call from a payphone to confirm, and the weapon was ordered. He would pick it up and pay for it – in cash – the following day.

Once that was taken care of, he had gone to work on the information he had intercepted a week ago between Morningstar and Simeon. Three ships were coming to the U.S. from Africa. Though he didn't know exactly why, where, or when, he had gotten the sense from the email that it was happening soon. What were they bringing? Who was navigating them? He had considered alerting the port authorities, but he had no specifics, and he couldn't share who he was or how he had acquired the information. They wouldn't take anything he said seriously.

One thing he did have, however, were a few well-placed friends; contacts he had nurtured over the years who would do anything for him. So, again using a payphone, he had reached out to five of those men up and down the eastern seaboard, asking each one to let him know the instant a ship from Africa arrived at a nearby port. *"Ships come in from Africa all the time,"* one of his friends had said. Henderson's reply: *"Just call me if you see something that doesn't seem right."*

He was now back in his room, eating a granola bar while he stared at his laptop. His next task was to figure how to unravel Morningstar's operation without jeopardizing Lili's safety. To do that, he would have to dismantle it from the inside out. How many soldiers were there? Did he refer to all of them as sons? Were they men like Henderson ... broken by life, ripe for the picking by a clever lunatic?

He typed Morningstar's name into his search engine. A series of articles appeared, the first with a photo attached. His stomach turned as he looked at the photo. He clicked it and read the biography. Most of it he already knew. Morningstar had been a part of government for the past twenty-six years, starting as an aide to General Alexander Daniels in the late 1970's. He had been with the general ever since, moving with him to the Pentagon in 1982. He had been involved in some of the more important military operations over the course of the last two decades, and Henderson cringed as he read words of praise for the man's contribution "...to the cause of freedom and the preservation of human rights around the world."

He closed the laptop. He couldn't read anymore. Morningstar had fooled everybody; it wasn't going to be easy to bring him down.

He narrowed his eyes. *But you, Phoenix, are a well-trained assassin.*

It was true, and, ironically, it was Morningstar who had trained him. But Morningstar wasn't the one who had shown him how to kill; he had acquired that skill in Latvia. He had spent most of his adult life as a Latvian Freedom Fighter. At the time that Morningstar had had him pulled from the fire, he was already a capable marksman. But Morningstar had taken him to the next level, teaching him everything from sniper skills to hand-to-hand combat. By the time he was done, Henderson could shoot a target a mile away, kill a man with his bare hands, and evade an entire battalion of soldiers. Why had Henderson gone along with it? *Because of Lili.*

He sighed as he leaned against the headboard of the twin bed that nearly filled his hotel room in the Overtown section of Miami Beach. The place was a dump, but he didn't care; he was comfortable there. It suited not only his lifestyle, but his worldview. He could barely remember the Ritz Carlton or the Park Hyatt. Those hotels were from a different time ... Martin Henderson was dead.

He pondered that fact as he thought about the Phoenix, his alter-ego for the past three-and-a-half years. Once he ridded the world of Morningstar, there would no longer be a need for the Phoenix. He, too would die. *So, who will I be then?*

He stood and walked to the window. There wasn't much to see. His room looked out on an alley, and, though it was nearly noon, the sun had yet to rise over the buildings. The shadows were hiding a scrawny black cat, and Henderson watched as the animal foraged through garbage for food. *We're not so different ... that cat and I.*

He was about to walk away, when he heard a voice from down the street.

"Here, kitty kitty."

He opened the window and leaned out, looking for whoever was calling the cat. It was a little girl's voice, soft and sweet; it reminded him of Lili. He looked left, then right, finally spotting her half-a-block away. A thin girl, she looked to be about eight or nine, with long stringy hair and dirty clothes. Though the hair was brown instead of blonde, she remined him of Lili. How old was she now? *Nine. She turned nine six weeks ago ... two days before she was kidnapped.*

He watched the girl, fighting tears as he imagined Lili calling for her cats. *Maybe it's her!* He was about to open the window wider and say hello, but he stopped himself. *Lili's gone, Henderson ... she was kidnapped ... in Latvia.* He tried to see the girl's features. What if it *was* Lili? What if her captor had dyed her hair and brought her to America? The girl had reached the alley; she started running toward the cat.

"You silly cat. There's nothing for you here. I have milk at home."

She looked up. Henderson gave a quick wave. She frowned as she picked up the cat and ran off. She wasn't Lili ... her face wasn't Lili's.

He turned from the window and walked to the bed, his heart sinking at the thought of what Lili might be going through. He fell back against the pillow, rubbing his temples as he stared at the ceiling and said aloud, "I miss you, Lili. I hope you're okay."

From nowhere, he heard a soft voice say, "I'm okay, Uncle Mart. Don't worry about me ... I'll be fine."

Chapter 6

THE TIBETAN PROVINCE OF CHINA

The image of Uncle Mart had come from nowhere, and had taken Lili Platacis completely by surprise. It was the first vision she had had of him in quite a while. It had to be her imagination; Mart had been killed four years ago in a hotel fire in America. Lili had actually seen him die ... she had felt his spirit leave. Though she had been thousands of miles away, she had witnessed his death as if she had been standing right next to him.

I'm just missing him, she thought, as she pulled a wool blanket to her chin. It was little help. Wind from the Himalayas blew in through the walls, every bit as cold as the icy squalls that used to sweep in from the Baltic in her hometown of Ventspils.

She missed those squalls. Even though they could freeze the whitecaps of the fierce Baltic Sea, she missed them. And she missed her bedroom ... with pictures on the walls and her treasures surrounding her. The only things surrounding her now were text books, old blankets, and the photo of her family she had grabbed at the last minute. She held it to her now as she stared at blank walls, doing her best to imagine pictures and posters and curtains on the window.

At least I'm no longer hungry. The two men who had kidnapped her that last day of November had eventually brought her to an old dormitory somewhere in Tibet, where a stern woman with short black hair had insisted she be given hot soup and a piece of fruit. That had been five days ago, and she had been well-fed ever since. Nothing extravagant, but she wasn't going hungry. She had been surprised there was running water; little else suggested any sort of modernization. The only heat came from vented fires throughout the building, and she was forced to wear layers of clothes given to her by that same woman, her caregiver, Ching Lan.

Ching was also her teacher, and Lili had become quite fond of her. Though she wasn't overly warm, she had a good soul; Lili could tell. After a brief introduction, Ching had started immediately with lessons on China. And, because they were in Tibet, Tibet was where they began. In spite of the circumstances, Lili enjoyed the lessons. She especially loved tales of the Dalai Lama. Ching would whisper when she came to that part; Lili wasn't sure why. She guessed it had to do with the fact that the Dalai Lama had been forced out of Tibet by Chinese leaders back in 1959. Ching clearly disapproved, but was afraid to say. Lili understood. There were just some things that shouldn't be said out loud.

Ching had made a point of sharing the Dalai Lama's wisdom; it was as if Lili was hearing the Truth of the Ages in the tinny, high-pitched voice of her teacher. Lili liked the Truth. She seemed to know it before it was said. She had told that to her teacher. Ching had nodded. *"Yes, my child, it is that way with the truth ... it doesn't need words."*

But the Wisdom of the Ages couldn't take away the ache in her heart. Lili missed her home. She missed the ocean, she missed her cats ... she missed her caregivers, Danil and Anna. She had lost too many. Her mother, her father, Uncle Mart ... all of them gone. She had spent quite a bit of time trying to get past it ... the feeling that everyone leaves in the end. Ching Lan had helped her with that, as well. *"People in our lives don't leave us, Lili ... they merely move to another plane. They are there; you can talk to them. You will hear their reply ... if you pay attention."*

So, Lili had tried it. In the middle of the night when everything was quiet, she had tried to talk to Danil, to Anna, to Uncle Mart ... and to her parents, Larissa and Albins. She had heard nothing from any of them ... until tonight.

For whatever reason, she had heard Uncle Mart, and had even seen him sprawled on a bed in a dark room, all alone. She had felt his grief as he mourned his life ... as he mourned her. *But he is dead!* She had felt him die in that hotel fire as if the flames were burning her skin, not his. She had ached for him ... for his pain, for the world he was leaving behind.

Though he wasn't her real uncle, he was every bit the same. He had kept an eye on her when her parents were away, which was often. Her mother had worked for the government and would be called away at a whim. Her father was often asked to go with her, and Lili would stay at the Henderson estate. Uncle Mart would look after her. He made her presents ... a sled for the snow, a special box for the rocks she found outdoors. Handmade gifts ... built with so much love.

She squeezed her pillow. She missed him. Danil had told her that Mart had gone to heaven ... just like her parents. She hoped it was true. She had tried to see him there; she had tried to see them all, but, for whatever reason, she couldn't. Though she was able to see so many things that others could not, she could never see heaven. But she believed in it. She wasn't sure why; just another feeling she had ... *like goodness hovering over us all.*

But tonight, she had felt Uncle Mart's presence ... *and he is sad.* How could he be sad when he was in heaven? Had he maybe *not* gone to heaven? Where else would he have gone? She shivered. She knew he hadn't gone to that other place ... he was far too good a man.

Regardless, she had sensed his presence and his pain, and it hurt her ... deep inside. *If only I could bring him comfort,* she thought. *If only that had been my gift.* She frowned. It didn't seem fair. A man should be freed of his misery once he left this earth. *Perhaps he has unfinished business.*

She snuggled against the pillow, sighing as she looked out the window at the full moon. Could Mart see the moon? Where was he? Why was he sad? Maybe she could help him ... maybe ease his pain as he struggled even in death with unstoppable sadness. What was it the Dalai Lama had said: *"I find hope in the darkest of days."*

As she stared at the bold bright moon, she vowed ... *From here on, Uncle Mart, I will do what I can to bring you hope.*

Chapter 7
COLUMBIA, SOUTH CAROLINA

Washington, DC

Amanda's afternoon was no better than her morning. She was over-booked and exhausted. She had tried to take a nap over lunch, but had spent most of the time staring at the empty spot next to her in the bed. She had been glad to go back to work.

But, from the minute she got there, it was crazy. Both her and Lorraine's schedules were packed. More addicts had come in, their symptoms exactly the same as those she had seen that morning.

She took a sip of lukewarm tea as she jotted notes in a chart. She tossed the chart in a pile and walked to the next treatment room. She again noted a black sticker on the chart, indicating a drug user. She frowned as she walked into the room and saw yet another emaciated woman lying on the table. She glanced at the chart; the woman's name was Gloria and she was forty years old. She looked much older.

"Good afternoon, Gloria. What can I help you with today?"

Gloria raised her head and tried to smile. Amanda saw the tell-tale bleeding gums, along with a tremor when she moved her hands.

"I'm ... really sick. Word on the street is that we ... got some ... bad blow."

Amanda had to agree; she had never seen anything like it. She did a quick exam, noting the same symptoms she had seen in the others. She wrote up a lab order. "We'll run some tests, Gloria; I'll see you back in a week."

Gloria nodded and got down from the table. She was unsteady, and Amanda helped her to the front desk, where Lisa took over. The next patient had failed to show, which gave Amanda a chance to go to her office, turn on her laptop, and pull up a medical website. She typed in the symptoms that plagued the addicts and waited. Several diagnoses appeared on the screen and she scrolled through them, looking for one that fit. She saw a few that were close, but none that included every complaint. She was about to give up when her eyes fell on a group of symptoms that included tremor, vomiting, headache, and – *there it is* – bleeding gums. They were found under the heading "Viral Hemorrhagic Fever," or "Lassa fever." *No way,* she thought, as she read the next paragraph.

"Symptoms of Lassa fever typically occur anywhere from a few days to three weeks after the patient comes into contact with the virus. Symptoms include fever, chest pain, cough, abdominal pain, vomiting, diarrhea, facial swelling, mucosal bleeding. Neurological problems include hearing loss, tremors, and encephalitis."

Amanda frowned as she read on, looking for a connection to IV drug use. There was nothing. *Why would Lassa fever suddenly show up in South Carolina?* It was endemic to West Africa; there was no mention of it ever being in the States.

She shook her head and sighed. *So ... if it is Lassa fever, how do I treat it?*

"The antiviral Ribavirin has been used with some success. It is most effective when given early. Approximately 20 percent of patients hospitalized for Lassa fever die. Death rates are especially high for pregnant women, and for fetuses, about 95 percent of which die in the uterus of infected mothers."

She still had no answer as to why IV drug users were so vulnerable, or how her patients might have gotten infected. As she was about to click off, the final paragraph caught her attention.

"Because of its easy spread from person to person, it is felt that Lassa fever would be useful as a bioterror weapon. Although it would require modifications, the changes could be made by any lab familiar with the virus."

"No," Amanda thought. *"There's no way I'm looking at bioterrorism in our small clinic."* She missed Andrew even more. She stuck her head out the door and caught Lorraine as she was coming out of a treatment room. "Come and look at this."

Lorraine walked into the office and Amanda showed her the screen. "I find it hard to believe, but it fits what we've been seeing, don't you think?"

Lorraine skimmed the article. "Wow."

Amanda nodded. "Do I report it? I don't want to overreact, but it would be worse if I didn't at least tell somebody, right?"

Lorraine nodded. "We should run it by someone who knows about these types of diseases. Maybe somebody at the CDC?"

Amanda immediately thought of her good friend – and Maddi's on-again, off-again boyfriend – Hank Clarkson. "I know a bioterror expert at Homeland Security."

"Perfect. Are we going to start using the special lab testing?"

Amanda was dialing Hank's cellphone. "Yes, and I'll stop by and have the pharmacy get some ribavirin ready, just in case."

Lorraine nodded and left the office. Amanda waited for the call to go through. After three rings, she heard the upbeat voice of her friend since medical school, Hank Clarkson. "Hey Amanda, what's up? How's Andrew?"

"He's fine," she lied. "Hank, I've got the weirdest thing going on down here. There's a cluster of cases involving our IV drug population, and the symptoms are consistent with Lassa fever." She hesitated. "No way ... right?"

There was a pause. "It would be an odd pathogen to see in South Carolina ... or anywhere in the States, for that matter."

"I know. But I've searched several medical sites and I've found nothing else that fits. And here's the thing ... it fits perfectly."

Another pause. "Let me talk to Hanover. He'll probably want me to come down." There was a pause. "You need to isolate the patients, Amanda; at least those you see from now on."

"How do I do that?"

"I'll talk to Hanover. We can designate someplace nearby as an isolation center."

"There's an abandoned warehouse right next door. It used to be a storage site for an old grocery store chain. Would that work?"

"I think so. Let me talk to the boss. I'll call you back."

Amanda ended the call and logged off the computer. She leaned back and closed her eyes. These responsibilities would normally fall on Andrew's shoulders, but he was gone. It was up to her. *You can do this, Amanda.* She pulled a piece of paper from a desk drawer and made a list. Number one: ask the local pharmacy to arrange for ribavirin. Number two: let the lab know that she and Lorraine were going to require specialized testing. Number three: have doctors and staff initiate steps to keep from being exposed. She thought of the patient who had vomited that morning and frowned. *A little late for that.*

Doctor Hank Clarkson stared at his phone. He set it on the desk and ran a hand through thinning black hair. *How would Lassa fever wind up in South Carolina?* He stood, his thick frame stiff from sitting so long. He had spent the entire day at his desk, wading through a seemingly endless barrage of biologic threats. None of them ever amounted to anything, but it was frightening to think how close a few had come.

He paced the office, stopping now and then to look out the window. A few bare trees and a parking lot; that was all he had for inspiration. He thought of Amanda and frowned. She was scared; he could hear it in her voice. *I should tell Maddi.*

He dialed Maddi's senate office. Her secretary answered on the first ring. "Hey Phil. Is Maddi available?"

"She just got back from a vote, Dr. Clarkson. I'll put you through."

Hank grinned as Maddi said cheerfully, "Hey, Deputy Director. How's it going in the world of toxic gas and bad bugs?"

"You'll never guess who just called me."

"Hmmm ... your ex-wife? An old girlfriend? Okay, I give."

He laughed. "Amanda. There's a weird virus at the clinic; she needs some help."

"That's kind of scary, Hank."

"I know. I'm going to talk to Hanover. I'll probably be heading down there."

"Maybe it's just a new flu strain or something."

"I thought of that. But I can't imagine Amanda calling me about a flu."

"You've got a point. When do you think you'll leave?"

"As soon as possible. Do you want to go?" The minute he said it, he regretted it; he already knew the answer.

"I ... I can't get away right now, Hank. Too much going on."

Hank flinched. "A chance to fight a battle outside the beltway and you're turning me down?"

"Hank, I–" She stopped. "Maybe I can find some time before I leave for the summit."

Hank knew she wouldn't; he could hear it in her voice. "Sure thing, Maddi."

They ended the call and Hank stared at the phone. *Go see Hanover.*

He rubbed his eyes and sighed. What was it Maddi had once said about them? *"They're the warmest eyes I've ever seen."* He scoffed and walked down the hall to Jason Hanover's office. He waited outside, grinning as he watched the large man pace behind his desk. He could hear him in a heated discussion on the phone, and he chuckled as the man tackled the problem with his usual gruff manner.

"I don't give a shit what you *think*. Get me facts ... now!" Hanover slammed down the receiver and motioned to Hank to come in.

Hank walked in and sat across from Hanover's cluttered desk. The director sat down and sighed, his lined face reflecting the strain of years of investigative work. His hairline had receded, but he still had plenty of thick, black hair, clipped close, military style. His dark eyes were kind, but tired, and the circles underneath reflected the tension of his role as the lead man in the fight against terror. He smiled as he said gruffly, "What the hell do you want, Clarkson?"

Hank grinned. He informed Hanover of the situation in South Carolina.

"The doctor down there thinks this could be a biologic agent?"

"She finds it hard to believe, but she's convinced it's some form of hemorrhagic fever ... not something we normally see in the States."

Hanover frowned, his large fingers drumming the top of his desk. "Most of the agency is involved with the subway explosion from last week. But it sounds like we should at least check it out."

Hank nodded. "Yes sir, I think so."

Hanover rubbed his chin. "I'll call local law enforcement down there. We'll need to isolate the patients."

"There's an empty warehouse next to the clinic."

"Sounds good." Hanover leaned back and sighed. "Hank, I hired you specifically because of your medical knowledge. I assumed, sooner or later, we would have a case of bioterrorism on our soil. This could be it. I'll send you down with a couple of agents." He paused. "We need to move fast, but I can't send you without having an isolation facility in place. We should be able to have it up and running by tonight." He frowned. "Be ready to go first thing in the morning."

Hank nodded. "Yes sir."

"And once you get there, you need to make a quick assessment. If it's bioterror, we can't waste any time."

"I understand, sir." Hank stood to leave. Hanover handed him a folder. "Keep notes." He narrowed his eyes. "And Hank, be careful."

Chapter 8

WASHINGTON, DC

Morningstar stormed into his office and tossed his briefcase on the desk. He had lost the entire day to running errands for his boss, General Daniels. Even worse: Simeon had yet to confirm the arrival of two of the three boats from Africa. Abid's boat had arrived three days ago at the Charleston Harbor, and, as far as he knew, there had been no attempt to stop or search it. But they would need the cargo from the other boats to create a crisis large enough to get the country's attention.

He walked to the window of his eight-by-ten office on the first floor of the Pentagon. He liked it there. He was in a back corner and, other than a nosy clerk who worked across the hall, he was pretty much left alone. He could see the dome of the Capitol in the distance, and, though it was only four in the afternoon, the fading sunlight cast deep shadows on the imposing structure. It calmed him as he admired the city that would soon be his. He opened his cellphone and dialed.

It was answered quickly. "Yes, Father?"

"Well?" he waited.

Simeon said nothing.

He sighed. "Have you found the other two boats, Simeon?"

There was a pause. "Not ... not yet, Father. They're likely just running late."

Morningstar bristled. "Running late? Running late is for children that are tardy to school! Now find them, dammit!" He paused. "What about Joseph?"

"No sign of him yet, sir."

"Find him, too ... and bring him in ... alive." He ended the call. *Is Simeon up to it?* Can he find two small fishing boats lost in the vast Atlantic? Can he bring in a world class assassin? Morningstar smirked. *The first task will be easier.* Henderson wasn't merely a highly skilled assassin, he also had nothing to lose ... *except for Lili.*

Morningstar grinned as he thought of the remarkable little girl hidden somewhere in western China. He had heard from her captors only once ... to let him know they had arrived. He didn't know where in Tibet they were keeping her; he didn't care. He had left that part of the mission to his contact in China. The orders had been clear: *"Prepare her for what's next."* Lin Chu would do it; he had proven himself many times over the last three years. Morningstar grinned. *And if he doesn't, he'll receive the same punishment his cousin got when he defied me in Tianjin.*

He laughed aloud, recalling Henderson's brutal assassination of Lin Chu's cousin – a diplomatic attaché – outside a Tianjin bar on a cold night in December. The message had been clear: *Defy Edward Morningstar, and you will pay the price.*

In return for Chu's help with Lili, Morningstar had promised him a seat at the table. Little did Chu know ... the table was far too small to accommodate Morningstar, his twelve sons, and the Chinese Minister of War. But, by the time Chu figured it out, Morningstar would have so much power there would be nothing he could do about it.

He shoved his laptop in his briefcase, threw it over his shoulder, and put on his coat. He left the Pentagon and searched the curb for a driver. He had called a meeting of the secret organization, the Bentley Group, for the following morning and would need the entire evening to prepare. He had strung the men along nicely. They had no idea what he was up to, nor would they until it was too late. As a matter of fact, there would soon be nothing anyone could do to stop him.

Chapter 9
COLUMBIA, SOUTH CAROLINA

Amanda finished the day with five more patients, two of whom had presented with the Lassa fever symptoms. Each was an IV drug user. She ordered the testing and kept them in treatment rooms, hoping she would hear from Hank about the isolation facility before the end of the day. She sat in her office reviewing charts, and, finally, at 5:30 he called and told her that the warehouse next door had been designated as an isolation site. He had arranged for two nurses from the local health department to staff it until Homeland could send in doctors and nurses from the CDC. Amanda assured Hank she would personally see to it that the two patients got to the warehouse. "But I don't know if I can find any of the ones we saw earlier, Hank."

"I'll have local law enforcement find them. I'll need their names."

She read off the names and addresses; most had listed the local shelter.

"I'll see what I can do." He paused. "You and your staff need to take precautions, Amanda."

"It's a little late for that, Hank."

"Do it anyway ... and start the ribavirin, okay?"

"Sure."

"I'll see you in the morning, Amanda."

"It'll be good to see you, Hank."

Amanda ended the call. It was hard to believe what was happening ... *and Andrew isn't here to help.* She grabbed her coat, walked out to the front desk, and asked Lisa to gather up the two patients who were waiting in the treatment rooms. "I'm taking them next door," Amanda said, as she put on her coat. She met both patients at the front door and walked them outside. It was already dark, and the air was cold. She wrapped her coat tighter as she walked them to the warehouse. They had only light jackets. *At least they'll be warm here.*

An armed guard had been assigned to watch over the facility; he checked Amanda's ID as she entered the building. She spoke to the RNs from the local health department and told them she would arrange for a delivery of ribavirin. "You'll need to take it, as well." She watched as the patients were led to a makeshift shower which had been set up to wash them down. She walked across the hall to a large room with several beds lined in a row. She frowned. Her patients would soon be lying in those beds, craving the cocaine that had made them so sick. The withdrawal would be tough, especially on top of the illness. She would make sure to have Valium available.

She left the facility and walked to her car. She got in, strapped on her seatbelt, and leaned against the seat. She was exhausted. *Keep going, Amanda.* She started the engine and pulled out of the lot, driving a block to the local pharmacy. She walked in, asked to speak to the pharmacist, and was told it would be a minute. She absently scanned the shelves, stopping when she saw the one-step pregnancy kits. *So, I'm late ... it's just stress.* Besides, she was on birth control pills. She started to walk away, then turned and grabbed a kit, along with a bottle of antacids.

"The pharmacist can see you now."

Amanda walked to the counter. "I'm Dr. McKinney-Madison from the clinic down the street. I'm afraid we'll be needing extra doses of ribavirin."

The pharmacist glanced at her over a pair of reading glasses. The phone was ringing and a tech was waiting to ask him a question. He nodded impatiently. "I'll take care of it."

Amanda thanked him, glad he hadn't been more curious. She purchased the items, left the pharmacy, and drove home. She walked into the townhouse and set the bag on the kitchen table. She pulled out the antacids and was about to take one, when she saw the pregnancy kit. Before she could talk herself out of it, she grabbed it, took it into the bathroom, and sat and gave a sample. The words from the computer article came from nowhere ...

"Death rates are especially high for pregnant women, and for fetuses, about 95 percent of which die in the uterus of infected mothers."

Amanda was afraid to look. She stood at the sink and took a deep breath. She picked up the test strip, looked for the telltale blue line, and grabbed the wall to keep from falling. The result was staring back at her, clear as could be ...

Positive.

Chapter 10
COLUMBIA, SOUTH CAROLINA

Tuesday, January 13th, 2004

Abid Mensah was sick. He had arrived in America four days ago, the trip across the Atlantic uneventful, in spite of storms off to the north. As instructed by the mysterious Simeon, he had traveled from Charleston to Columbia, and had sold his wares near the bus station in the heart of the city. He had been fine until a few hours ago, when he had begun to feel pains in his stomach and a throbbing in his head. He couldn't afford a hotel; he had yet to be paid, and the money from four years ago was long gone. So, he had gone to a shelter downtown. It was cold in January, even in South Carolina, and the shelter was full. He had been lucky to find a cot in the corner, away from the others. He had been lying there for the past two hours, fighting nausea, trying to sleep. He felt a stab to his gut and grabbed his stomach, wincing as he tried to keep from crying out. He couldn't draw attention.

His head was pounding. He felt like he was dying. If he didn't get help soon, he just might. *I don't want to die here ... not without my money.* His hard-earned cash was waiting for him at his boat at the Charleston Pier. *I need to go.*

He sat up, wiping sweat from his forehead as he strained his eyes to see. It was dark; dawn was hours away. He stood and, using the wall for support, took a few cautious steps. *I need to get help.* The moonlight through a window guided him as he traipsed over sleeping bodies. He made it as far as the doorway and stopped. He thought he might vomit. *Not here ...*

you can't draw attention! His eyes fell on a sheet of paper hanging near the door.

"Free Clinic ... Broadway and Main. Doors open Monday through Friday at 8:00 a.m."

Abid checked a clock on the wall. *Five a.m. I will go when the sun comes up.* He memorized directions and then clung to the wall as he trudged back to his cot. He would get help from the clinic. And then he could return to his boat, get his money, and wait for Jacob to give him a home in America. He grinned. Within days, he would be a very rich man. *Jacob has promised me.*

Chapter 11

WASHINGTON, DC

Morningstar sat in the back of a cab on his way to the Morgan Building. He didn't like to meet with the Bentley Group in the middle of the week, but it needed to be done; he had received important information from his analyst at the Pentagon; it was imperative he let them know. He grinned. He couldn't wait to see their faces.

It was still dark outside, though he could see a hint of sunrise through the window. The cab let him off in front of the building; he paid the fare and got out. Ignoring the cold, he trotted up the stairs and through the door. He walked to the elevator and stepped inside. He put his key in the slot and waited while it carried him to the top. He nodded at two agents by the door as he strode into the elegantly appointed meeting room. Instead of going to the credenza to get a cup of coffee, he went straight to his chair. The other six members were already seated.

The leader of the group, referred to as Chief, glared at him, his cigar smoke forming a misty haze over his wild gray hair. "It's your meeting. What've ya got?"

Morningstar reached into his brief case and pulled out a document. "May I?"

Conner nodded.

Morningstar read from the sheet of paper.

"One week ago, Phoenix was observed killing three men in downtown Savannah. Though likely threatened, his response was excessive. All three had their throats cut. He is escalating. Suggest intervening or severing all ties."

Morningstar looked up. "Our man is unstable. We need to bring him in."

Chief frowned. "How was he spotted?"

"Closed-circuit TV."

"FBI?"

"No, my man pulled the feed before they could see it."

Chief nodded. "Did you try to bring him in?"

Morningstar flinched. "No."

"Why not? I thought you said we could use him."

"We can ... but only if we leave him alone."

Chief bristled. "What the hell sense does that make?"

Morningstar hid a sneer as he crossed his hands on the table. "In his former life, Phoenix associated with some very important people. They all think he's dead; it has made him quite useful to us." He paused. "Since his transformation, he has never tried to contact any of them," he leaned back, "...but I think that may have changed."

Chief eyed Morningstar. "What do you mean?"

"Last week you asked me to keep Senator Madison out of our hair. Starting three days ago, we began monitoring all correspondence going in and out of her office, hoping to undermine her credibility in some way. Yesterday, we came across an anonymous email asking for her help with an upcoming court trial involving the City of Providence versus Rocky's Restaurant."

Chief said curtly, "So?"

Morningstar stiffened. "I have this computer guy who works for the Pentagon, but lately I've had him working specifically for me." He paused. "He has software that links seemingly random events through a common denominator. I asked him to be on the lookout for a link between Madison and our man Phoenix, thinking, just maybe, he might try to make contact."

"Why would he contact her?"

Morningstar hesitated. "I've learned recently that prior to becoming a CIA assassin, the Phoenix had worked with Madison on some sort of legislative effort."

Chief's eyes widened. "Then I must know him."

"No. It was back-room sort of stuff. I don't have the details, but I think the guy might have had a thing for her." He paused. "So ... on a hunch, I thought he might try to get in touch with her ... especially now that he's 'in the wind.'"

Chief frowned. "So ... was the email from him?"

Morningstar nodded. "I think so. The question about Rocky's restaurant triggered a response."

Chief shook his head. "Why would a restaurant trigger the software?"

Morningstar grinned. "I've just learned that Rocky's is where our Phoenix took the senator when she visited him in Providence four years ago."

Chief's eyes widened. "I see. What was Madison's reply?"

"It appears she tried to email him back, but it went nowhere. We attempted to trace his e-mail; it was futile. The sender clearly wants to remain anonymous."

Chief puffed on his cigar. "Okay. So how is this useful?"

Morningstar reached into his briefcase for a second item, an article from a Providence newspaper, dated that morning. He laid it on the table and began reading.

"The case of Rocky's Restaurant v. the City of Providence will likely go to trial this spring. A prominent senator has recently shown interest in the case, citing its impact on the discussion of Eminent Domain. Senate Majority Whip, Cynthia Madison, has indicated that she'll be submitting a brief on behalf of Rocky's restaurant, claiming that the owner, Marco Solvino, has sole authority over the use of his property. She goes on to say that he should never, under any circumstance, be forced to give up his property simply because a government entity deems it in the public interest. The senator hopes this case will serve as an opportunity to spur debate and force a change to the law that allows the

government to steal the property of its citizens."

No one said a word. It was Chief who broke the silence. "So, you think Madison's responding to the request from Phoenix?"

"It's certainly a strange coincidence that she's all of a sudden involving herself in the case, don't you think?"

Chief narrowed his eyes. "Have there been any more emails?"

"No. The article was in this morning's paper, so I'm guessing he'll respond later today."

"Okay. Keep monitoring all contact to and from her office."

What do you think I've been doing, dumbass? Morningstar nodded. "Yes sir."

Chief said, "What do we do if he's trying to reach her?"

"The attack in Savannah would suggest that he's escalating. He's unpredictable." Morningstar leaned forward, stared at each face at the table, and said coolly, "I'm worried he might make an attempt on her life."

The room fell silent. Chief's eyes narrowed and he took a puff on his cigar. "I don't want any part of this shit, Morningstar."

Morningstar shook his head. "Me either, sir. But it's out of our control."

"What do you mean?"

"The guy's nuts. We can't be responsible for what he might do."

Chief stared at him. After several seconds, he chuckled. "You're right. We can't control the actions of a madman."

Morningstar nodded. "No sir. That's why I think we should issue a memo indicating that the CIA agent has "gone rogue." But there are steps I'm forced to take for such a release. It might take a while for it to reach the proper channels. Who knows what will happen in the meantime."

"Yeah ... who knows?"

Dan Lawford, the chairman of the Senate Arms Committee, shook his head. "Look, I hate that bitch as much as the rest of you, but I can't be a party to murder."

Morningstar smirked. "Who said anything about murder? I'm simply saying that we have a rogue agent on our hands. We can't be held responsible if a man goes crazy, now can we?"

Lawford said, "Who exactly does Phoenix work for ... I mean, besides us?"

"He's listed as CIA. But even the guys at the Agency don't know about him. I've managed to lead each branch to think he's the responsibility of another branch. He's so top secret that no one's questioned it. The director, Jack Miley, doesn't know shit about him. He's ours, boys, and we can use him however we want." He grinned, "...just like we've done for the past three years." Several of the men lowered their eyes; a few shook their heads disapprovingly. Morningstar ignored them.

"I think whatever happens to Madison can easily be tied to Phoenix. But I'll need to issue the alert that he's gone rogue in order to make our case." He paused. "Which means that our 'secret weapon' will suddenly be Public Enemy Number One." Again, he stared at each of their faces. "The outcome will be this," he leaned closer, "...both Phoenix and Madison will be out of the way, and we can carry on without interference."

Chief feigned a frown. "Now, you know we don't condone violence." The others looked around uneasy. Chief laughed. "Make it happen, Morningstar."

A few of the men chuckled nervously. Morningstar sat back and nodded. "Yes, sir."

Chief rose from his chair, prompting the others to do the same. They walked to the elevator and, two by two, headed to the lobby. Morningstar stayed behind, waiting for the last man to leave. As the elevator closed, he lifted the receiver of a secure phone sitting on the table, and dialed.

The call was answered by a low, male voice. "Yes?"

Morningstar whispered, though there was no one to hear. "It's a go, Josh ... start drafting an alert."

He ended the call and dialed another number.

"Yes?"

"Pocks, it's me. I have an assignment for you."

There was a pause. "Another assignment?"

Morningstar sneered. *Yes, dumbass.* A week ago, he had given Pocks the task of keeping an eye on the senator. It was Pocks who had helped with her abduction in Jacksonville. "Remember your subject from last week?"

There was a pause. "Yes sir."

"She's back in DC I need you to figure out her next move … quickly."

"Her next move, sir?"

"Yes. What's she's planning for the next couple of days." He paused. "Can you handle it?"

Another pause. "Um, sure … yes sir."

"Good. Get busy." Morningstar hung up the phone. He would have Pocks monitor Madison, learn her plans for the next week or so, and then have her killed. He would make sure it was Phoenix who got blamed. But, in spite of what he had told the others, he wouldn't let Phoenix be captured or killed. He couldn't. The man was his son … his Joseph. He felt certain that once Henderson realized he was a wanted man, he would seek out Morningstar's protection. *The prodigal son will come home.*

He grinned and reached for a cigar. He leaned back, lit it, and took a long, slow drag. He exhaled, creating a perfect smoke ring that rose to the vaulted ceiling of the room with no windows. "Here's to us, Joseph … and the battle we're about to fight … together."

Chapter 12

COLUMBIA, SOUTH CAROLINA

Hurry home, Andrew. But, even as she wished it, Amanda wondered how he would take the news. She had spent the night worrying ... afraid of how he would feel about the fact that she had somehow gotten pregnant. *He'll think I did it intentionally.* She stood and grabbed her white coat from a hook on the door. *What if he hates me for this?* She put a hand to her belly. *What if he hates ... this?*

She combed through her hair and grabbed her stethoscope. She had no idea how she had gotten pregnant while on the pill. It was rare; almost unheard of. She had had a bout with the stomach flu in early November and had missed a couple of pills. Had that been it? *It has to be.* But they had been careful; Andrew had insisted. It had spurred the argument about starting a family.

She had been sitting in her clinic office for the past few minutes, trying to ward off the queasiness she had been fighting since dawn. She stood and was about to go to the first treatment room, when the nausea won out and she ran to the bathroom. She made it just in time. She went to the sink and rinsed her face. As the cool water comforted her, she thought back on what she had read about Lassa fever and its effect on pregnant women and their babies. *Don't think about it.*

She walked to the first treatment room. She skimmed the chart as she opened the door. *Thank God, not another addict.* Sitting on the table was a short, overweight man, with dark hair and eyes. He appeared to be of Arab descent, though Amanda couldn't be sure. She glanced at the name on the chart. "Hello, Abid."

The man looked up from the table. He spoke in broken English with an accent Amanda couldn't place. "I sick. Chills. Cough. Headache. And, look." He pointed to his mouth, where Amanda saw the now-familiar bleeding from the gums.

Her heart sank. *It's spreading.* He was the first non-drug user to have the symptoms. She listened to his heart and lungs, doing her best to not get too close.

"Abid, I need to know where you've been. What you've done recently that may have exposed you to a virus."

The man shifted uncomfortably. He looked up at Amanda. "I ... I from Africa. I bring ... clothes to sell."

Amanda frowned. *Africa ... where Lassa fever is endemic.* "Abid, you must be honest with me. Why are you in Columbia?"

He looked down. "I come here by the bus."

"From where?"

He paused. "Um ... DC"

"How long have you been in America?"

"A few days."

Amanda frowned. Did he arrive in America infected? *He must have.* What was his connection to the IV drug users? She stared at him, knowing that his role was significant, whether he knew it or not. She checked both of his forearms. "Abid, have you ever used IV drugs?"

He pulled away. "No! Never!"

Amanda closed the chart. "Okay. We'll do blood work and start you on medicine. You'll need to check in next door; there's a temporary hospital that has been set up to take care of you."

Abid frowned, his eyes darting back and forth.

"You need to be isolated, Abid."

He stared at her, his dark eyes hard to read. Was it anger she saw ... or fear?

"It's okay, Abid. I'll have one of my staff walk you over there."

She gave him a mask to put on, and then wrote out the prescription and the lab order. She helped him down from the table. She walked him out to the hall and pointed to the front desk. "Lisa will walk you next door. You'll hand the nurses your script and the lab sheet. Okay?"

Abid gave a reluctant nod.

She walked to her office and sat at her desk. She yawned and rubbed her eyes. Never had she felt so tired. She was tempted to lay on the sofa and take a nap, but she couldn't; there was too much to do. Hank was scheduled to arrive later that morning; she had to have all the charts ready for him. She closed her eyes and rested her head on her hands. *But Abid is the key.*

Suddenly she sat up ... *but he wouldn't have crossed the ocean by himself!*

She grabbed the chart to see if he had listed a contact. Nothing. She frowned. Whoever had come with him was likely sick as well ... *and is spreading the virus!*

She jumped to her feet and ran out to the reception area, hoping to catch Lisa before she took Abid to the isolation facility. She needed to find whoever had come with him from Africa. Lisa wasn't at her desk. Amanda went to the front door to see if she and Abid were on their way to the warehouse. She didn't see them. She was about to grab her coat and run over there when she turned and saw Lisa coming from the bathroom. "Did you take Abid next door?"

Lisa frowned. "He said you told him to follow up; that he wasn't sick enough to go to the isolation ward. I made him an appointment for next Thursday." Lisa's shoulders slumped. "You ... you didn't say that at all, did you?"

Amanda ran out the door, hoping to catch him before he got far. Ignoring the cold, she ran one direction, and then another, looking everywhere for the chubby man from Africa. He said he had come by bus. She went to the bus stop; there was no sign of him. She walked back to the clinic, frowning as she stepped inside.

"I am so sorry, Doctor."

Amanda nodded. "It's okay, Lisa." But it wasn't. The man who could shed light on a horrible illness had just walked away.

Amanda went to her office and fell into the chair ... *and he'll likely infect others.*

Chapter 13

WASHINGTON, DC

This time the e-mail was brought straight to Maddi. Phil had knocked, walked in, and set it on her desk. "Another one, Senator."

"Thanks, Phil. Still no word on who's writing these?"

He shook his head. "Should I pull in the FBI?"

"No. Hold off for now. Just have our guys stay with it."

Phil nodded and left the room.

Maddi picked up at the e-mail.

My dear Maddi, so glad you're looking out for Mr. Solvino. He remembers you. He asked that I thank you. He hopes to see you soon.

She dropped the note. Her hands were shaking; she rubbed them on her skirt. Whoever was writing the emails was paying close attention; he knew she had filed a

brief. *Who would take such an interest in Solvino's case?* Maddi tried to think who else had known that she had been in Providence four years ago and had gone to dinner at Rocky's. *And would refer to me as 'my dear Maddi!'* She tucked her hair behind her ear and thought back to that night. She had flown to Providence to meet with Henderson. They had planned to discuss legislation that would have combined federal health care dollars with Henderson's insurance company. He stood to gain greatly, which had made Maddi skeptical. She had needed to hear how he thought the proposal would benefit the American people. He had seemed to welcome the challenge of selling her on the plan. *"Let's discuss it over dinner. I know a restaurant that serves an out-of-this-world filet."* They had gone to dinner at Rocky's, and afterward he had taken her back to her hotel—she stopped. She couldn't go on. She felt like she was smothering. She stood and walked to the window. She tried to open it, forgetting that the Secret Service had nailed it shut after 9-11. She stared at the brown grass and dormant rosebushes outside the window, recalling with stunning clarity the warmth of Henderson's breath on her cheek ... the feel of his hand against her skin. *Stop it, Maddi.* She walked to her desk and sat down.

The explosion had taken place a week later, killing senators, VIP's ... *and Henderson.* She closed her eyes. *But what if he didn't die?* It was impossible. The hotel had been destroyed. Homeland Security had had Urgent Cares and emergency rooms monitored for months following the explosion. He had not shown up at any of them. *He's dead, Maddi.* So, who else could have sent the emails? Who else knew about dinner at Rocky's? She frowned. *Maria Harvey.*

Maria was the former VP and current CEO of Marker Health; the insurance company Henderson had built from scratch. She might have known where Henderson had taken Maddi for dinner. But why would she care about Mr. Solvino or Rocky's?

Maddi pushed the intercom. "Phil, could you get Maria Harvey on the phone? She's the CEO of Marker Heath Insurance Company in Providence."

She sat back and stared at the email. She picked it up, her hands shaking as she held it in front of her. *"My dear Maddi ... he hopes to see you soon."* Maria Harvey would never say that. So, who else could it be? *It has to be him.*

"I have her on the line, Senator."

She picked up the phone. "Is this Maria Harvey?"

"Yes Senator. It's good to hear from you. We haven't spoken since the memorial."

Maddi's jaw tightened. *Henderson's memorial.* "It's good to hear your voice, Maria." She paused. "I'm looking into the Eminent Domain case involving Rocky's Restaurant."

There was a pause. "I haven't been to Rocky's in ages. I didn't think they were still in business."

That eliminates Maria. "The city of Providence is apparently trying to take the restaurant's land to expand the jail."

Another pause. "I certainly hate that for the restaurant, but it's hard to argue against expanding the jail. We clearly need more room."

She's not even on the right side of this! "I respect your point of view, Maria, but I want you to know that I'm proceeding with a brief on Mr. Solvino's behalf."

"Oh, by all means, Senator. I won't weigh in. I appreciate the heads-up."

"Good to talk to you, Maria."

"You too, Senator."

Maddi hung up the phone. There was no one else who would have known that Henderson had taken her to Rocky's. *So, who is writing these emails?* Was it Solvino himself? No ... he would have simply asked Maddi for help. *There's only one man it could be!* Though Maddi knew it was impossible, there was no other explanation.

She stood and paced the room. "Don't be ridiculous, Maddi. He died ... no one could have survived it at the end." But, even as she said it, she wasn't 100% sure. After all, they had never found his body.

She returned to her desk, trying to think of a way to prove to herself, once and for all, that Henderson was dead. *I'll reach out to him.* Whoever had written the email was paying attention; they knew she had filed the brief. If it was Henderson – *which is impossible* – he would reply.

She closed her eyes, trying to think of something she could do or say that only he would recognize. What had happened during that weekend – the only weekend they ever shared – that was just between the two of them? *The nights we spent in the hotel.* She picked up the email, her eyes burning as she read it again. She would go to that same hotel ... and stay in that same room. If he was alive, he would find her. *If he doesn't, then I have my answer.*

She pushed the intercom. "Phil, I've decided to go to Providence to look into the Eminent Domain case. But I'm flying to Monterrey tomorrow for the summit; I'll be there through Saturday. Let's make it Monday morning." She paused. "Please don't tell anyone I'm going." Another pause. "Oh yeah, and Phil? Make sure to book us in the penthouse suite of the downtown Westin. Agent Moses will travel with me; Collins can fly in that evening." There was silence. "Phil? Did you get that?"

"Uh ... yes, Senator. I'll take care of it."

~ ~ ~

Morningstar had stopped for breakfast after his meeting and was walking into his office when his cellphone vibrated. "Yes?"

"It's me ... Pocks." He was whispering. "I'm outside the uh ... subject's office, and–"

"You're what?"

"I'm outside her office ... in the men's room down the hall. I'm using a digital intercept device that my uncle gave me, and I just overheard a conversation between our ... uh ... subject ... and her secretary."

Morningstar's eyes widened. "That was quick. What did she say?"

"She's going to Mexico ... tomorrow, sir ... some sort of summit. She'll be back Saturday or Sunday."

Morningstar frowned. He knew what summit Pocks was referring to. It was the Monterrey Summit of the Americas. The U.S. President was also attending; there would be no way he could get to her there. "Did you get anything more?"

"Yes sir. She's flying to Providence, Rhode Island, on Monday. Staying at the downtown Westin."

Morningstar grinned. *That's more like it.* "Good job, Pocks." He ended the call and leaned back in his chair. *Now I've got you both.*

Chapter 14

COLUMBIA, SOUTH CAROLINA

Hank had made the trip to South Carolina on many occasions, but never quite like this. The military jet supplied to the Department of Homeland Security was far more convenient than the airlines. Instead of a one-hour flight taking three, the trip took about 55 minutes, and there was a car waiting on the tarmac to take Hank and two agents to the clinic in downtown Columbia.

As he left the plane, he looked at the black sedan and shook his head. He had come a long way. In a few short years he had gone from a family physician in Strongsville, Ohio, to an insurance executive in Chicago, Illinois, and, finally, to his current role as Deputy Director of Homeland Security's bioterrorism unit in Washington, DC The changes had been rapid, but good ... at least up to now. He hoped he was ready for whatever he was about to face.

He buttoned his overcoat and walked to the car. He slid in the back seat, and one of the agents climbed in beside him. The other agent sat in the front passenger seat. Hank gave the driver directions and they drove away.

He sat back, soon recognizing the streets and buildings of downtown Columbia. He and Maddi had come there many times to visit Andrew and Amanda, but they hadn't made the trip in over a year. He rubbed his neck and looked away, reminded of how much things had changed.

The car pulled up in front of the small, single-story clinic building, and he got out. He threw his bag over his shoulder, and he and the agents walked inside to the front desk. He pulled out his badge. "Good morning, Ma'am. I'm Dr. Clarkson from Homeland Security; these are agents Smith and Rangel." He watched her smile fade.

"Just a moment, sir. The doctor is expecting you. I'll see if she's available."

Just then Amanda walked out of a treatment room. "Hank!" She ran to him and hugged him.

He hugged her back, letting his bag fall to the floor. "Amanda, it's good to see you!" He frowned as he noted the dark circles under her eyes. "Are you okay?"

She sighed. "Come with me, Hank. I have a lot to tell you."

He turned to the agents. "Rangel, you and Smith check on things next door."

The agent nodded, and he and his partner left the clinic.

Hank grabbed his bag and followed Amanda into her office. She closed the door and stared at him, her brown eyes almost black in the dimly lit room. "Andrew's at a conference in Charleston, we're barely speaking, I'm pregnant, and one of the patients died last night."

Hank found a chair. He had already heard about the death of the patient. The rest of it was a complete surprise. "My god, Amanda. Andrew should be here. I'm guessing he doesn't know about the clinic death." He paused. "Or the pregnancy?"

"No. He doesn't know any of it." She paused. "And I don't want him to. I'll wait until he gets back."

Hank frowned. "Are you two okay?"

Amanda hesitated. "I don't know. You know how they get sometimes."

She was referring to Maddi and Andrew, and Hank nodded. He did know; better than most.

Amanda turned her computer screen so he could see it. "I've been keeping track of the cases we've had so far." She cleared her throat. "In this column I've listed symptoms, next to it is treatment, and here are the outcomes."

"Wait a minute. Back to you. Are you feeling okay?"

"I'm fine, Hank ... really." She forced a smile. "But I can't say the same for these patients. Whatever this is ... it's bad."

She pointed to the last column. There had been five patients next door; now there are four, all worse despite the antiviral.

He shook his head. "It doesn't look good."

"I know. And there's more. About an hour ago, I saw a patient with the same symptoms ... who came here from Africa."

Hank raised his eyebrows.

Amanda nodded. "He swears he's not a drug user, and I saw no evidence to suggest that he was, but he presented just like the others." She paused. "I tried to get him to go next door, but he ... sort of ... escaped."

"Escaped?"

"Yeah, he had agreed to walk over with my receptionist, but he lied and told her I had released him." She looked down. "I have no idea where he went."

"He's got to be the source."

She nodded. "I knew you'd want to talk to him." She paused. "He's scheduled for next Thursday, but I'll be surprised if he comes back."

"He might. He's probably scared. It's what brought him here in the first place." He paused. "Did you give him a prescription for the ribavirin?"

She nodded.

"We can check with area pharmacies. I'll put Rangel on it when he gets back." He paused. "Let me see the charts."

Amanda grabbed the stack of charts and set them in front of him. She walked to the door. "I have a few more patients to see. I'll help you when I'm finished."

"Okay."

She left and Hank immediately dialed Maddi's cellphone.

She answered on the first ring. "Hey Hank, did you get down there okay?"

"Yes, but Maddi, things aren't good here. I'm worried about Amanda."

"What do you mean? Where's Andrew?"

"He's at a conference in Charleston. Not expected back until Friday."

"Why are you worried?"

Hank sighed. "Things don't sound good between them, and Amanda doesn't look well." He paused. "Maddi ... she's pregnant."

Silence. "Pregnant? Does Andrew know?"

"No ... not about the pregnancy or the sick patients."

"Has Amanda tried to reach him?"

"She says she wants to wait until he comes home."

"No ... he needs to be there, Hank. I'm going to call him."

"I'm pretty sure Amanda didn't want me to say anything."

"I'll be discreet."

Hank laughed. "Yeah, I'll bet." He paused. "I'll let you know if anything changes." He ended the call and pulled the stack of charts closer. He sifted through them, and then sat back and stared at the pile. There were charts for nine patients; each one was a known addict except Abid. Two of the isolation patients were in critical condition, and the three she had seen before the facility was in place were likely wandering the streets of Columbia ... *if they're not already dead.*

Hank dialed Hanover's private cell.

The director answered quickly. "What've ya got, Hank?"

"I think this is big, Hanover. I'm not sure it's bioterror, but it's deadly and it's spreading. We need a team down here right away."

He heard a sigh. "I guess I could pull a couple of guys from the subway bombing." There was a pause. "I'll issue an alert, and then I'll probably come down there myself."

"Great. The sooner the better."

Hank ended the call and leaned back in the chair. He crossed his arms as he looked back and forth between the computer screen and the stack of files. He reached for the last chart, Abid Mensah. He read it through. Symptoms, onset ... everything just like the others ... *except that he doesn't use drugs, and he came here from Africa.* He had listed his U.S. address as Washington, DC *So ... why is he in Columbia?* Was he the only one from out of town? Hank grabbed the other charts, looking for addresses. Some had listed a half-way house downtown, and a few had put other local addresses. Every one of them was local, except Abid. Which meant that Abid had somehow spread Lassa fever to drug addicts in Columbia. *The question is ... how?*

Chapter 15
MIAMI BEACH, FLORIDA

"**H**ave you ever wondered, Mart, when the first moment of a battle begins?" Henderson sighed as he looked out at the Atlantic Ocean. His good friend, Albins Platacis had asked that question their last day together. His words had foretold the battle that was to come ... a battle that was still underway.

Albins had died that day, and his death had changed everything. Not only was one of Henderson's dearest friends gone, but the man's daughter, Lili, had suddenly become Henderson's responsibility. Not that he wasn't up to it; he was. As a matter of fact, he had welcomed the idea of caring for the remarkable little girl. But it wasn't to be, for Albins' death was soon followed by his own.

He rubbed his eyes and pulled his stocking cap lower on his forehead. *Clearly ... the first moment of a battle begins with death.*

He tightened his scarf around his neck. Though it was warmer in Miami than it had been in Jacksonville, the winter breeze from the Atlantic still held a chill. But it wasn't the cool ocean air that was making him shiver. He was worried ... about Lili. And he missed her. Hearing her voice yesterday had only made it worse.

He knew he hadn't really heard her. Yes, Lili was a remarkable girl with extraordinary gifts, but he didn't believe for one second that she had mastered the art of telepathy. He had likely heard what he hoped was true ... that she was fine wherever she was. Nonetheless, his call to Rozenblats later that night had held a bit more hope. Unfortunately, like every other night since he had come back to the States, he had gotten the same report. *"I've not found her, sir, but I've got a promising lead."*

Henderson leaned against the shed across the street from his hotel, his long frame blending with the shadows. Through high-powered binoculars, he watched the sea pound the shoreline. It was late afternoon, and the sun was glistening on the water. Someday soon, three African boats were coming to America on that very same ocean. Or, maybe they had already arrived. He didn't know why and he didn't know where; all he knew was that they were part of Morningstar's plan ... which meant they needed to be stopped. He had heard nothing from the five men he had reached out to who had agreed to let him know if a suspicious boat came in from Africa.

He turned from the sea and angled the lens on a warehouse two blocks away. He might not be able to stop the boats, but at least he could disrupt the shipment of arms headed for Yemen. Maybe that would be enough ... a first strike in his war against Morningstar. A war that had started over three-and-a-half years ago in a remote hospital room in Novosibirsk, Russia ...

"Good morning, Henderson." Morningstar strode into the Siberian hospital room where Henderson had lain since being pulled from the blast. The short man with a limp lifted the blinds, letting in sunlight for the first time since Henderson had arrived. He covered his eyes and Morningstar grinned. "How are you today, son?" It had been hours since Henderson had had a dose of the painkiller, Dilaudid; he was craving it and he moaned. Morningstar ignored him as he put up a stand in the center of the room, doing his best to balance it on the uneven linoleum. He set a laptop on top and turned it on; it threw a white square onto the far wall. He went to the window and closed the blind, returning the room to darkness. He stood behind the laptop and cleared his throat. "You're about to see images you'll recognize, Henderson."

Henderson pulled himself up against the back of the bed, the effort draining him. A series of pictures flashed on the screen; dozens of images of him at work, at home, both in Boston and Latvia, as well as in DC The pictures were from his life before the explosion, and, as he stared at each one, his heart ached for the life he was leaving behind. He wondered why Morningstar had so many ... had he been surveilling him? If so, why? Henderson was about to ask, when another image filled the screen. It was his parents. They were holding glasses of champagne. Henderson tightened his jaw. He wanted to look away, but couldn't; he needed to see the photos ... all of them. They were like the drug ... comforting, yet offering their own sort of pain.

The next slide showed charred bodies lying among fallen pillars and broken chandeliers, decrying the once-beautiful ballroom of a notable DC hotel. He saw the broad-beamed column that had trapped him, and he turned away, grateful when Morningstar clicked to the next slide. It was a picture of Lili Platacis, and, again, Henderson tightened his jaw. Long blonde hair, blue eyes gleaming as she looked out at the sea. He frowned, curious how Morningstar knew about Lili.

Morningstar turned to face him, chuckling as he sang off-key, "She's the Lily of the Valley, the bright and Morning Star, the fairest of ten thousand to my soul." He turned back to the screen and said coldly, "I hope nothing happens to her."

The next slide showed two pictures at once. The first was Henderson with his parents at his Harvard graduation. The three of them shared the same smile, and Henderson flinched as he put a hand to his bandaged jaw. The second picture showed Lili with one of his best friends, Danil Latkovskis, whose back was turned as he looked over his shoulder outside his home in Ventspils, Latvia.

The screen went dark. Morningstar walked to a corner table and turned on a lamp. Henderson said nothing as he tried to piece together what he had just seen.

Morningstar pulled a vial from his pocket and rolled it between his fingers. He walked over and took a seat by the bed, his voice unnervingly calm as he said, "The funny thing about Dilaudid, son, is it makes you remember. It takes you to places in your mind you didn't know existed; things you had forgotten ... or maybe buried away." He crossed his legs and moved the vial to his other hand. Henderson needed the drug; he reached for it. Morningstar batted his hand away. "Not only do you remember, son, you talk; you say things you normally wouldn't say."

Henderson was starting to feel sick, and not only because of his need for the drug. He suddenly understood. Morningstar hadn't saved him; he had infiltrated him.

He buried his head in his hands. His very life depended on a man who was willing to drug him to get him to talk. And, clearly, he had done plenty of talking. He had put nearly everyone he loved at risk, all because of his need for a drug ... a drug that Morningstar was all too eager to give.

The more he thought about it, the madder he got. He threw off his covers and stretched his legs over the side of the bed, ready to choke the life out of Morningstar. He tried to stand, but fell to the floor, weakened by months of bed-ridden recovery.

Morningstar stood over him, laughing at the helpless man lying broken before him. "It didn't have to be this way. But, you were never going to appreciate the opportunity you've been given." He knelt beside him. "You're weak, Henderson. Because of it, you've put those you love in danger. Soon you'll recover, like a phoenix rising from the ashes. You'll be stronger, more skilled than ever before. You'll learn to steal, to lie ... to kill. You'll do whatever I ask. If at any time, you choose to defy me, the people on these slides will be at risk; especially that little girl." He moved closer. "One phone call and she's gone, Henderson ... taken from Ventspils and the devoted Danil. Then, who knows what will happen to her." His mouth was at Henderson's good ear. Henderson could feel his breath hot against his neck as he whispered, "How did the Bard put it? 'A lily that festers smells far worse than weeds.'"

Morningstar stood and threw the vial of Dilaudid to the floor, laughing as it broke into pieces. He walked out of the room, locking the door behind him.

Henderson lay amidst the shattered glass, his hospital gown halfway up his legs. His IV had been pulled with the force of the fall, and blood had begun to trickle, outlining a portion of his body like the chalk of a crime scene.

He drifted in and out of consciousness. When he awoke, he could see that the sun had shifted. Only a glimmer of daylight was visible through the blinds. He tried to get up but he couldn't. He replayed Morningstar's words. "You're weak, Henderson. Because of it, you've put those you love in danger." Henderson wanted to kill him for saying it, but he couldn't ... he didn't have the strength. Besides, he knew the words were true ...

There were pieces missing; parts of the slide show Henderson couldn't recall because of the Dilaudid. It didn't matter; he remembered enough. Morningstar had taken away his power ... *along with any dignity I might have had left.*

The one person who had been left out of the slide show was Maddi. Why? Had Morningstar been saving her to use later? He didn't think so; Morningstar would have gone after Maddi before he went after Lili. What was more likely was that Henderson had used her nickname; Morningstar had no idea who *Maddi* actually was.

Regardless, she had become a target. Had Morningstar finally figured it out? Henderson stiffened, repulsed to think that, along with Lili, he may have put Maddi in danger, as well.

He once again angled his lens to the shoreline. He was searching ... for what? Boats? Forgiveness? All he saw was the gray-blue ocean blending easily with the sky. He thought again about the man who had saved him, then enslaved him. Though he hated Morningstar for what he had done to him, the man had shown him an important truth: *Any man who suffers enough will lose his soul. Then, he's capable of anything.*

Henderson lowered the binoculars. The ocean mist bathed his skin as he took off his cap and ran his hand through his hair. He thought again of Albins' question. *"Have you ever wondered, Mart, when the first moment of a battle begins?"* He popped his collar and put on his cap, bristling as he turned and walked away. *The battle has begun.*

Chapter 16

WASHINGTON DC

Maddi sighed as she leaned back in her desk chair and ran her hands through her hair. She looked out the window, surprised to see that it was dark. She hadn't left her office since the call from Hank. Her concerns about the emails had been set aside at news that a strange virus was infecting patients in South Carolina ... *and Amanda is pregnant.*

She had tried calling Andrew's cellphone three times now; it had gone straight to voicemail. She had finally resorted to calling every major Charleston hotel chain, and had determined that he was staying at the downtown Marriott. A clerk had rung his room; he hadn't answered. That was about an hour ago. She pulled out her phone and dialed it again. They put her through, and this time a sleepy voice said, "Hello?"

"Andrew? Did I wake you? It's only eight o'clock."

He chuckled. "I had a little wine with dinner ... it hit me hard, I guess."

Maddi frowned. "Is everything okay?"

"Yeah, I'm fine."

"Why aren't you answering your cellphone?"

"I forgot my charger."

Maddi rolled her eyes. "Andrew, you need to go home."

"Why? Is something wrong?"

"No. Well ... yes. There's a virus infecting several of your clinic patients."

"Is Amanda sick?"

"No." Maddi paused. "But ... she's pregnant."

There was silence.

"Andrew?"

"Yeah."

"Are you okay?"

A pause. "I'm great."

"Really? You don't sound great."

There was a chuckle. "I'm great. And I'm on my way. I'll leave here as

soon as I call Amanda."

"Wait. Hank is there ... investigating the virus; he's the one who called me." She paused. "I don't think she meant for him to tell me, and I'm sure she wouldn't have wanted me to call you."

"So, what do you think I should do?"

"Leave in the morning. Tell her the conference ended early."

Another chuckle. "Okay. I probably shouldn't drive tonight anyway."

"Are you sure you're okay, Andrew?"

"Yeah." She heard a sigh. "The anniversary is in four days, you know."

Maddi closed her eyes. She did know; she had tried not to think about that day in January, thirty-two years ago, when her father was killed and her mother fell completely, mercilessly apart. "Leave the past in the past, Andrew."

"Like you do?"

They both laughed. "Point taken. Call me when you get home."

"Will do. Love ya', sis."

"Love you, too."

Maddi pushed the intercom. "Phil, could you come in here please."

He walked in and Maddi handed him a sheet of paper. "These are a few notes I made on Mr. Solvino's Eminent Domain case. Could you include them when you speak with the lawyers?"

"Certainly, Senator."

"And I'll need you to cancel my meetings through next week."

"Yes, Senator."

"Oh yes, and Phil?"

"Yes ma'am?"

"Go home!" He chuckled and left the room.

Maddi gathered up her papers and stuffed them in her briefcase. She pulled on her coat and tossed the red scarf Andrew had given her a few Christmases ago loosely around her neck. Her Secret Service agent, Larry, was waiting outside her door and the two of them walked to a waiting sedan. They climbed in and the car pulled away.

"Home Senator?"

"Yes, please."

They arrived at her house just as a light snow began to fall. She walked inside and hung her coat and scarf on a hook by the door. She skimmed through the mail. Nothing important. She tossed the letters on a table and walked into the bedroom. She heard the doorbell and listened as Larry said a few words to his relief agent, Jeremy Collins. She threw on sweats and a sweater and walked into the living room. Larry had left and Collins was standing by the door.

"Can I get you something, Jeremy?"

"No Ma'am. I'll go back to the study."

The study was a small room in the back of the house where Collins stayed each night when he took over for Larry. He would stretch out on her recliner, and eat cookies and drink tea. She followed him as he walked into the room. He sat in the chair, switched on a lamp, and pulled a Patterson novel from his briefcase.

Maddi took a blanket from the closet and handed it to him. "Are you hungry?"

He nodded. "A cup of tea and a few of those cookies of yours would be great, Senator."

Maddi grinned as she left the study and walked into the kitchen. She put on a kettle of water and waited for it to boil. She made two cups of tea, set one on a tray with cookies, and took it to Collins. She came back for her tea, which she carried into the living room and set on the coffee table. She went to a cabinet, pulled out a well-worn Rickie Lee Jones album, and placed it on a turntable. As the music filled the room, she walked over to a steamer trunk sitting against the wall. The trunk, given to her by the grandson of a wealthy banker who had taken it on safari in the early 1900's, had been a show of appreciation for her help on a matter years ago. It was made of rich leather with dulled seams, and had copper studs along the edges. She rubbed the leather and stared at the lid, hesitant to open it. She finally did, but had to force herself to look at the quilt on top. Her eyes filled with tears. Sewn from pieces of faded cloth, it was filled with thick batting, and, as she reached for it, she could feel her heart stop....

"Here, Maddi. Though Martin and I hadn't had a chance to talk about it, I know he cared for you." Dora Henderson cleared her throat. "I sensed from your comments at the Memorial, that you must have felt the same." Her eyes glistened as she handed Maddi the quilt. "Our housemaid, Nelly, made this for him. Several years of saving shirts from his childhood, the pieces sewn together with the love of a woman who had watched him grow." She fought tears. "But I'm sure you knew nothing of Nelly; you two hadn't had enough time to know any of the things you should have known about one another." She whispered, "There just wasn't enough time..."

Maddi hugged it to her chest and eased to the floor, her eyes burning. How many nights had she fought the urge to curl up in that quilt, comforted by nothing more than the woeful words of a song? And how many nights had she failed?

She wrapped it around her and walked to the couch. For the longest time, she could smell Henderson on the quilt, and had refused to wash it, thinking he would disappear. But finally, in a valiant effort to put it all behind her, she had forced herself to wash it and tuck it away inside the chest. That had been nearly two years ago; this was the first time she had taken it out.

She closed her eyes and pulled it tighter around her, imagining him ... his face, his smile, the touch of his hand on her cheek. She could almost hear him telling her where he had been ... what he had been doing for the past four years.

She sighed and looked out the window. The snow had completely consumed the night, and it brought tears to her eyes. *Are you alive, Martin Henderson?*

Chapter 17
MAIMI BEACH, FLORIDA

Henderson checked his watch. *Ten-forty-five*. The night was pitch-black as he looked through the scratched glass of an abandoned church, focusing on the warehouse across the street. It was raining, making it even harder to see what was happening inside. He would need to wait for the rain to slow, but he was in no hurry. Tonight, he would take care of this one small detail, and then he would leave Miami.

He sat in a chair watching the rain, his eyes focused on the warehouse, as his mind wandered to the moment when he had known he couldn't do it anymore; when he had known he had to leave Morningstar – and the killing – behind. Six weeks ago, in New York City ... the night had been wet and cold. *Much like tonight*. He had taken the same steps he had taken so many times before to prepare for the murder of the Yemen leader, Al-Gharsi. What he hadn't expected was that Maddi would be sitting right next to the man. Each second of that seven-minute assassination played in his mind like a recording, running from beginning to end and then repeating. One minute, Maddi had been laughing with Al-Gharsi; the next she had looked on as her friend's bloodied forehead fell onto the table. Her horrified expression was carved in his mind far deeper than any of his scars. He could still see the white tablecloth ... still smell the mix of garlic and fine wine. And he could still feel the heat from Maddi's presence; the closeness of being only a few feet away from the woman he had not stopped loving since he met her in Providence nearly four years ago. It had taken only seven minutes for everything to change ... to finally see what he had become.

He straightened as he saw a light come on in the warehouse across the street. He stared through the binoculars. The rain had slowed and he watched as two men organized the cargo: rifles, grenade launchers, ammunition ... all of it headed for Yemen. He had once been on the other end, just like those two men, arranging to move weapons overseas.

Were they sons of Jacob? Or were they merely drifters, hired solely for this mission? He looked closer. They were dirty ... and poorly dressed. He frowned. They weren't sons of Jacob; they had no idea what they doing ... who they were about to hurt ... or kill. *I will spare them.*

They finished tying up the last box for delivery, and then stepped outside for a smoke. Henderson reached for his AK-47 and attached a grenade launcher. He opened the window, aimed at the shipment, and fired. The grenade pierced the window of the warehouse, landed in the cache of weapons, and exploded in a deafening fireball. It quickly consumed the rifles, along with much of the warehouse. The men bolted away, looking over their shoulders, their wild eyes revealing their shock. Henderson rubbed his neck as he watched them, thankful they hadn't been touched by the flames. *No one should have to go through that.*

He broke down his weapon and removed the grenade launcher, sliding both items into a canister. He put the canister in his backpack, along with his binoculars. He spotted a scrap of paper at the bottom of the pack; a letterhead from a piece of Maddi's stationary. He had taken it from her trash soon after he had begun killing for Morningstar ... a way to remember who he had been ... and who it was that kept him alive. He took it out and rubbed it tenderly.

Another explosion shook the church he was standing in, and he shoved the scrap of paper into his pack. He tossed the bag over his shoulder, stole out the door and down an old staircase, leaving through a side door. As he walked to the street, he looked over his shoulder at the warehouse. Flames were everywhere. He shook his head and kept walking. *Always, I leave by fire.*

Chapter 18

WASHINGTON, DC

Wednesday, January 14th, 2004

Long before the sun rose, while the streets of DC were still fast asleep, Morningstar got out of bed and walked to his desk in the living room. He sat in his swivel chair, the one that made him feel like Star Trek's Captain Kirk, and he turned on his computer. He went to the Pentagon website and scanned the posts, looking for Josh's handiwork.

INTERNAL MEMO: CLASSIFIED. There is strong evidence to suggest that a CIA agent, known only as the Phoenix, may have gone rogue. The Pentagon is trying to corroborate. We will keep relevant agencies informed. Required action: NONE AT THIS TIME.

He chuckled. *Perfect.* Though the report had been issued through the Pentagon, Josh had made sure it couldn't be traced to a particular department.

He cracked his knuckles and stared at the screen. *And now for the next item.* He typed a few sentences, read it through, and grinned. *That ought to do it.*

"A West African militant group has claimed responsibility for a series of deaths from a biologic agent. Though there is no confirmation, the Pentagon is advising it be taken seriously. Homeland Security will be made aware."

He issued the report through a series of cyber pathways within the Pentagon, hiding the source. So many threats were issued each and every day ... *why not make one of them actually turn out to be true?*

The Lassa fever operation was just one of many plans Morningstar was about to launch. He had sons everywhere ... preparing to overthrow leaders in nearly every corner of the globe. But it wasn't random ... there was order to it; a symmetry that would allow for each event to build on the one before it, resulting in a cascade of calamity that would eventually topple the world. The next task couldn't take place until the one before it had been completed. The terror attack couldn't happen until the Middle East was in chaos ... which, thanks to Henderson, was well underway.

He turned off his computer and clicked on a lamp. As shadows filled the room, he found a half-smoked cigar in an ashtray on the desk and lit it. He puffed several times, breathed in, then exhaled a perfect ring of smoke. He spun his chair and looked out the window at the darkness. *I am brilliant.* Not only had he come up with a way to force Henderson to come home, but he was about to simulate a terror attack on a group of disenfranchised Americans.

He laughed as he recalled telling Simeon of the plan. The man had been skeptical. *"Why would we kill a bunch of druggies, Father? They're insignificant."*

"Only to you, Simeon."

"But what is the purpose?"

"To start a war."

Simeon had frowned. *"With Africa?"*

"With everyone."

Simeon had then asked how the virus would be delivered. *"It's not like it's in an envelope we can mail."*

That had been the stroke of genius that Morningstar had put into place years ago. He had learned of the tragic Abid, who had lost his family and left his home with little more than the clothes on his back. Morningstar had flown to Guinea-Bissau in West Africa, and – a mere ten thousand dollars later – had gotten Abid Mensa to join the team. *"A meek, unsuspecting fisherman will bring the virus to America, my son."*

A few weeks ago, Morningstar had had his girlfriend, Edi order three vials of Lassa fever virus from a Saudi lab. *"Nothing special, babe ... just your run-of-the-mill killer virus."* She had balked, but had given in when he told her it was for a secret research project being conducted by the Pentagon. *"You'll be helping me make this country – and our entire world – a safer place, babe."*

A few days later, Morningstar had sent Simeon to Saudi Arabia to pick up the vials, and then on to Africa. With the help of a Libyan lab technician, he had changed the virus to a powder, and had mixed it with batches of cocaine. He had then hidden the cocaine in stacks of shirts. Using the same offer of cash, he had recruited two more boats with a crew of two each from the ports of Dakar and Conakry, not far from Guinea-Bissau. Like Abid, the captains had been told they were taking clothes to sell in America. They had been instructed to sail to either Rockland, Maine, Charleston, South Carolina, or Ft. Lauderdale; which meant – within days – the entire Eastern Seaboard would report outbreaks of Lassa fever. This would create a panic, which would be followed by action against the West African militants, similar to Iraq and Afghanistan after 9-11. *"As I said, Simeon, we need to start a war."*

Morningstar stood and walked to the window. The sun was beginning to rise, though it was hard to see through an endless parade of thick, dark clouds. He sighed. He hated DC, especially in the winter. *Why couldn't we have put the U.S. capital somewhere like the Florida Keys?*

Abid had landed in Charleston days ago. The other two boats should have docked at about the same time. Morningstar was getting antsy. It would take all three to create a panic weighty enough to get the U.S. to strike back at Africa.

He turned from the window and was about to walk to the bathroom, when his phone vibrated. He checked the caller ID. The call was from China. "Yes?"

"We have problem." There was a pause. "This little girl ... she not ordinary."

"What do you mean ... not ordinary?"

"She very bright—"

"We knew that, asshole. It's one of the reasons we took her."

"Yes, but ... she knows things."

"She knows things? Like what?"

There was a whisper. "Things she should not know."

Morningstar frowned. "What are you talking about, Chu?"

"She ... knows ... about you ... about who you are, what you do."

Morningstar shook his head. "She's nine years old, for Christ's sake!"

"Yes sir. But she knows ... I swear."

Morningstar sighed. It was ridiculous. He was aware of Lili's eidetic memory; Henderson had shared it while under the influence of the Dilaudid. And the man had alluded to the fact that Lili could see things that were happening miles away. But to know the truth about someone she had never met or heard of? *Ha! It's bullshit.* But, she had clearly said or done something that had gotten his Chinese friend up in arms. "Why do you think this, Chu?"

"We listen ... when she go through lessons with her teacher."

"What did she say?"

"She tell teacher that morning star is not what it seems. She say 'It lights the sky as it darkens the world.'"

Morningstar narrowed his eyes. "What did the teacher say?"

"She just chuckle."

Morningstar paced the room. "There's nothing revealing about that, Chu. Call me if she says anything more."

He ended the call, pondering the girl's words. *"The morning star ... lights the sky as it darkens the world."* Suddenly he laughed. "I couldn't have said it better myself."

Chapter 19

COLUMBIA, SOUTH CAROLINA

"This is Marlene Reynolds for TV 5. I've just arrived outside the bus station here in Columbia, where early this morning two drug addicts were found dead behind this building. Several Homeland Security agents are here, which makes the deaths even more alarming. We'll keep you updated as information becomes available."

"Crap." The Director of Homeland Security, Jason Hanover opened three bags of sugar and poured them in his coffee. He had arrived the night before and Hank had brought him up to speed. Another drug user had died; four more had been diagnosed and taken to the quarantine facility next to the clinic. "This might complicate things."

Hank nodded. "I'd hate to see a panic before we even know what we're dealing with." He had been awakened at five a.m. by a call about the addicts found behind the bus station. He had called Hanover and they had gotten to the site before the sun came up. They had stayed about two hours, overseeing setup of a makeshift forensics lab and talking to a few of the locals. Hank had spoken with the coroner, who had agreed to call him the minute she had information on cause of death.

They had left the site, keeping two agents there to process the scene with local investigators. They had then driven to a diner, which was where they were now finishing eggs and toast, along with several cups of strong black coffee.

Hanover's phone rang. "Yeah," he said, through a mouthful of food. He nodded, but said nothing, ending the call with a gruff, "Got it. Keep me informed."

"Who was it?"

He stirred his coffee. "The Pentagon. They're saying that a West African militant group has claimed responsibility."

Hank stopped halfway through a sip of coffee. "For what? Killing a couple of drug addicts with a virus?"

Hanover shrugged his shoulders. "I guess so."

"Is it credible?"

"Seems to be. They're looking into it."

Hank shook his head. "That would change things."

Hanover nodded. "Yes, it would."

Hank finished his coffee and set the empty cup on the table. "It doesn't make sense, Hanover. If it's terrorism, why aren't there more dead bodies?"

Hanover sighed. "I don't know." He leaned back, his large frame straining the chair. "Maybe it didn't go the way they planned. That would be good news. We've got plenty to do, without chasing down some half-assed bioterrorism plot."

He reached for the check, threw a twenty on the table, and the two men stood and left the diner. It was spitting rain as they climbed into Hanover's rental car. They drove back to the bus station and parked the car, saying nothing as they jogged to the terminal in the pouring rain. Hanover stopped just inside the door to talk with one of the clerks, while Hank went to the lobby, looking for the familiar coats of the Homeland agents. He spotted an agent standing off to the side. "Hey, Tom."

Tom was a small man in his early thirties. He looked up from his notebook and smiled. "Hey, Dr. Clarkson."

"Anything new?"

"No sir. We've been looking for anybody who might have known one of the victims, but no one's willing to talk."

Hank nodded. "They're scared. Even for drug users, these deaths are weird."

"Yeah, I guess so. Speaking of weird, I found something a few minutes ago I think you'll want to see."

Hank followed Tom down a hallway and out the back door. The rain had slowed, but hadn't stopped, and they sprinted to the temporary work station. A blue tarp had been pulled over a table, and a heater had been set up so the men could work without freezing to death. Tom grabbed a bag from the table and opened it, pulling out a white button-down shirt. "See this?"

"Yeah."

"I found it in a garbage can out back. I've never seen anything like it."

"What do you mean?"

Tom held up the shirt and lifted one of the arms, revealing a tear from shoulder to cuff. He teased apart two layers of material. "Look closer."

Hank leaned in, and then pulled on gloves and wiped the inside of the sleeve. A white powder covered the fingers of the glove. "Cocaine?"

Tom nodded. "We're still waiting for the spectrometry report, but yeah, I think so. Pretty clever, huh?"

Hank frowned. "Yeah." He pulled off the gloves and threw them in a biohazard container. "I'll be right back, Tom."

He went to the front of the terminal and found Hanover finishing up with one of the clerks. Hank pulled him aside. "I think we've got a lead. Tom found a shirt with a double layer of material inside the sleeve. Guess what's between the layers."

Hanover frowned. "What?"

"Cocaine. I think the shirts might be the connection. Amanda's patient from Africa told her he came to the U.S. to sell clothes. What if he smuggled in the cocaine using the shirts, and somehow the cocaine made them all sick."

Hanover narrowed his eyes. "That doesn't explain how Abid got sick ... he claims he didn't use the drugs."

"Maybe he's lying. Or, more likely, he was sick before he left Africa."

Hanover nodded. "So maybe he spread it to the druggies?"

Hank frowned. "I don't see how. Lassa fever is spread by close human contact ... a typical drug deal doesn't provide that."

"So, we're back with the shirts."

Hank sighed. "I guess. But the virus can't survive without a host."

"What are you saying?"

Hank shook his head. "If the virus was spread using the cocaine, it would've needed to have been altered."

"Is that easy to do?"

"No."

Hanover frowned. "So ... we have a drug dealer who's sick with the virus, but didn't spread it, and shirts full of cocaine and an altered virus. Have I got it right?"

Hank looked at him and sighed. "Yep."

"Then we'll need to know more about the cocaine. We also need to know more about the militant group that might be behind this." He paused. "I'll put an agent on the militant group. You and Tom need to work with the coroner and the forensics lab."

Hank nodded. "Will do."

Hanover added, "We need to see if we can tie the African group to the man selling the shirts. What did you say his name was?"

"Abid ... Abid Mensah."

Hanover nodded. "We have to find him. I'll let the agents know that he's our top priority." He started walking toward the door. "We need to get back to DC, Hank. I've got a plane waiting. Get Tom squared away. I'll meet you at the car."

Hank nodded, and walked to the back of the terminal. It was still raining, so he pulled up his hood as he ran to the make-shift lab. He gave Tom his orders, and then jogged to the car, dialing Amanda on the way.

"Hey Hank." Her voice sounded tired.

"Is everything okay, Amanda?"

"No. Another patient just died, and I've had three new cases this morning."

"All of them drug users?"

"Yep. The ribavirin isn't working. It's kept my staff from getting sick, and it seems to slow progression of the disease, but those who do get sick ... they die."

Hank could hear her despair. "Are you taking good care of yourself?"

"Yeah, I'm doing better since Andrew's here."

"When did he get back?"

"This morning. About an hour ago."

"Are things okay with you guys?"

"Yes ... he took the news better than I thought he would."

Hank grinned. "Good. You need to make sure you get plenty of rest."

"Sure Hank. Anything new in the investigation?"

"That's why I called. Two things. A West African militant group is claiming responsibility." He paused. "And, I think we may have figured out the connection between Abid and the addicts. We found a shirt with cocaine hidden in the sleeve."

There was a pause. "Abid said he brought clothes to sell."

"Exactly. But what we don't know is how the virus was spread, or if Abid is working for the militant group. I need to talk to him. My men haven't had any luck finding him. Didn't you say he had a follow-up appointment?"

"Yes," Hank could hear her rummaging through charts, "... next Thursday afternoon ... at 1:30."

"Okay, if my men don't find him, let's hope he keeps his appointment."

He heard a sigh. "If he's even still alive."

Chapter 20

MIAMI BEACH, FLORIDA

The noonday sun cast shadows on the bleak wallpaper and the ragged bedspread as Henderson checked the Miami hotel room one last time. He tossed his backpack over his shoulder and walked out. As he went downstairs, he reached in his pocket for a ticket he had gotten that morning. It had a four-digit number printed on the front; on the back, he had scribbled a phone number. He pulled out his cellphone and dialed. A woman's voice answered, her Vietnamese accent unmistakable.

"Harry's Pawn Shop. How I help you?"

"Tuyen, you must listen carefully to what I'm about to tell you."

"Who is this?"

"A friend. Leave your shop immediately. You're in danger if you stay."

He waited. She said nothing. He went on. "Before you go, I want you to grab—" he looked at the ticket "—item #B417. When you and your husband are safely away, I want you to look inside. Will you do it?"

There was a pause. "Why?"

"Please, you have to trust me."

Another pause. "I talk to my husband."

Henderson hung up, praying she would do what he asked.

It was time to go. Someone was watching him; he had sensed it that morning when he went for a jog. Though he hadn't seen the man's face, he guessed he was one of

Morningstar's goons. *Who else would make such an effort to find me?*

He left the hotel and walked down a back alley. He tucked his head under his hood as he neared the pawnshop. He picked up his pace. He had planned the next three minutes precisely; there could be no mistakes.

He looked across the street, relieved to see the Vietnamese woman and her husband running to the alley; she was carrying a duffel bag over her shoulder. He took his gloved fist, broke through a window of the shop, and tossed in an explosive. Within seconds it detonated, spewing flames in every direction. The small store was quickly consumed by fire. He cringed. He had talked to the shop owner and his wife only yesterday; this store was not only their livelihood, but their life. They had come from Vietnam in the seventies and, starting with nothing, had worked hard and done well. They were good people. But he needed a diversion; something big enough to let him get away without being followed. *Collateral damage,* he thought sadly.

It was noon and shoppers filled the nearby stores. At the sound of the blast, they ran into the square. Police arrived, sirens blaring, lights flashing. Henderson ducked behind the pawnshop, flinching as he felt the heat from the fire and saw the bright orange flames from the corner of his eye. *Just keep moving.* He slipped into a diner. It was empty; the patrons were outside in the square. He walked through the kitchen and out the back door, his head hidden beneath the hood of his jacket.

He crossed the street to an auto garage. Cars were sitting on the lot, and he walked up to a black 1996 Honda. He had seen it dropped off the night before, and had overheard the driver tell a mechanic that it needed an oil change and a tune-up. *A perfect get-away car.* He couldn't take the pickup truck; it would die before he made it out of Florida. Besides, whoever was following him had likely seen it.

He opened the driver-side door, slid into the seat, and grabbed wires beneath the steering column. He connected them and the engine came to life. He pulled away, careful to hide his face with his hand. A mechanic looked up from an old Volvo.

"Hey, that car hasn't been looked at!"

Henderson ignored him and left the lot. He turned onto 10th Avenue and drove down several back streets, eventually reaching the highway. He checked the rearview mirror; no one was following him. He merged onto the highway and traveled north. It was quiet in the car, but the blast from the pawnshop reverberated in his head, and he covered his good ear to try to block the sound. He was thankful the owners had gotten out before it went up in flames. He hoped they would survive the loss. He started to say a prayer, but then stopped mid-sentence. *God doesn't listen to people like me.*

~ ~ ~

"He just said to go! Come on!"

Tuyen had believed the man. She wasn't sure why, only that she had sensed genuine concern. And he knew her name. She had run to the back of the shop and had found the item marked B417. It was hidden behind several other pieces, nearly invisible to anyone who might have been strolling through the store. A blue and white vase about a foot high. Tuyen remembered it; she had thought it beautiful when the man had brought it in a few days ago. And she remembered the man. He had spoken softly, his voice like gravel, and had worn his cap low on his forehead, but not low enough to hide the scars on one side of his face. She purposely hadn't stared.

She had tucked the vase between layers of clothing that she and her husband had thrown hastily into a bag. It reminded her of how they had left Vietnam; quickly, in a panic. They had nearly reached the alley behind the store, when she had suddenly been propelled backward by the force of an explosion. She had failed to notice a man in a hooded sweatshirt jogging to the nearby diner.

She now stared in horror as their pawn shop burned to the ground. Tears covered her carved cheeks as she tried to imagine what they would do; the shop was all they had. She pulled the vase from her bag. *Why would I want this silly pot when I've lost everything?* She spun it around and, in spite of her sorrow, was impressed by beautifully-etched dragons and brilliantly-painted birds. She looked inside. There was an envelope. She reached in and grabbed it. It was blank, front and back. She opened it and took out a note card. A cashier's check fell to the ground; she picked it up. Her jaw dropped. It was made out to her and her husband in the amount of two hundred and fifty thousand dollars. She clutched her husband's arm and showed him the check. He looked at her, puzzled. She read the note, shaking as the words became real, finally having to lean against a rusted trash can to keep from falling.

This vase is from the sixteenth century and was believed to have been a part of the Le Dynasty. It is treasured by the Vietnamese people, and was thought to have been lost forever during the Vietnam War. It was found recently during an archaeological dig. I was able to pick it up while on a recent trip overseas. It is worth a considerable amount of money, along with its significant historic value. Forgive me for the damage to the pawn shop. Please allow the check and the vase to make up for it.

Sincerely, a friend.

Chapter 21

COLUMBIA, SOUTH CAROLINA

Abid shivered as he pulled his coat tighter around him. The rain was coming harder, and he had nothing but the coat to keep him dry. He had left the shelter. He couldn't stay there; he was too sick. Soon the attendants would notice and would send him to the hospital. He couldn't go to a hospital ... they might figure out what was in the shirts he was selling. He hadn't known it at the time; he hadn't known he was bringing narcotics to America. *Why did I let that man talk me into it?* He knew why: Thirty thousand dollars ... in cash.

He had been lying on a park bench since dawn. Though it had nothing more than a slatted overhang, it was hidden by trees, and sat across the street from a pharmacy. He reached under his coat and patted the prescription in his pocket. He had yet to fill it. He had walked up to the door of the pharmacy three times now, but each time had stopped himself, knowing that the pharmacist might turn him in.

He grabbed the arm of the bench and forced himself up. *I will only get sicker if I don't get out of this rain.* His head was spinning and he closed his eyes to make it stop. He had eaten only a little, but had managed to keep down Gatorade. He fought the urge to vomit as the dizziness nearly overpowered him. It eased and he was able to open his eyes. Droplets of rain brushed down his cheeks and into his beard. The air was cold and he shivered even more. He needed to do something or he would die.

Again, he patted the prescription. *Just get the medicine, Abid.* He stood, using the back of the bench to keep from falling. He took a few steps, keeping his eyes on the pharmacy. He crossed the street and was about to walk up to the door, when he saw two policemen go in ahead of him. *I can't go in now! What if they are looking for me?* He turned and walked the other way, stumbling down the street in search of a YMCA. He would go there and rest; at least it would be dry. *I will go to pharmacy later ... when it is safe.*

Chapter 22

WASHINGTON, DC

Morningstar paced the hotel room, furious as he shouted into the phone. "What do you mean the other ships are lost?"

"I think the one heading to Maine was caught up in a storm, Father."

"The losers can't even navigate an old-fashioned Nor'easter?"

"I guess not. Neither one of the boats has been heard from since Monday. The ship heading to Lauderdale must have been taken by pirates or something. There's no sign of it."

"That's just swell, Simeon."

"Um, there's more, Father."

Morningstar gritted his teeth. "What!"

"The arms shipment intended for Yemen was destroyed last night ... blown to bits."

"By who?"

There was a pause. "I don't know, but I have my suspicions."

"Who do you think it was?"

"Phoenix."

Morningstar was seething. "Why do you think it was him?"

"You told me to find him, so I decided to use NSA software to monitor police scanners along the coasts of Florida and Georgia, guessing that Phoenix couldn't have gotten far." There was a pause. "Anyway, the explosion of the shipment in Miami came across the scanner, so I focused my attention there, hoping to get a lead on the bastard who did it. A police dispatcher said that a bystander had seen a man walking away from the scene carrying a backpack. He described the guy as over six feet tall, and wearing a hoody," another pause, "...and he thought he saw scars on his face."

Morningstar cracked his knuckles as he paced the floor. "What did you do?"

"I was in Jekyll Island at the time, so I rented a car and drove to the site."

"And?"

"I got there early this morning. I spotted Phoenix jogging and followed him back to an old hotel on West Third Street."

"So, have you got him?"

"Here's the thing," he paused, "...he ... sort of ... escaped."

Morningstar closed his eyes. He was doing his best to maintain control. He said evenly, "Where did he go, Simeon?"

Another pause. "I ... I don't know, sir."

"You don't know?"

"No, Father. He created a ... diversion. I lost him. Don't worry; I'll find him."

"Forget it. Just get your ass to Providence. I'm pretty sure he'll be there by Monday."

Another pause. "Providence ... as in Rhode Island?"

"Yes. I think he might be meeting someone ... someone you know."

"Who?"

"Senator Bitch."

Morningstar heard a laugh. "Thank god! I'll nab them both. Two for one."

"Simeon, you're not the point man on this. You need to contact Levi once you get there. He'll tell you what to do."

"But sir, I—"

Morningstar ended the call. He was losing patience with Simeon. *How many tasks can you screw up before I kill your skinny ass?*

He sighed and stared out the window. He had gotten home from work an hour ago, and was on his second Manhattan. But, with the news he had just gotten, he should probably move on to Scotch. He heard a groan in the next room. Edi had arrived about ten minutes ago, and had immediately strutted to the bedroom. He was tempted to go in and rough her up a bit; it often helped when he was frustrated. His warped little Edi would probably like it. He would give it another few minutes. What was it Ike and Tina Turner used to say? *"Make 'em wait."*

He looked out at the DC skyline. The sun had begun to set; he watched as his town was slowly cloaked in gray. All at once, he pounded the sill with his fist. "Dammit!" Two of the three ships had vanished, the shipment to Yemen had been blown to bits, and Henderson had gotten away ... again. Not only that; the little girl, Lili, had made references to a morning star. His contact in China, Lin Chu, was getting nervous. Too many things were going wrong. *I have to do something!*

He opened his phone and dialed the number to his Chinese contact.

"Yes?"

"It's me. I'm moving up the timeline. Do what we talked about ... now."

There was a pause. "It will take couple days to get things ready."

"Then get busy, dammit!" He paused. "And send me proof."

He ended the call. *That oughta' get things going in the right direction ... at least in one part of the world.*

He pulled a cigar from a pocket of his smoking jacket and rolled it between his fingers. The leathery casing seemed to calm him. He lit it and breathed in the cherry scent, sneering as he looked out at the dusky night. Edi had recently scolded him for lighting up in the hotel room; he didn't care. *I smoke where I want.*

He walked to the bar, grabbed a bottle of Scotch, and filled a glass half full. He drank it, poured another, and carried it to the window. Things weren't all that bad. One of the ships had made it, the Middle East was still in chaos, and Henderson would soon be in Providence, where Levi and Simeon would create such a mess for him that he would have no choice but to come in. Morningstar forced a grin as he raised his glass and said, "Here's to you, Henderson." He was about to chug the Scotch when his phone vibrated. He checked caller ID. "Yes, Josh."

"Hello, sir. You asked me to keep you updated on the response to the Lassa fever outbreak in South Carolina." He paused. "Homeland is apparently buying the West African claim; the threat level has been raised."

Morningstar grinned. "Excellent. Let me know if you hear anything more."

"I will, sir."

Morningstar looked out the window and chuckled. It had begun. In spite of the loss of two of the boats, step one of his master plan had begun. Would it be enough? Would the deaths of a bunch of junkies in South Carolina be enough to compel the U.S. to wage a war against West Africa? He hoped so. *If not, I'll have to figure out a way to do it myself.*

He gulped down the Scotch and threw the glass against the wall, ignoring the thud as it landed on the carpet unbroken. "Are you ready, World? Are you ready for what I'm about to do to you?"

He heard another groan from the next room and grinned. *Perfect timing.* As he turned and walked toward the bedroom, he yelled, "Are you ready, Edi? Are you ready for what I'm about to do to you?"

Chapter 23

MACON, GEORGIA

The rain felt good, as if it was washing off the scars both inside and out of his tired, broken body. Henderson stood there letting it soak him as he watched the car tumble down the embankment. The sound of crushed metal and breaking glass blended with the rush of the rain. It wouldn't take long for whoever was hunting him to identify the car he had used to leave Miami. From here, he would either hitch a ride or walk, never along main routes; only through small towns and back roads.

It was nearly ten p.m.; the darkness was complete. He liked it … he felt at ease in the dark with the rain on his face. As he walked away, he began to feel a sense of freedom. It was a feeling he had known before, and, like before, he knew it wouldn't last. Because he wasn't free. He would never be free. Like the scars on his face and hands, he knew … he would never be able to leave behind the assassin he had been for the past three years, let alone the man who had made him that way…

"First, you must learn to kill without thinking." Morningstar spoke the words calmly, as if he was talking to a group of kids at summer camp. "You should look at your target the way you once looked at the Russian separatists you killed as a young man. They are a threat and must be removed."

Henderson's injuries had healed, but the internal wounds showed no sign of going away. Morningstar had given him back his life, but had stolen away everything important to him

... his dignity, his self-worth, and his desire to live. He had forced him to hone valuable skills to do terrible things. And Henderson had had no choice: Morningstar had threatened Lili. With a simple phone call, he would have her taken, and Henderson knew; Morningstar wouldn't hesitate to murder a little girl.

So, if he was to be a killer, he would become the best there was. Everything had been taken from him; what did it matter? He had been left for dead by everyone he had ever loved, and Morningstar reminded him of it whenever he got a chance.

"They've forgotten you, Phoenix ... it's time you do the same."

Henderson had barely spoken to another human being since arriving at the outpost in Novosibirsk, Russia. Morningstar had become his whole world. The man had changed his bandages and had taken nearly every meal with him ... and now he was spending each and every day training him for what was to come.

"And, when you choke a man, remember my son, to do it quickly, without remorse. That man is your enemy. Everyone is your enemy..."

After a mile, the rain eased, and a sliver of moonlight found its way through the clouds. Henderson was nearly to Macon, Georgia, but he didn't head into town. He turned instead down a bypass road which took him to a small farmhouse outside the city limits. He was going to one of his safe houses; a place where he could spend days at a time without anyone knowing he was there. The houses were in different parts of the country, and the absent owners knew nothing about him. He snuck in and snuck out; they never even knew he had been there.

He had found the hideouts during his years with Morningstar. He had used them to escape; not only the authorities, but Morningstar. He would read and sleep; he would recover. But he couldn't stay long; a few days at the most. Morningstar would have Simeon hunt him down if he wasn't in DC by the allotted time.

He moved cautiously toward the house. As expected, there were no lights on inside. The family travelled during the month of January; they had done so for at least the last three years. Still, he had to be careful. It was possible they had changed their plans, or that someone was staying there while they were away.

As he neared the front door, he saw the glow of a porch light. It had likely been timed to come on at dusk to imply that someone was home. He crept around the entire house, hiding in bushes as he looked in each window and made sure every room was empty. When he was satisfied, he sprinted to a clump of trees about thirty feet away. Using predetermined landmarks, he counted twenty paces, and then began to dig. Within minutes, he uncovered a bag he had hidden months ago. He replaced the dirt, and, with the bag under his arm and his backpack on his shoulder, he ran to the house. He took off his coat and shoes and left them by an outside cellar door. He broke the door's padlock and crept down the steps in stocking feet. He stood silent for well over a minute, listening for footsteps. When he was satisfied no one was upstairs, he turned on an overhead light. There were no windows in the cellar; no one would see it if they drove by.

He opened the bag and spread out the contents: satellite access, scanning gear, packs of dry food, bottles of water. He grabbed a granola bar and a water and opened his pack. He pulled out his laptop and linked to the satellite. He now had access to the government's entire telecommunications network, which could scan everything from phone calls and texts to email exchanges. He was focused on one man: Morningstar.

He went to sites they had used in the past, looking for information. Who was the man after? What was he planning? *And who the hell tracked me to Miami Beach?*

He skimmed every site, looking for veiled comments or outright threats; he found nothing. After an hour, he changed his focus. Was Morningstar still targeting Maddi? If so, why? And where had he taken Lili? Was he hurting her?

He found nothing, but he knew, sooner or later, Morningstar would reach out to him. *He can't stand not to.*

He clicked to Maddi's Senate webpage, flinching when he saw her picture on the screen. He wondered if she had responded to his latest email. He scanned the page, and then read every entry ... no new posts. He clicked to the website of the same Providence newspaper that had run the article the day before. Nothing. He went to a courthouse website to see if there had been any further legal action concerning *'The City of Providence v. Rocky's Restaurant.'* Nothing there, either.

He sighed. *Talk to me, Maddi.* He went to Marker Health's website – *his website* – on the off chance that Maddi might have contacted the CEO to arrange a meeting; anything to suggest she was following up on his email. He struggled as he stared at the site; it was his past, a company he had loved and had worked hard to create, and his imprint was everywhere. Marker Health remained the number one health insurance company in the United States. *It's still standing ... but I'm not.*

He found nothing, so he left the site and went to a City of Providence webpage. He clicked a link to area hotels. He scrolled through the list, stopping when he came to the Westin; the same hotel where he had booked a room for Maddi nearly four years ago. He stared at the screen. He should do it again; he should book her a room and invite her to Providence. Would it be too obvious? He frowned. Maybe he wanted it to be. *Maybe I'm tired of hiding.*

With a few quick clicks, he hacked into the hotel's website, and then into reservations. He was about to book a room for some time next month, when he stopped. The name Larry Moses was listed among the reservations. *Maddi's Secret Service agent!* The reservation was for Monday, January 19th, in the same suite she had stayed in four years ago. Coincidence? Maddi's agent simply taking a trip to the magical city of Providence? *And staying in the penthouse suite?* He stared at the reservation and began to shake. *Maddi is going to*

Providence ... in five days! Should he meet her there? *Of course, I should!*

He stood and paced the cellar; there was a lot to do. He had to book a room; not in the same hotel, but somewhere close, where he could keep an eye on her. He had to figure out how to get there without being followed. He needed to come up with an excuse to see her. *I'll take her to dinner.* He could call his old friend Marco to reserve a table. He would need a new suit ... and a place to take her afterward.

Suddenly he stopped. He put a hand to his cheek. He felt the jagged scars and the battered jaw. *I can't let her see me ... not like this.* He stood there, rubbing the scars that he knew would repulse her. *I'll wear a disguise; just like with the Al-Gharsi hit ... a beard and a pair of glasses.* He nodded. Maybe, if the room was dark enough and the wine strong enough, he could find a way to hide. *Even if it's only for the moment before she realizes what I've become.*

He frowned. Though he knew it was necessary, he hated to wear a disguise with Maddi. She was the one person who should always see him honestly ... how he really was. But he would have to ... at least at first. *If for no other reason than to spare her the horror.*

He knelt down, shut off his computer, and slid it in his backpack. He folded the satellite equipment and returned it to the bag. He turned off the overhead light, sat on the floor, and leaned against the wall. He sighed as he rubbed his disfigured jaw. Clearly, she wanted to see him ... she had booked the same hotel room. Right? *Or ... maybe she chose it simply because she had stayed there before.* He shook his head. But what if that wasn't the case? What if she had heard his request, and had replied. What if, in spite of the fact that she had thought him dead for the past three-and-a-half years, she was going to Providence ... to see him.

He stifled a grin. *Then you need to get your ass to Providence, Henderson.*

Chapter 24
THE TIBETAN PROVINCE OF CHINA

Thursday, January 15ᵗʰ, 2004

Lili liked this time of day. Early morning ... before anyone was awake. Not that there were many people in the old warehouse outside Ngari, China. From what she could tell, it was only her, her caregiver, a cook and a maid, and two men with guns. They weren't the same men who had brought her from Latvia; these men were quiet. And, unlike Mr. Chin on the train, they never hit her. They never smiled, either, and they never spoke. It was as if they were statues keeping watch.

But it wasn't like she had anywhere to go even if she did escape. She was in the middle of nowhere in the vast outreaches of western China. She had learned that much from her teacher. Lili didn't think she was supposed to know it. But Ching Lan had wanted Lili to know she was safe. *"No one will hurt you here, Lili, and no one will take you away. We are miles from civilization ... just like the Dalai Lama."*

Lili liked stories about the Dalai Lama. She could relate to his exile from his homeland. She, too, felt exiled. Maybe someday she would get the chance to talk to him ... or, better yet, to listen to what he had to say.

She had not forgotten her vision from two nights ago. She had felt Uncle Mart's presence, and she could tell that he was hurting. She had yet to figure out why or how he could be hurting when he was in heaven. She had spent the last hour going through every memory she had of him, and, though it upset her, it also brought her joy. Playing in the snow, stories around the kitchen table, Christmas carols in the big room at the mansion. Thinking of those days – before everyone was dead – gave her the sense that they were still there ... that they hadn't died after all.

She was sitting in her bare room at the back of the dormitory, looking out the only window at the far-off peak of Mount Kailash. She could barely see it in the early morning darkness, made worse by a ring of clouds that hung over the mountain like a rattan hat. Lili had learned about Kailash ... its elevation, its status as one of the highest mountains in the world. She had asked if she could climb it; Ching had merely laughed. *"Such lofty goals for such a little girl!"*

Which had then made Lili certain; she would climb it ... someday ... and she would visit the Dalai Lama, too. She would invite Ching Lan to come with her.

Lili liked Ching Lan. The woman was kind and wise, and, over the past week, Lili had felt comfortable enough to tell her about her special gift ... her ability to recall the past, including every story she had ever heard and every book she had ever read.

Ching Lan had merely nodded. *"I know of it, Lili ... it is why you are here."*

Lili didn't speak of her other gift, however. For one thing, she wasn't quite sure how to describe it. For another thing, she felt certain that Ching Lan would laugh at her. After all, to claim to know what was happening – to be able to *feel* what was happening – to a person in a place far away, seemed impossible. She imagined her teacher scolding her. *"Don't spin fantasies, Lili."* That was what she had said when Lili shared that she had seen a vision of the Dalai Lama at his home in McLeod Ganj, India. The old woman had frowned and said, *"The sky, the trees, the walls around you are all that you see, my child ... it is all any of us see. That gift you speak of belongs to God."* But then Lili described – in detail – the Dalai Lama's house and the land around it. Ching Lan had stopped what she was doing and had stared at her for quite a long time. Lili never brought it up again.

Ching Lan refused to tell Lili exactly why she was there or what they had planned for her. But she had told her enough. *"You are being groomed, my dear."*

"Groomed ... for what?"

"It doesn't matter. Just know ... your role is important."

That was the end of it.

Ching talked a lot about Tibet and China, and the cultural differences that had come between the two. *"Remember, Lili ... you must never go against China."*

Lili had simply nodded, not quite sure why it mattered.

Then, two days ago, the lessons changed. America had become the focus ... its past, its present, even its politics. Lili found it interesting, but she was confused. *"Why must I know of America, Ching Lan?"*

The old woman had frowned. *"It is not for me to know why, my child ... it is only for me to teach."*

So, teach she did ... all day, every day, from sunup to sundown. On rare afternoons, they would go outside. Lili cherished those days. The Tibetan landscape was magnificent, and the chance to breathe fresh air was a balm to her soul.

But her favorite time was now ... the early morning hours before anyone was awake ... when she would know that back home Danil and Anna were preparing to sleep. She felt as if she could talk to them during that mystical hour ... when they were ending their day and she was beginning hers. And she would tell them she was okay. *"I have food and clothes. I am learning a lot ... I miss you, Uncle Dan and Aunt Anna."*

She had never spoken to Uncle Mart that way; he was dead. But, now that she had seen him in a vision, she felt obligated to reach out to him. What should she say? She wanted to give him hope, but, the more she thought about it, the more she decided it was useless. *He can't hear me ... he's dead.*

She leaned back and stared at the ceiling, wondering about heaven. Were there thrones and angels and fluffy white clouds? Or was it more like Ching Lan had told her: *"Heaven is not a place, Lili ... it is a passage to Nirvana ... an end to suffering."*

Uncle Mart wasn't in heaven; he couldn't be. He was suffering, which meant he hadn't gone to Nirvana. *So, where is he?* She closed her eyes. *Go to sleep, Lili ... Mart is dead.*

Then, suddenly, she saw him ... clear as day. She opened her eyes; he didn't go away. He was sitting in a truck. *Are there trucks in heaven?* His face was hidden by a hat and a sweatshirt, but she knew it was him; she could feel it. And, once again, she could feel that he was hurting. He turned to say something to the man behind the wheel; she saw his face. She sat up, unsure whether to laugh or cry. His jaw was disfigured, and he was scarred over the left side of his face. She knew the scars hurt; she could *feel* them. His eyes, though still bright blue, looked sad and empty. Tears came to her own eyes. She rubbed them as she said aloud, "Uncle Mart is alive!"

Week #2

"Lizzie Bordon took an axe
And gave her mother forty whacks
When she saw what she had done
She gave her father forty-one."

Chapter 25

PROVIDENCE, RHODE ISLAND

Monday, January 19th, 2004

The plane landed amid a fog-laden runway. Maddi looked out the window, watching as the wing sliced through the mist. She and Larry had chosen a military transport to fly to Rhode Island, and she was now glad they had. Domestic flights had been grounded, and her plane was the only one moving on the runway.

She had gotten back to DC two days ago, glad to have the summit in Mexico behind her. But it had kept her busy, which had kept her from dwelling on the possible outcome of this trip. She had never *felt* like Henderson was dead, but she had been forced to accept it ... and this trip was finally going to prove it. Was she ready for that? She sighed. *One way or another ... it's time.*

She stepped off the plane and breathed in the ice-cold air, thankful for the car waiting on the tarmac. Larry was next to her, scanning the landing strip through the dense fog. It was only the two of them; Collins was flying in later that night.

They walked to the sedan and climbed in back. It took thirty minutes to get from the airport to downtown, and, by the time they arrived, the fog had begun to lift. Maddi looked out tinted windows, remembering the landmarks from her visit years ago. But then, instead of Larry, it had been Henderson sitting next to her. He had told her the history of the buildings and the stories of the people who owned them. She had instantly felt a connection, both with him and the city. She had asked why he had chosen Providence to locate his company.

"It has close ties to the East Coast," he had said, adding, *"...and it's a sister city to Riga, Latvia."*

Maddi had wanted to ask why that mattered, but had simply nodded, letting the moment, and the chance to know more about him, disappear.

They arrived at the Westin and the driver pulled beneath the awning. He came around, helped Maddi with her bag, and walked her and Larry into the hotel. Her knees suddenly felt weak; she stumbled. Larry helped her to a chair.

"Are you okay, Senator?"

She nodded, trying to hide her anxiety. "I'm ... I'm fine, Larry." But she was not fine as she stared at the table in the center of the lobby; it looked exactly the same, down to the Ming vase filled with pine sprigs and a splash of red poinsettias. She could see it all so clearly, and, though some of the furnishings had changed – a bigger couch, different chairs – it felt exactly like it had when she and Henderson had walked through those doors four years ago. As she stared at the vase, she remembered the questions that had spun in her head back then: *Who is Martin Henderson? What drives him? Who's important in his life?* The same questions she had now, but with different answers, she was sure. *If he's even alive.*

"Just tired from so much traveling," she said as she brushed a strand of hair behind one ear. Larry gave her a minute, and then walked her to the counter. The reservation was in his name, so he checked in and was given key cards. He handed Maddi a card, and they walked to the elevator. A bellman joined them as they stepped inside. She watched as he pushed the same button she had pushed years ago. The elevator rose and she felt her stomach drop, the feeling staying with her even after they reached the top floor. They walked to the suite. She was finding it hard to breathe. She fumbled with the key card; the bellman reached out to help. She closed her eyes, recalling the same gesture from a different man so many years ago. He opened the door and the three of them walked into the suite. He set their luggage in the bedrooms, Larry handed him a five-dollar-bill, and he left.

Maddi stood in the front room, her hand against the wall as she did her best to keep it together. The last time she had been in that room it had changed her life. *So, what's going to happen tonight?* She walked to a bay window that covered an entire wall. There were the same gray curtains pulled back on each side, and the same view of downtown, with Narragansett Bay in the distance.

Larry made a search of the entire suite and then walked up to her and nodded. "Everything looks good." He paused. "You okay out here, Senator?"

"I'm fine. Thanks, Larry." He turned and went to his bedroom. She soon heard the muffled sounds of a TV news program coming from behind his closed door.

She walked into the kitchen, opened the refrigerator, and found a bottle of water. She poured a glass and carried it to the sofa. She stared down at the familiar gray stitching with pillows to match. She set the water on the coffee table, and then fell onto the sofa, grabbing one of the pillows and hugging it to her chest ...

"I like these pillows," Maddi said nervously as she stroked one with her hand. "They're softer than most ... more inviting somehow."

Henderson grinned as he pulled her closer. "They just look like pillows to me."

Maddi feigned a frown. "You've failed to see their uniqueness."

He kissed her neck. "No ... I'm just distracted..."

She closed her eyes, trying to remember the feel of his hand on her cheek, the hint of salt on his lips as he kissed her. She could smell his cologne as she hugged the pillow to her chest. How many times had she done it; made love to him in her memories with nothing more than a pillow in her arms? *But this is the first time I've been back ... to where it happened.*

She was startled by a knock at the door. *Henderson?* She stood, letting the pillow fall to the floor as she smoothed down her jacket. *Should I get Larry? No ... I'll be fine.* She walked to the door, stopping at a mirror in the hall. "Just ... just a minute." She brushed bangs from her forehead and opened the door. It was the bellman.

"For you, Senator," he said as he handed her an envelope.

"Thank you." She closed the door, staring at the envelope as she walked to the couch and sat down. She was afraid to open it. Was it from Henderson? What if it was? She frowned. *What if it isn't?* Finally, she tore it open and pulled out a folded card, blank on the front except for a stylish letter 'H'. Her hands trembled as she opened it.

Dinner ... tonight. Mr. Solvino is looking forward to it. I'll be waiting for you ... the same table in the back. Six o'clock. I've missed you.

Oh my god, Maddi thought. *He's alive!*

~ ~ ~

Sometimes, between night's darkness and the light of early dawn, Henderson would remember. The images would come never by choice, but simply be there ... like loneliness. Or, better yet, like the spark of hope one feels before they face the end ... *the final breath before we die.*

At first, he had fought the images, thinking if he did, the hurt they brought would disappear. He soon learned, however, he couldn't fight memories of Maddi any more than he could fight the pain as he struggled with the aftermath of the fire on his skin. Over time, he grew used to the ache in his chest as he longed for something he could never have. But it never got easier.

As he looked across the street through his high-powered lens, he could see that she looked the same. Her blonde hair barely brushed her shoulders, a slight curl framed her face, and her blue eyes still glistened like the ocean at dawn. She smiled as she stood at the window and it overwhelmed him. He closed his eyes, shaking as he realized, for one weekend, that smile was his ... one perfect weekend that had gone by far too quickly. There was so much they didn't say, so much he didn't know about her. Like where she grew up or what kind of music she listened to. He didn't even know her favorite food. He had assumed there would be more weekends, and had failed to appreciate that one chance to get to know Cynthia Madison.

Had he fallen in love with her then, or was it later, when a conflict halfway around the world took him away from her? When he realized that his longing for her was like nothing he had ever felt, bringing his entire world to a halt as he eagerly awaited the chance to see her again. Or had it been the first time she stepped out of the hotel – the same hotel he was now staring at – and approached his car for their first night together? Henderson felt like he had always loved her, like she had touched him from the beginning. Before he had ever seen her, he loved her.

And she had been there through it all ... through the terrible days after the explosion, when the pain from his burns made him long for death. Images of her had encouraged him to hope, to hold on ... *and she didn't even know I was alive.*

He watched her walk to the kitchen, and then the couch, and he saw her fall into it and grab a pillow. It was as if he was sitting next to her ... as if she was hugging him and not the pillow. His need to be with her was physically painful ... but he couldn't look away.

She stood and walked to the door. *She's getting the note.* He watched as she carried it to the couch. He swallowed; his heart felt like it was in his throat. *What if she just tosses it on the table?* He focused the lens as she opened the envelope, his hands shaking as she pulled out the card. She tucked her hair behind one ear, her face blank as she read the note and then read it again. What did she feel? *Joy? Anger? Fear?* Suddenly her eyes lit up, and she hugged the card to her chest.

He laughed. Like a child, he laughed as he turned away from the window. He paced the room, eager to see her, knowing he would no longer be alone. After four long years, he had found a way back. *Maddi and I ... together.*

He stopped. He had caught a glimpse of his reflection in the window. He stared at it, the laughter vanishing as he realized how different he was from the man she had known. Maddi was overjoyed to hear from a man who no longer existed.

And it wasn't just the scars. Martin Henderson was broken ... and dead.

He threw the lens to the floor. Why had he let himself run with it? He was a freak, not a man Maddi could love. She was the same, but he had changed ... a lot.

His hands were shaking as he picked up the lens and looked at Maddi. She was still holding the note. Suddenly he flinched. The angle of the sunlight had let him see something else; a reflection from another window, not far from his. He adjusted the lens and looked closer. He felt sick. Standing somewhere nearby, watching Maddi from his own window, was a man Henderson knew all too well ... *Simeon.*

He ran to the desk and opened his laptop. *What are you up to, Morningstar?* His hands were still shaking as he logged onto sites where he and Morningstar had communicated in the past. Starting first with the Pentagon, and then moving to the Department of Defense, he looked for something ... anything ... an email, a message. There was nothing. He checked Navy Seals, Green Berets, other Special Forces sites: Nothing. Finally, on a Delta Force site abandoned years ago, he saw it....

Committee meeting: 6:30 PM, Monday
Subject: interdepartmental cooperation
Location: Phoenix Hotel, Levi St, Providence, RI
Participants: Pentagon and Congressional
Representatives
Not present: Senate Majority Whip, Cynthia Madison

Henderson stared at the screen, reviewing the code in his mind. Those requesting a hit were listed as "participants." The agent performing the hit was listed in "location." The object of the hit was listed as "not present." Anyone glancing at the website would read the information and see it as nothing more than a routine summary of government business ... but he knew better; he knew exactly what was being said in that paragraph. Maddi was on Morningstar's hit list. And, at 6:30 PM, tonight, he, Martin Henderson, the *Phoenix,* was to be her assassin.

Chapter 26

WASHINGTON, DC

Providence, Rhode Island

"Simeon, are we ready?"

"Yes, Father. I got in late last night. I've been watching her. Is he coming?"

"He'll be there, don't worry. I checked the restaurant ... dinner's at six. I've scheduled the 'event' for six-thirty." He paused. "Have you spoken to Levi?"

"The minute I got into town."

"Good. Call me once they leave for the restaurant. Follow them. Your job will be to get a photo of our two targets together. Got it?"

"Yes, Father."

"We'll talk when it's done." Morningstar ended the call. He grinned as he looked out the window of his first-floor office. There wasn't much to see; it was a gray Monday morning in the nation's capital. His eyes fell on a black and white photo sitting on a table near the window. It was a picture of his father as a Green Beret captain. Anyone who walked in would think it a gesture of homage to the man; the truth ... it kept Morningstar's anger – his hate – alive. Those emotions had served him well through the years ... he certainly didn't want to lose touch with them now.

He stared at the photo, remembering well what his father had taught him. *"Never stray from your objective, Edward. Self-discipline and perseverance are your obligations to yourself, your family, and your country...*"The fact that Morningstar had only been six at the time had been lost on the old man.

He leaned back, clasped his hands behind his head, and chuckled. The plan was coming together well. He had called Rocky's restaurant earlier that morning acting as Madison's secretary, and had learned there was a reservation for the senator and a guest at 6:00 p.m. He didn't know Henderson's whereabouts, but was almost certain he was either in Providence or on his way, and would join Madison at the restaurant. Which meant, by 7:00 tonight, Morningstar's problems would be solved. The annoying Madison would be 'murdered' by the rogue agent, Phoenix ... *and, with nowhere else to go, Henderson will be forced to come back to me.*

~ ~ ~

Maddi stared at the note. *Henderson is alive.* She knew it now. The note with the simple "H" on the front had referenced the seat in the back of the restaurant, and had spoken of their dinner years ago. There was no one else it could be. She ran a finger over the H, and then stared at the writing inside ... *his* writing. It was the closest she had been to him in four years; *his* hand had written those words ... *his* thoughts were staring back at her. She tucked the note in her pocket and walked to the window. She tried to imagine what it would be like to see him again. Would he look the same? *Of course not.* Would it matter? *No.*

But how could he be alive? She had run out of the burning hotel ballroom, thinking he was right behind her. He wasn't. So where had he gone? How had he lived through such a thing? *And why didn't he tell me?*

She pulled out the note and read it again. It didn't matter why. She could tell from his words that he felt the same. She would have her answers in—she checked her watch—seven hours. She ran her hands through her hair as she stared out the window. *So ... how does a woman prepare to meet a man she thought was dead?*

She walked to her bedroom and opened her suitcase. She unpacked the few things she had brought, taking care as she hung up a navy Jovani dress; the same one she had worn four years ago. *Will he notice?* It didn't matter; she wanted to feel what she had felt then ... she wanted to fall in love with him all over again.

So, what do I do for the next seven hours? She slid her suitcase in the closet and walked to the smaller bedroom. She knocked on the door. "Larry?"

"Yes Senator?"

"I feel like going out." She chuckled as she added, "I'll be fine on my own, if you'd like to stay here."

The door swung open. "No." Larry turned off the TV and grabbed his jacket from the back of a chair. "Wherever you go, I go."

"Whatever you say. But I'm going to the courthouse. You might get bored."

"It's my job, Ma'am."

Maddi grinned as she walked to the door. "So you've said, Larry ... a thousand times."

She grabbed her coat and purse, and Larry fell in behind her as she walked out of the suite. They took the elevator to the first floor. Larry had vetted a specific cab company prior to the trip, and he pulled out his phone to call them as he and Maddi walked to the front door. All at once, the concierge called out, "Senator, wait! Don't bother with a cab. There's a driver already here for you."

Maddi stopped. She looked at the concierge over her shoulder. "A driver? Who arranged for a driver?"

"I don't know, Ma'am, but we've been instructed that he's to take you wherever you want to go."

"Instructed by whom?"

The man shrugged his shoulders. Maddi looked at Larry, who frowned and said, "It wasn't me, Senator."

She walked over to the concierge. "I need to know who arranged for the car."

He frowned. "Apparently a man stopped by late last night; I wasn't here. He indicated that a driver would be available to take you anywhere you wanted to go."

"Do you know what the man looked like?"

He shook his head. "As I said, Ma'am, I wasn't here."

Maddi thanked him and walked away. *Who sent the driver?* She stared at the Ming vase in the center of the table and grinned. *Henderson ... it had to be.*

~ ~ ~

Morningstar pulled out a cigar and was about to light it, when he changed his mind. "Not until the bitch is dead," he said, and slid it in his pocket. *I'll blow smoke rings in Chief's face.* He couldn't wait to see the man's reaction when he informed him of the success of the mission. *He's such an idiot.*

~ ~ ~

Morningstar had always been a little disappointed with the Vice-President, never understanding why such an uninspired man had been given command of the Bentley Group. *The guy's just a stupid politician.* Like so many in Washington, he lacked vision, and vision was what was needed now. America's enemies had grown stronger over the last decade, and he and his sons were the last chance to save not only America, but the world. Chief just wasn't up to it. *Only I, God's Chosen One, am prepared for such an undertaking.*

~ ~ ~

He checked his watch. *Eleven-thirty.* He pulled out his phone and dialed. The call was answered by a low, even voice. "Yes Jacob?"

"You spoke to Simeon?"

"Yes sir."

"Six-thirty tonight. Got it?"

"Don't worry, Jacob. It'll go down exactly as you've instructed."

"The reservation is for six o'clock. You should pick her up at 5:40. But go to the hotel now ... be available in case she wants to go out this afternoon."

"I'm already there, sir."

"Good. Whatever she wants, Levi, anything at all."

~ ~ ~

Maddi turned to Larry. "I think we'll be fine with whoever the driver is."

The agent shook his head. "This isn't a good idea, Senator."

She walked to the door and looked outside. There was a dark sedan parked under the overpass, and a tall, well-groomed man was standing by the car. He looked up as he put his phone in his pocket. Suddenly her fears were gone; she recognized him. "Molinaro!" she said aloud. He had been Henderson's driver four years ago and he looked the same; his dark hair recognizable under his cap, his muscled frame obvious beneath his black driving coat. He had been polite and professional back then; she felt certain she could trust him now. *And maybe he can tell me about Henderson.* She turned to her agent. "It's okay, Larry. I know this guy. He works for Marker Health Insurance Company ... or at least he used to."

Larry shook his head. "With all due respect, Senator, I can't let you get into a car with a man I haven't vetted. Let me make a call. What'd you say his name was?"

"Molinaro." She paused, trying to envision the nametag on his lapel from four years earlier. "Clint Molinaro."

Larry dialed his phone and waited. "Hello, sir, it's Larry Moses. I need to run a check on a man by the name of Clint Molinaro. He used to work for a company called Marker Health. I don't know if he still works there but he's currently standing outside the Westin Hotel here in Providence, prepared to serve as a driver for the senator." Larry waited and Maddi watched him, grinning at his professionalism. He looked at her and pretended to scowl. "Former military?" His eyes widened. "The Pentagon?" He nodded. "Yes sir, thank you." He turned to Maddi. "He checks out. He's military. Apparently, he's been doing work for the Pentagon, and was assigned to drive you because of his familiarity with Providence."

"Assigned by who?"

"The Chairman of the Joint Chiefs ... Alexander Daniels."

Maddi frowned. "How did General Daniels know about this trip? And why weren't you notified?"

He shook his head. "My boss said it all happened at the last minute. They were about to call me, I guess."

Maddi frowned. *The Pentagon? General Daniels?* It didn't make any sense. *It doesn't matter,* she thought; she was certain Henderson was somehow behind it.

"Works for me," she said, as she walked through the door and waved. "Hi, Mr. Molinaro. It's good to see you again."

Clint Molinaro had ended the call with Morningstar and was putting his phone in his pocket when he saw Senator Madison walk out of the Westin. He would do as Morningstar had instructed. *"Whatever she wants, Levi, anything at all."*

She waved and said hello, and he stepped forward and nodded. "It's good to see you, as well, Senator."

She introduced him to her agent. He forced a smile as he escorted the two of them to the back seat. He would need to do something about the agent.

He walked to the front and slid behind the wheel. He glanced at Madison in the rearview mirror and smiled. She was a beautiful woman. He understood what Henderson had seen in her. Such a shame he had to kill her.

"Where to, Senator?"

Chapter 27
PROVIDENCE, RHODE ISLAND

Maddi's a target! Henderson had paced the room for the past five minutes, trying to come up with a way to stop whatever was being planned. The easiest solution would be to cancel dinner, but he couldn't do it. *Not yet, anyway.* He grabbed his lens and walked to the window. He looked for the reflection he had seen only minutes ago. It was gone. Simeon was gone.

He looked across the street. Maddi was gone, as well. He couldn't see her or her agent, and he began to panic. *Have they gone out?* He looked down and noticed a black sedan parked under the hotel's covered entryway. Had she called for a car?

Then he saw her. She stepped through the door, waving at someone as if she knew him. Henderson leaned closer to the window. *Who does she know in Providence?* He watched as she walked to the car, her agent beside her. He tensed. Was Simeon somewhere nearby, waiting to kill her? *No ... the hit isn't until tonight.*

He saw a man step away from the sedan and walk toward her. He tightened his lens; the man looked familiar. As he helped Maddi into the car, Henderson caught a glimpse of his face. "It's Molinaro!"

Henderson felt a flash of joy at the thought of Clint Molinaro, his assistant from years ago, coming to pick up Maddi. *Just like before, only then it had been me who had sent him.* Who had sent him this time? Did he still work for Marker Health? Perhaps Maria Harvey had arranged it. Maybe she and Maddi were meeting for lunch.

But why would Maddi meet with Maria? Henderson went to his laptop and typed in Marker Health's website. He scrolled the page, searching for something that might explain a meeting between Maddi and Maria. There was nothing. He searched an employee directory to see if Molinaro still worked for the company; he wasn't listed. He grabbed his cellphone and dialed the number he knew so well.

"Marker Health Insurance Company. This is Miranda, how may I help you?"

Miranda. Henderson remembered her; she had worked there from the beginning. He wanted to shout into the phone, *"Miranda, it's me! Your boss! The guy who started the company!"* Instead, masked by his raspy voice, he said, "Yes ma'am. I'm trying to locate a driver by the name of Clint Molinaro. I know he used to work there; I'm wondering if he's still employed." There was a pause. He continued. "I'm aware you might not be able to give me that information; could you simply confirm or deny it? I have a message from his mother in Genoa. It's urgent I speak with him."

Miranda seemed to soften at the mention of Molinaro's mother. "Sir, I can't really reveal details, but Mr. Molinaro has been gone for nearly four years."

Henderson thanked her and ended the call. If Maria Harvey hadn't sent him, then who had? He typed Molinaro's name into his search engine. There were dozens of Clint Molinaros and none of them seemed to match the man who had been his one-time aide. He went back to the Marker website, shook his head, and sighed. "I hate to do this, Marker Health, but I've got to know." He hacked into the company's private records and found Molinaro's name in a list of former employees. Beneath it he saw the man's last known address. He wrote it down and logged off. He pulled up a surveillance program, courtesy of the U.S. government, and looked for everything he could find on Clint Molinaro at that address. He scrolled through information about the man's parents, his siblings, and his prior employment. Then he saw it.

Clinton Molinaro, United States Army, Marine Corp. Commissioned, 1972. Re-commissioned, March of 2000, the Pentagon.

"Shit!" Molinaro was now working for the United States Army, or, more likely, for Morningstar. Henderson frowned. How could it be that his once-trusted aide was now working for his enemy? *Morningstar must have something on him.*

He thought back to the memo: *"Location: Phoenix Hotel, Levi St, Providence, RI."* He typed the street name into his search engine. He frowned as he stared at the screen. *No such street.* He leaned back and sighed. *"How do you fit in, Molinaro?"*

After a minute, he leaned forward and typed in "Sons of Jacob." He checked the list. His eyes widened. There it was; son number three, right after Simeon: *Levi.* Was Molinaro the Levi in Levi Street? Henderson frowned. *He has to be.*

Henderson closed the laptop and returned to the window. The sedan was gone. He checked his watch. *Eleven-thirty-five.* He had about seven hours before the hit on Maddi was to take place. There was a lot to do. But, at least now he knew ... *Clint Molinaro is to be her assassin.* And the man had just helped her into his car.

Chapter 28
PROVIDENCE, RHODE ISLAND

Maddi asked that they be taken to the courthouse so she could research the Eminent Domain case. As she sat in the back seat, she stared at the driver, wishing she could ask about Henderson. *There are so many mysteries the man up front could likely solve.* But she had to wait until the time was right; she couldn't just blurt out comments about a prominent man whom the world had buried years ago. *Maybe I can find a way to talk to him alone.* She looked over at her agent. *Fat chance.*

They arrived at the courthouse and Molinaro parked the car. He came around and opened the door. "The courthouse, Senator."

"Thank you. We won't be long."

She and Larry stepped out of the car. The air was cold and she pulled the red scarf Andrew had given her over her chin as she climbed the steps to the courthouse. She wore a pair of dark sunglasses, which she would keep on until she was well inside the building. She didn't want to be recognized.

Once inside, she found the department she was looking for on the second floor. She located the records she needed and carried them to a desk in the back. Larry stayed with her, pretending to be her aide. She scrolled through files for the next hour or so, taking notes as she went.

They walked out of the courthouse just after 1:00. The black sedan was still at the curb. Molinaro got out, opened the back door, and Maddi and Larry climbed in. Molinaro slid behind the wheel and pulled away.

Maddi leaned forward. "I'm hungry. What about some lunch?"

Molinaro nodded. "Where would you like to go, Senator?"

"I don't know. You decide."

Molinaro drove Maddi and the agent to a diner in a part of Providence Maddi had never seen. As the driver helped her out of the car, he stopped short of walking her to the door. Maddi said, "Won't you join us?"

"It isn't customary, ma'am."

"Mr. Molinaro, I rarely worry about what's customary. Please, join us."

He hesitated, and then fell in beside them as they walked into the diner.

Larry's phone rang and he excused himself. The hostess led Molinaro and Maddi to a table by the window. Maddi looked at Molinaro and shook her head sadly. "It was so tragic about Mr. Henderson."

Molinaro nodded. "Yes, it was. We all mourned him for quite some time."

Maddi watched him; he seemed truly grieved. She nodded. "He touched a lot of people." She waited; nothing. "So, tell me … who sent you to drive me today?"

Without hesitation, Molinaro said "The Pentagon."

Maddi nodded. "I wonder who at the Pentagon would know – or care – that I–"

"Maria Harvey. She called them. She heard you were coming to town and insisted you be taken care of." He added, "In honor of Mr. Henderson, of course."

"Of course." Maddi tried to recall if she had told Maria she was coming to town when she had spoken with her last week. *I didn't.* "How did she know I was visiting Providence?"

He hesitated. "She must have read it in the newspaper."

Maddi nodded.

Larry returned and took a seat by Maddi.

"Everything okay?" she asked.

He nodded. "Just the boss checking in."

A waitress came and took their order. Molinaro gave them a quick history of the diner, and Maddi was reminded of Henderson's tour four years earlier. The waitress brought their food, and they ate slowly, the conversation covering everything from the weather to sports to politics. Molinaro insisted on paying the bill. He then drove Maddi and Larry back to the Westin, and escorted them to the lobby. Maddi thanked him and said, "We're having dinner at Rocky's at 6:00."

Molinaro tipped his hat. "I'll pick you up at five-forty, Senator."

He left and Maddi and Larry walked to the elevator. They stepped inside and Larry pushed the button to the penthouse. As they rose to the top, Maddi wrestled with an unsettled feeling that had been with her since her first bite of lunch. She was rubbing her neck when suddenly it came to her. She had specifically asked Phil to keep her visit to Providence out of the news. She felt a chill up her spine as the elevator door opened and she and Larry walked to her suite. Molinaro had lied.

Chapter 29
COLUMBIA, SOUTH CAROLINA

"Andrew, they're dying!"

It was three in the afternoon and Amanda was standing in front of the makeshift isolation facility next to the clinic. She brushed her hair from her face, chilled by a bitter wind that seemed far colder than the day before. She watched, disheartened, as the medics put another patient into an ambulance, and then drove off to a hospital she knew couldn't save him.

The facility next to the clinic was too small to handle the number of sick patients, so the decision had been made an hour ago to pull in the help of a nearby hospital. St. Vincent's had an isolation ward within their Intensive Care Unit. There would be a lot more room, and far more staff available.

Andrew removed his mask as he wrapped his arm around her and walked her to the door. "We'll figure it out, Amanda."

She lowered her mask and took a breath of cold, clean air; it felt good to breathe something other than the stale odor of the mask. She looked up at him and nodded, not at all convinced.

They walked inside and went to their office in the back. She sat on a stool by the doorway while Andrew grabbed two waters from a small fridge, handed one to Amanda, and then used his to take another dose of ribavirin. He sat at his desk and resumed work on a press release for the evening news. He looked at her and smiled.

"At least we haven't seen any new cases today."

Amanda suddenly ran from the office holding her hand to her mouth. She got to the bathroom just in time, losing most of her lunch. She hung over the toilet, tired of vomiting, tired of people dying around her. She walked to the sink and splashed water on her face. She looked in the mirror, shocked by the dark bags under her eyes. The vomiting was taking its toll. She cupped water in her hand, rinsed her mouth, and spat into the sink. She was reaching for a paper towel, when she stopped. There were droplets of blood in the spit. She opened her mouth and stared at the mirror. *Bleeding gums!* She held onto the sink, suddenly dizzy as she looked again to be sure.

She walked out of the bathroom, clinging to the wall as she made her way to the office. She stumbled through the doorway and Andrew helped her into a chair. He shook his head and frowned. "I need to take you home, Amanda."

She put her head in her hands and began to cry. Andrew put his arms around her. "It'll be okay. You're just tired … and pregnant. These cases are working on you."

Amanda pulled away. Her voice shook as she said, "I'm … I'm bleeding … from my gums."

Andrew stared at her. "You took the antiviral. How could you be bleeding?"

She looked down, refusing to look at him.

Andrew lifted her chin. "You took the medicine, right?"

She turned away.

Andrew slammed his fist on the desk and walked to the corner of the room. "Why the hell wouldn't you take the medicine?"

She looked at him defiantly. "Because of the baby. Ribavirin is a powerful drug. I was afraid it would hurt the baby."

"So, you think it's okay to expose yourself – and *our baby* – to *the virus*?"

"Of course not. I just didn't think I'd get sick. I've been careful."

Andrew walked from one end of the office to the other. "Dammit, Amanda! Now you're both likely sick with this thing!"

Amanda ran to the door. She opened it and had one foot through the doorway when she felt Andrew's strong arms around her.

"I'm sorry." He turned her to face him. "Amanda, I'm so sorry. I didn't mean to yell at you." His voice was shaking. "I'm ... I'm taking you to the hospital."

Amanda shook her head. "We can't leave. What about the clinic patients?"

"Lorraine can handle them. There's not that many now that most of them have either gone to the hospital or–" He stopped.

Amanda stared at him. What had she done? In her effort to spare the baby the possible side effects of ribavirin, she had now exposed both of them to a deadly virus. She fell into a chair and put her head in her hands.

Andrew knelt beside her. "It's okay, Amanda. You're going to be fine. You're both going to be fine." He helped her up and walked her to the reception area.

"Amanda isn't feeling well." He forced a chuckle. "Morning sickness is now all-day sickness, I guess. I'm running her home."

They walked outside and Amanda took a long, deep breath, forcing the cold air into her lungs. She laid her hands on her stomach, as if protecting the baby from the dreaded disease. Neither she nor Andrew said a word as they walked to the car, but she knew they were thinking the same thing.

... Lassa fever has a 95% fatality rate for a developing fetus....

Chapter 30
THE TIBETAN PROVINCE OF CHINA

Lili's heart ached; for what, she wasn't sure. It had been that way ever since she had seen the vision of Uncle Mart in the truck. She had been unable to tell where he was, but she had seen enough to know ... he had lived through a terrible ordeal, and it had hurt him ... badly. And not just on the outside.

She needed to help him. It was the vow she had made only a few days ago ... before she had known he was alive ... when she thought he was in heaven. But now she knew the truth: Uncle Mart was alive ... *and he's hurting.*

She had tried to stay with him ... to stay in the truck and travel with him to wherever he was going. With her eyes glued to the ceiling, she had done all she could to preserve his image. But, after only a minute or two, he had disappeared. She had continued to stare, hoping he would come back, but he didn't.

She had gone through the last four days with no further sense of him. But her lessons with Ching Lan had taken on a new meaning. America suddenly held far more significance, especially Boston and Washington, DC Uncle Mart had told her about those places; one was where he grew up, the other was where he went *"...to see the powerful."* Lili hadn't understood it at the time, but now she did. Washington was the home of America's government. And she was fascinated by it. Never had she heard of a place with such promise, such hope. *Maybe someday I will go there.*

It was three in the morning and she was once again awake, enjoying the quiet. She turned on a lamp by the bed and reached for a book that Ching Lan had given her. It was a history of China and she had gotten as far as the Ming Dynasty. She pulled it to her lap and opened it to where she had left off the day before. She was about to start reading, when, suddenly, she saw him ... *Uncle Mart.* Her eyes widened. He was running through streets she didn't recognize. His heart was racing and his grief was heavy; it made her heart hurt. She tried to hear his thoughts; to see what he was seeing. She had done it before ... when he was dying in the hotel ballroom. She had mourned with him there as he had said goodbye to those he loved.

She set the book on the bed, brought her knees to her chest, and closed her eyes. He was still running; she ran with him in her mind. He stopped. Her eyes flew open. She could *hear* him, and not just his thoughts. Actual words, said in despair as he stared at houses in the distance. But it wasn't the voice she recalled; the kind voice of Uncle Mart. This voice was harsh and gravelly; it made her throat sore.

"I am so sorry, Maddi ... so sorry I got you into this. I hope someday you can forgive me."

His image began to fade. She reached for him, hoping to keep him with her. Her outstretched arms grasped nothing but air. She let them fall beside her.

She stared out the window, her heart aching. She remembered the name Maddi. She was the Special Lady Mart had spoken of after he had buried Lili's papa. Months after Mart had burned in the fire, Lili had sensed the woman's grief and had tried to reach out to her. What had Mart done to her that was torturing him so?

The moon snuck from behind thick clouds, and Lili watched as it lit up the sky. It was like a light had been switched on. "It doesn't matter what he's done," she said aloud. "He needs this woman to forgive him. I will do what I can to make it so."

She sighed and picked up the book. She tried to read, but her mind kept drifting to Uncle Mart and his despair over Maddi. Suddenly, she heard a noise in the hall. She checked a clock by the bed. *Three-fifteen ... everyone should be asleep.* She stood and put on her robe. She walked to the door and listened. She heard nothing. She tried the knob. It was locked; it was always locked. "Is ... is anyone out there?"

She waited. Within seconds, she heard the sound of a key in the lock. She stepped back and the door flew open. She was relieved to see Ching Lan, but she could tell instantly that something was wrong. Instead of the colorful cheongsam her teacher normally wore, Ching Lan was dressed in dark pants, with an even darker smock. Her eyes were sad ... and frightened. She had a heavy coat draped over one arm, and she was carrying a tote bag filled with clothes. There was a loaf of bread sticking out of the top. "Get your coat, Lili. Come ... now!"

"Wh – why? Where are we going?"

"No questions! Come!"

Lili grabbed her coat and a pair of boots and ran out the door. She stopped. "Wait!" She turned and ran back in the room. She grabbed the picture of her parents, and then lifted the mattress and grabbed the black journal Danil had given her. She shoved the picture and the journal into the pocket of her robe and ran out the door.

Chapter 31
PROVIDENCE, RHODE ISLAND

Maddi had immediately gone to her bedroom to rest, but had been unable to do anything but lie on the bed and stare at the ceiling. She had spent the last hour wondering if she should tell Larry that Molinaro had lied. She had finally concluded that she shouldn't; Henderson was somehow involved, and he clearly wanted to stay hidden. But why would Molinaro lie? To protect Henderson? That had to be it. Molinaro didn't want Maddi to know that Henderson was the one who had hired him. But how had Henderson gotten a Pentagon general to do his bidding?

All at once, she sprung out of bed. *What if Henderson is a government spy?* It would explain so much ... why he told no one he had survived; why he was going to such lengths to stay hidden. She checked the clock. It was 3:30 ... still over two hours before she was to be picked up.

She walked out to the living room to get her laptop. She nodded at Larry, who was sitting in a chair with his feet on the coffee table, a service manual propped on one knee. "Larry, I'm going to try to get some work done before we go to dinner."

He nodded. "Five-forty, right?"

"Right." Maddi grabbed the laptop and walked back to her bedroom. She opened it, laid it on the bed, and typed in her password. Her senate webpage came up and she typed "Senate Intelligence Committee." She was taken to a page that listed members of the committee. She skimmed the list. Who did she know well enough to ask about a "secret agent" that had begun working for the government sometime in the year 2000? She looked at the names and sighed. It was useless. His need to stay hidden had clearly bypassed Congress; otherwise she would have known about him. Maddi was a high-ranking senator; he couldn't be part of any agency without her having at least some knowledge of it. *Which means he's beyond top-secret.* It was likely she would be putting him at risk just by pursuing it. *I'll let it go ... for now.*

She scanned Senate news, looking for information about the bioterrorism case. She wondered how Hank was holding up. This was his first big case since starting at Homeland. Was he making progress? She hoped so ... for his sake. *Hank hates it when things are left hanging.* She found a few bills addressing "the lack of oversight of the ports and borders," but that was it. Nothing about Homeland ... nothing about Hank.

She closed her computer and lay back on the bed. She stared at the ceiling. How would Hank handle the news that Henderson was alive? *Not well.* Henderson had 'died' saving him, and Hank carried the guilt of it as if he, himself, had killed him. But there was more to it than that: Hank knew that Maddi had fallen in love with Henderson, and he despised Henderson because of it. *How troubling, to feel so grateful – and so hateful – toward the very same man.*

But it wasn't just Hank who would struggle with the revelation that Henderson had survived; it was the entire world. After the dust had settled, and so many had died, the story of Henderson and Maddi running inside the burning building to save others had made them heroes. Maddi had run from it; she had refused to take credit for something that had ended so badly. But she had made sure everyone knew of Henderson's bravery; he had been celebrated not only in America, but overseas, as well. How would the world deal with the resurrection of the hero? *And why hasn't he told anyone – not even me – until now?*

Henderson closed a file drawer and checked his watch. *Four-fifteen.* He needed to hurry. He had jogged down side streets and alleys to Molinaro's home, had made sure no one was there, and – wearing gloves –had jimmied a back window.

He had crept inside and had sifted through every file, every drawer, every cupboard, looking for something to confirm that Molinaro was working for Morningstar. Though he had found nothing, he knew it was true; he could feel it. His former aide, now employed by his enemy, was about to kill Maddi. Had Morningstar hired him only for this hit? Or was he one of the sons … one of Morningstar's minions, hell-bent on ruining the planet, one war at a time.

He found a computer and used a military-grade decoder to log in. He sifted through data; he found nothing. Same with a safe he discovered behind a row of shirts in the closet. Other than stacks of hundred-dollar-bills, a fake ID, and two hand guns, it was empty. He checked his watch. *Four-forty.* He needed to get back to the hotel.

He gathered his gear and snuck out through the same window, making sure to leave it as he found it. He ran two blocks and hailed a cab, arriving back at his hotel just after five. He raced up the stairwell to his top-floor suite and checked to be sure that the hair he had placed in the jamb was undisturbed. Satisfied, he opened the door, walked in, and went to the window. He pulled out his lens and looked across the street into the living room of Maddi's suite. He saw no one. His heart started to race; where was she? Had she left the hotel? Had Molinaro come earlier than planned? Henderson couldn't let her leave. He would have no way of saving her once she stepped into Molinaro's car.

He stared at the empty living room and cursed. He prayed she was simply resting in her bedroom and that her agent was doing the same. He checked his watch. *5:14.* He needed to see her and know that she was okay. He pulled out his phone and stared at it, desperately wanting to call her, to hear her voice, to tell her he loved her and that she was the only reason he was alive. Instead, he sent a text message, routing it through two different numbers to keep it from being traced. He waited. He stared through the lens, praying she would emerge safe and sound from the bedroom. *Come on, Maddi, come out where I can see you.*

Maddi's phone vibrated and it startled her. She had just gotten out of the shower and she looked at a clock by the bed. *5:15. I need to hurry.* She reached for her phone and looked at the message.

You're in danger. Don't go to dinner tonight. Leave Providence, but don't tell anyone you're leaving. Molinaro is not your friend.

Maddi's hands began to shake. Who sent it? It couldn't have been Henderson. He was the reason she had come to Providence in the first place. Should she believe it? *No ... I won't leave.* She had to go to dinner; she had to see Henderson. But what if the text was true? What if she was in danger?

She threw on a pair of pants and a shirt and walked out to the living room. Larry wasn't there so she went to his bedroom. She failed to see a small note card lying on the floor in front of the door. She could hear a shower running. She would wait for him to finish. She began pacing the suite. She wasn't sure what to do. She needed to think. She needed to talk to someone she trusted. But there was no one; no one knew about Henderson. And she couldn't tell anyone. Not until she knew for sure what had happened to him, why he had stayed hidden ... why he continued to hide.

She glanced at a clock. *5:20.* Molinaro was picking her up in twenty minutes.

~ ~ ~

Henderson saw her walk into the living room and breathed a sigh of relief. But where was her agent? Had she told him about the text? Obviously not; otherwise, he would have rushed her out of there. Maybe she didn't believe the message. She was stubborn; she would want to ignore it. He couldn't let her. He had to convince her the threat was real. He watched as she paced back and forth, and he paced right along with her. It was just the two of them, separated by panes of glass and a one-way street, both faced with the same dilemma: how to keep Maddi safe.

134

Henderson stopped; he had an idea. He went to his computer and typed in an address; he searched the site, and then typed in another address. *Where is it?* After three more sites, he typed in the address to an obscure webpage and clicked on a link. After a few more clicks, he found it. He attached his phone to the computer and downloaded the photo on the page. He glanced at his watch. *5:23.*

He typed Maddi's number, sent the picture, and then added, *"Maddi, it's me. You have to believe me. Leave now. We'll find another way to meet."*

~ ~ ~

Maddi's phone vibrated; she opened it. She was stunned as she stared at the photo. She recalled the exact moment when it had been taken, the very second when everything had changed, and it was over nothing more than a stumble by a waiter ...

"I think that might have been the best salmon I've ever had," Maddi said as she patted the napkin to her lips.

Henderson smiled. "I told you; I deliver only the best."

Mr. Solvino walked up carrying a large tray of desserts. "Chocolate cake? Bananas foster?"

Henderson looked at Maddi and she shook her head. He grinned at Solvino. "We're good, Marco. We'll take a rain-check on dessert."

Solvino nodded. "Certainly, Mr. Henderson." He snapped his fingers and a man with a camera walked over. "May I have a picture of the two of you? It would be wonderful publicity for my restaurant. What do you say?"

Henderson looked at Maddi and she smiled. "It's okay with me."

Henderson slid closer and put his arm on the chair behind her, allowing his hand to gently squeeze her shoulder.

The photographer stood ready to snap the picture. "Okay now ... smile." Just then, a waiter side-stepped their table, bumped against a chair, and dropped his tray, spilling a large pitcher of water. The photo was snapped, capturing them with their mouths open and splashes of water on their hair, their

faces, their clothes. They laughed until they cried as they blotted the water with their napkins. Mr. Solvino apologized endlessly, but Henderson grinned and said, "Don't worry about it, Marco. Just make sure I get a copy of that picture ...
"

Maddi hadn't thought about the photo since that night, but there it was in front of her ... the two of them with their mouths open, their eyes wide, and their hearts warm. *It's from Henderson ... it has to be.* She scrolled down and saw the warning.

She walked to the closet, grabbed the few items of clothing she had brought, and stuffed them in her suitcase. She did the same with her laptop. She then went into the bathroom and got her toiletries, threw them in the suitcase, and walked the bag to the front door. She went to Larry's bedroom, this time noticing the note card on the floor in front of the door. She could still hear the shower running. She leaned over and picked up the card, her shaking hands barely able to hold it.

Senator, I didn't want to bother you while you were resting. I'm not feeling well. I'm going to take a shower and then stay in for the evening. I'm so glad you have Mr. Molinaro to look after you. Have a good evening. I'll see you when you get back.

Maddi was terrified. It was handwritten, but it wasn't Larry's messy scrawl. *Besides, Larry would never let me leave the hotel without him.* She knocked on the door. "Larry! Can you hear me?" Nothing. She pushed open the door, walked to the bathroom and knocked. "Larry, are you okay?" There was no reply. Her stomach was in knots. "Larry!" Still no answer. She pushed on the door and peeked in, not wanting to invade his privacy. Water was hitting the door of the shower; it was covered in steam. Maddi could vaguely make out the figure of a man standing behind it. "Larry!" The figure didn't move. Maddi began to tremble ... something was wrong. She walked to the door and grabbed the handle. She closed her eyes, not wanting to see whatever was behind it. She pulled it open and felt water splash against her face as a rush of steam poured out. She opened her eyes. She couldn't breathe. Larry was hanging from the nozzle of the shower with a bullet in his forehead and a rope around his neck. His eyes were open; Maddi knew instantly he was dead. She left the shower door ajar as she ran from the bedroom, shaking so hard she thought she might fall. *Keep moving, Maddi.* She had to get out of there. *But where can I go?*

Her phone vibrated and she jumped.

I'll have a car out back in five minutes.

It was as if he was watching her. She had never been so afraid. *Is the killer still here?* She had to leave the room and the hotel without anyone seeing her. She grabbed her suitcase, forgetting her coat as she hurried out the door and did her best to walk calmly to the elevator. She pushed the button and waited. Within seconds, the door opened; she stepped inside. She pushed the button for the third floor. The door opened and she looked down the hall. *No one.* She pulled the bag behind her as she walked from the elevator to the stairwell. She lugged the suitcase down three flights of stairs, past the lobby exit, to a door a half-floor lower that led to a service lot in the back. She opened the door, checked to make sure the lot was empty, and then gripped her bag and ran to a nearby dumpster. She knelt behind it. *This wasn't how tonight was supposed to go.* Her entire body was trembling. *Who killed Larry?* She clenched her jaw, holding back tears as she saw the image of the murdered agent in her mind. *How could anyone do such a thing?* She balled her hands into fists to try to stop them from shaking. Who was picking her up? Would she know him? Should she trust him?

Within minutes, a car pulled up. A black man stepped out and scanned the area. Maddi stepped hesitantly from behind the dumpster. The man looked at her and frowned. "Senator?"

Maddi nodded.

"I've come to get you. I was told it's an emergency. Is everything okay?"

Of course, it's not okay. I'm a U.S. Senator hiding behind a dumpster in the back lot of a hotel. Her teeth were chattering as she said, "Who ... sent ... you?"

"The man said he was your agent. Is he with you?"

"No." Maddi's knees were weak. *What if it's a trick?* "I ... I need to know that you are who you say."

The man shifted awkwardly. "Would it help if I told you the caller said there is only one copy of that photo? I'm not sure what that means, but he insisted I tell you that if you seemed unsure."

Maddi stared at him. *Henderson. It has to be.* She nodded. "Yes, that helps."

"Good. Let's go."

She ran to the car; she had no other choice. The driver took her bag and helped her into the back seat. He set the bag beside her, and then slid behind the wheel. He pealed out of the lot to Market Street, and headed away from the city.

When Maddi could stand it no longer, she said, "Did ... did the caller tell you where to take me?"

The driver nodded. "Yes, to DC"

To DC? He's sending me home. "Won't that take forever?"

The man nodded. "About seven hours, Ma'am. We can stop along the way if you'd like."

"No, that won't be necessary." Maddi sat back, fighting tears. *He's sending me away ... we're not going to meet.* She pulled out her phone and stared at the last text. She tried to reply; it didn't go through. Whoever it was wanted to remain hidden. It had to be Henderson; no one else knew about the photo from the restaurant. But how had he known she was in danger?

Another vibration caused her to jump. She looked down at the text.

Turn off your phone.

It *was* Henderson. It was like he was watching her, looking out for her, anticipating her every move. She clung to the phone as if it was him. *This may be as close as I get.* Her chance to see Henderson was gone; her chance to *be* with Henderson was gone. Larry was dead, she was on the run, and, if Henderson was smart, he would disappear ... like he had done for the past four years. She had never felt so frightened ... or so alone. She would do as he suggested and turn off her phone, but first she had a call to make. She dialed and Hank answered after the second ring.

"Maddi! How's it going in Providence?"

She said nothing.

"Maddi? Are you there?"

Maddi sighed. "Yeah, I'm here. Hank, there's something I need to tell you."

"What's that?"

Maddi heard a TV newscast in the background. "Where are you?"

"In my office. Things are a mess."

Maddi said, "What do you mean, a mess?"

"I'll tell you when you get back." He paused. "When is that, by the way?"

"I'm not sure."

"Is everything okay?"

She hesitated. "Yeah ... things are fine. I'm just tired. I'll see you soon, Hank."

Maddi ended the call and laid her head against the seat. She couldn't do it. She couldn't tell him that her agent had just been murdered and she was on the run, saved by the man who had died saving Hank. It was too much.

She turned off the phone. She would turn it on at 6:00, just long enough to call the restaurant and let Mr. Solvino know that she had needed to leave unexpectedly.

She checked her watch. It was 5:35. Molinaro was scheduled to come for her in five minutes. Would he still come? Did he kill Larry? Did Henderson know that Larry was dead? She thought about Larry and all they had been through, and she choked back a sob. Larry had been a good agent; he had always put her safety first. He had recently gotten engaged, and Maddi's heart broke as she thought about his fiancée and the loss she would feel. She knew that kind of loss. She clenched her jaw to keep from crying. *Keep it together, Maddi.*

She looked out the window, watching as the trees whisked by ... just like her life, moving so fast it made her head spin. In the blink of an eye, her world had changed completely. Henderson was alive, and her agent was dead ... *murdered* ... by some unknown killer. *I need to tell someone.* But who? She couldn't call anyone – she had obediently turned off her phone. *Why didn't whoever killed Larry, kill me?*

"Are you okay, Ma'am?" The driver was looking at her in his rearview mirror.

She did her best to smile. "Y – k yeah, I'm fine. Just a little shook up."

"Should we try to locate your agent?"

"No, it's ... okay. He'll catch up to us."

The man frowned, likely not believing a word of it. She didn't care; it was the best she could do. She closed her eyes and tried to calm down. She needed to stop shaking and get her emotions under control. How good it would feel to cry ... to let it all go in an avalanche of tears. But she couldn't. No matter what, she wouldn't cry....

"Stop crying, Cindy!" Her mother jerked her arm to make her stop, but she couldn't. The graveside service was nearing an end and people had begun to walk away. She, Andrew, and her mother remained at the site as the gentle rain that had fallen throughout the day suddenly became a downpour. Maddi was glad for the rain. She hoped it would hide her tears, because – regardless of what her mother wanted – she couldn't stop crying.

Why, she wondered. Why was she crying? It wasn't sadness, though there had been plenty of that. So, what was it? She looked at Andrew standing obediently on the other side of their mother. He was frowning, his dark eyes angry as he stood alone and stared at the casket. Suddenly she understood. Their world had changed. Nothing would ever be the same again. Maddi was crying because she was afraid ...

As she sped along in the back of a car with a driver she had never seen before, her agent murdered, Henderson lost to her, she was afraid ... but, no matter what, she wouldn't cry.

Chapter 32

PROVIDENCE, RHODE ISLAND

Using his lens, Henderson had followed Maddi as she had hurried to the door of the suite with her bag. He had seen her stop and leave the bag, and then walk into the agent's bedroom. He had seen her run out in a state of panic, and had immediately texted her that a car would be waiting. He had then dialed the pre-set number of a private transport service that had promised him earlier that day that they would wait near the hotel and be ready immediately if the need arose, "... *no questions asked.*" Henderson had prayed he wouldn't need them; he had hoped the night would end far differently. But he had learned the hard way; always be ready for a fast getaway. The transport service had answered his call and Henderson had practically yelled into the phone, *"I spoke to you earlier. I need a car in back of the Westin ... now!"*

He had added that the driver should tell the woman – a senator – that there was only one copy of the photo if she seemed unsure, and had given a destination.

He had then thrown on a Westin bellman's jacket and cap confiscated the day before and had sped out of his room. In less than a minute, he had descended the stairs, crossed the street, and was now crouched behind the Westin, hidden by a row of overgrown boxwoods.

He was thankful for the setting sun as he pulled his cap low over his forehead and popped the collar of his jacket. He kept his eyes glued to the back exit of the hotel. He sank deeper in the brush as he saw Maddi burst through the door and run behind the dumpster. He was angry as he looked at her frightened eyes ... *my fault, once again.* Not since the Al-Gharsi hit had he been so close to her, and not since that night had he seen her so afraid. But this time, he wasn't the one responsible. Morningstar had put out a hit on her ... again. The question was ... why?

A car with a Motor Way Transport logo pulled into the lot and he watched as Maddi exchanged a few words with the driver. He breathed a sigh of relief when she slid into the back seat. He watched the car pull away, staring at the taillights until they were no longer visible. He stood from his hiding place, brushed down his coat, and walked calmly, but quickly, to the front of the hotel. Within minutes, Molinaro would come for her, prepared to take her to the restaurant ... to kill her.

He bristled. *Not on my watch, you son-of-a-bitch.*

Chapter 33
PROVIDENCE, RHODE ISLAND

It had been so simple.

Molinaro checked his watch. *5:38*. He was pulling into the drive to pick up Senator Madison for dinner, and was almost disappointed at how easy it had been to kill her agent. After he had dropped him and the senator at the Westin after lunch, he had driven around back to an alley and had parked out of sight. He had waited, and, at 4:45, he had taken off his jacket, and had walked into the hotel through a service entrance door. Hiding his face from the cameras, he had climbed the stairs to the top floor. A cart had been waiting in the hallway where he had put it earlier in the day. Still hiding his face, he had moved it out of sight of a wall-mounted camera, and had then knelt beside it and pushed aside the tail of a table cloth hanging over the side. He had pulled a duffel bag from underneath and had carried it into a bathroom. The bag contained clothes and a hairpiece. He had hidden in a stall and had put on the disguise, stuffing his clothes in the bag. He had walked out, and, making sure no one was watching, he had shoved the bag under the cart.

Dressed as a hotel clerk, he had slid on a pair of white gloves, walked to the Senator's suite and knocked on the door. There had been no answer. Using a master key-card he had stolen from the front desk the day before, he had opened the door and stepped into the suite. Neither the agent nor Madison had been anywhere in sight. He had heard water running in the smaller bedroom and guessed the agent was taking a shower.

He had figured Madison was likely in the larger bedroom preparing for the night ahead. *Perfect!*

With his hand on a pistol in his jacket, he had slipped into the smaller bedroom, heartened to see that the bathroom door was closed. He had pulled out the gun, slid on a silencer, and crept to the door. He had knocked.

A muffled voice had said *"Maddi?"*

"No, it's housekeeping. I have clean towels for you."

"I'm taking a shower!"

Molinaro had stepped into the bathroom, his pistol raised. He had opened the shower door and – before the agent could reach for his gun by the sink – Molinaro had shot him in the forehead. He had then taken a piece of rope from his pocket and, with the shower still running, had wrapped it around the agent's neck. He had then hung him from the top of the nozzle. He had closed the shower door, the steam on the inside making it look as if the man was simply taking a shower.

He had been wringing wet, so he had grabbed a towel and had dried himself off. He had then knelt and mopped the floor by the tub. He had taken the towel with him and had walked out of the bathroom, closing the door behind him. He had left the bedroom, leaving a note card on the floor in front of the door, indicating that poor Larry didn't feel well. He had smiled at the irony as he thought of the agent hanging by a rope in the shower. *No, I'm sure he doesn't.*

He had been tempted to go into Madison's room and do the same to her, but he had been given specific instructions: *"The hit on the senator must take place at the restaurant."*

He had left the suite as quietly as he had come and had walked back to the cart. He had grabbed his bag from underneath and had returned to the bathroom. He had removed his gloves, hairpiece, and damp clothes, and had put them in the bag, along with the wet towel. He had then dressed and walked down the stairs and out the back door, taking the bag with him to throw into the river miles away. Yes, it had been so simple. He grinned as he pulled into the drive. *And you sure can't beat the pay.*

Chapter 34

PROVIDENCE, RHODE ISLAND

Henderson looked at his watch. *5:40 ... any minute now.* The sun was fading as he stood outside the entrance to the Westin, wearing the bellman's uniform with the cap pulled low to hide his face. He edged away from the door, using shadows from an awning to hide him even more. He reached his hand to his back pocket, satisfied as he felt his pistol with the silencer attached. He wouldn't need his SG-550 for this task. This was going to be up close and personal.

A black sedan eased into the breezeway. Henderson tensed and slid further under the awning. He put his gloved hand over the left side of his face to hide the scars.

The sedan came to a stop and Molinaro stepped out. Henderson's jaw tightened as he watched the man walk to the entrance. He had to fight the urge to beat him to death right then and there. Molinaro nodded casually as he walked through the doorway, clearly not recognizing the scarred man hiding in the shadows. Henderson watched him as he strode confidently to the concierge desk. He was eager to see his expression once he realized Maddi was no longer in the suite.

Molinaro said a few words to the concierge, who nodded and picked up his phone. He dialed and drummed his fingers on the desk as he waited for an answer. Henderson grinned as he saw the concierge shake his head, puzzled. Molinaro sprinted to the elevator, and Henderson had to fight not to laugh.

He walked inside, avoiding eye contact, keeping his cap low over his forehead. He strode behind the elevator and slipped into the stairwell, racing up the stairs two at a time. He had timed the elevator; he knew he could beat it.

His legs were throbbing as he reached the top floor. He grabbed his chest, winded as he stepped into the hallway and walked to the elevator. It was coming to a stop. He was glad to see that there was no one in the hall, but he saw a camera angled at the elevator. He kept his head down, letting the bill of the cap hide his face. The door opened. Henderson was relieved to see that his former employee was alone.

"Hello, Molinaro."

The man's eyes widened with stunned recognition. He reached for his gun, but, before he could fire, Henderson put four bullets into his chest. Molinaro fell to the floor. Henderson leaned in to confirm that the man was dead, and then pushed the button for the floor below. He stepped back as the door was closing.

He wouldn't have much time before Molinaro's body was discovered, but he needed to know what had happened to Maddi's agent. He ran to the suite and picked the lock. He walked into the first bedroom, heard the shower, and ran into the bathroom. The shower door was open. He ignored the water as it sprayed his face and clothes. He stared at the dead agent; it took all he had not to pound his fist through the wall. *Morningstar ... you prick!*

He gritted his teeth as he tore out of the suite and ran to the stairwell. He took the steps two-at-a-time to the utility exit a half level below the lobby. He threw open the door – the same door Maddi had opened only minutes before – and walked outside, yanking off the water-soaked bellman's jacket and tossing it, the gloves, and the cap into the dumpster. Underneath he was wearing a button-down shirt, and he pulled a tie from his back pocket, along with an Irish cap and a pack of cigarettes. In less than ten seconds, he had changed from a hotel bellman to a visiting executive who had snuck outside for a smoke.

The sun had set; the moon was barely a sliver. Other than the occasional lamppost lighting the parking lot and the street, it was pitch-black. Keeping to the shadows, he pulled the cap low over his forehead, tied the tie loosely around his neck, and popped his collar. He lit a cigarette and walked away. He could hear commotion inside ... *they've found Molinaro.* He picked up his pace, eager to get back to his hotel room and see how Morningstar would handle the turn of events. *The first of your sons has been killed ... by your very own creation.*

Chapter 35

WASHINGTON, DC

Hank had been disturbed by the call from Maddi. Though she had said she was fine, he could tell that she wasn't. One thing he had learned through the years was how to read between the lines with Maddi. And it was clear ... something was wrong. But she wouldn't tell him until she was ready, which was another thing he had learned over the course of their six years together. He would simply have to wait. Fortunately, he had plenty to keep him busy. The country was under attack. Or, at least a dozen or so cocaine addicts were under attack.

He checked his watch. *5:50.* He was sitting at his desk, where he had been most of the day, trying to sort out who was behind the terror plot – if it was a terror plot – and how vulnerable the rest of the country might be. He leaned back and looked out the window of his DC office on the corner of 12th and C Street, watching as streetlamps lit up the city. *Why aren't there more dead bodies,* he wondered, as he stared at the Capitol's dome in the distance. His phone rang and he jumped.

"Clarkson here."

"Dr. Clarkson, this is the Richland County Coroner calling from Columbia. I have preliminary results from the autopsies."

"Great. Fill me in."

"It was Lassa fever, alright, but the virus had not been weaponized."

"Good news, right?"

"Not exactly. The amount of the viral load was so great ... there's no way it could have happened by accidental spread."

Hank frowned. "What are you saying?"

"We found traces of the virus in the sleeve of the shirt that your agent found at the bus terminal. It had been altered."

Hank frowned. "Altered?"

"Yes ... converted from liquid to powder." There was a pause. "Dr. Clarkson, there's no doubt about it; Lassa fever was transmitted to those victims intentionally."

Hank thanked her and ended the call. He dialed Hanover's number. The gruff voice answered immediately. "What's up, Hank?"

"I just got off the phone with the coroner."

"Yeah?"

"The deaths were from Lassa fever. But the stuff wasn't weaponized."

"So, it wasn't a terrorist attack?"

"Well, that's the thing. It wasn't weaponized, but it had been altered to mix with the cocaine." He paused. "Hanover, someone *put* that virus in the shirts."

There was a pause. "Like maybe West Africa militants?"

"That would be my guess. But they would have had to work with a lab. Altering viruses is tricky business."

"Any way to trace the lab through the sample we have?"

"Unfortunately, no."

He heard a sigh. "Okay. I'll issue a statement about the militant group."

Hank frowned. "It doesn't make sense, Hanover. How many have been infected ... maybe twelve? Even if it's twenty, that's hardly enough to justify a terror attack."

"I don't know, Hank ... twenty deaths from a virus we never see. I find that pretty terrifying."

Hank sighed. "Maybe so, but I have an idea. What if we issue a statement saying we've concluded the virus was spread by an infected African drug dealer?"

Another pause. "You mean lie?"

"Not exactly. We just won't reveal the whole truth. With so few deaths, it would be easy for us to assume it was unintentional; we can leave out what I just learned from the coroner. The terrorists gain nothing if we dismiss it as nothing more than a sick man making a few others sick."

Another sigh. "How about this: I'll issue a statement, but I'll only imply what you've said. I'll say we're holding back some of what we know in the name of national security."

"Works for me. Maybe if these guys think they failed, they'll give up."

"I doubt it, but it's worth a try. I'll get it out immediately."

They ended the call. Hank stared out the window, thinking through what the coroner had told him, and then pondering his question to Hanover: If this was a terror attack – which he now had every reason to believe that it was – why were so few targeted? He sighed as he leaned back in his chair. *Maybe the terrorists aren't done.*

Chapter 36

WASHINGTON, DC

Morningstar checked his watch. *5:58.* He was becoming inpatient. Though the hit on Madison wasn't scheduled until six-thirty, he had expected a confirmation call from Simeon once Levi picked her up at the hotel. Something must have gone wrong. His phone vibrated and he screamed into the receiver, "What's happening?"

"He's dead."

"What do you mean, he's dead? Who's dead?" Morningstar stood from the bed and paced the floor.

"Levi."

Edi, lying naked in bed, looked up at him as she wrapped the sheet around her. She mouthed the words, "What's going on?"

Morningstar ignored her as he tightened his jaw. He screamed into the phone. "Jesus, Simeon, what the hell went wrong?"

"I don't know, Father. The concierge found him in the elevator. He'd been shot several times in the chest."

Morningstar walked to where his pants were hanging over the back of a chair. He pulled them on, his ear still glued to the phone. "So, where's Madison?"

"She's gone, sir."

"What do you mean, she's gone? Where did she go? Did she check out?"

Edi got up with the sheet still around her. She grabbed her clothes and ran into the bathroom. When she came out, he was still yelling into the phone.

"Find her, dammit! And find Phoenix!" Morningstar hung up the phone and sat down in front of his computer. *How the hell did Madison know to get out of there? And how did she leave without being seen?* He typed in a website, entered a password and waited. He stared at the screen, not even noticing when Edi walked out of the hotel room.

It took only seconds for the information to appear. He was looking at the same site where he had posted the hit the day before. He glared at the monitor and his hands began to shake. "That son of a bitch!" There was the same notice of a meeting, and the same cast of participants. Senator Cynthia Madison was still listed as "not in attendance." But now, written below her name, in bold, capital letters, were the following words:

NOT AS LONG AS I'M ALIVE.

Chapter 37

SOUTH OF PROVIDENCE, RHODE ISLAND

Maddi checked her watch. *Six o'clock ... I'm supposed to be sitting beside Henderson at this very moment, ordering a glass of Chardonnay.* She sighed as she turned on her phone, dialed information, and asked them to connect her to Rocky's restaurant. The phone was answered by a pleasant female voice.

"Rocky's. May I help you?"

"Could I – could I speak with Mr. Solvino, please?"

"May I ask who's calling?"

"Senator Cynthia Madison."

"Certainly, Senator, I'll get him."

Soon a pleasant voice with an Italian accent said, "This is Mr. Solvino. Is this Senator Madison?"

"Yes, it is."

"Ah, yes! We are waiting for you! Is there a problem?"

Maddi paused, "Mr. Solvino, I am so sorry, but I was suddenly called back to Washington to handle an urgent matter in the Senate."

"Oh, that is too bad, but I understand. You are an important woman." Maddi could hear his disappointment. "Perhaps another time, then?"

"Absolutely. And don't think I've forgotten about your case against the city. I will continue to work on it, and I'll be there for you when it goes to trial."

"I am so grateful. Perhaps I can treat you and your companion to dinner at that time?"

Your companion. Maddi sighed. "I'll look forward to it, Mr. Solvino. Thank you for understanding."

She was ready to end the call, when Mr. Solvino said quickly, "Senator? Do you know whether your gentleman friend will be coming to dinner?"

Does he know about Henderson? "My gentleman friend?"

"Yes. Mr. Marker."

Marker ... as in Marker Insurance. "I'm ... I'm not sure. I've not been able to reach him."

"All right, then. I'll be prepared, just in case."

Before Solvino could hang up, Maddi said, "Mr. Solvino, this Mr. Marker, have you seen him before?"

"Seen him? Well, no. But he told me on the phone he was a good friend of Mr. Henderson. That is enough for me."

"Thank you, Mr. Solvino. I'll be in touch." Maddi turned off the phone. *Mr. Marker.* What had compelled Henderson to hide not only from her, but from his old friend, Mr. Solvino? The notion that he might be a government spy popped back in her head. But even then, why couldn't he tell her? After all, she had kept far bigger secrets during her time in the Senate.

She leaned against the seat, trying to imagine where Henderson had been and what he had done since she had last seen him. Suddenly she realized ... *it doesn't matter.* The man she had loved, lost, and mourned for nearly four years was not dead after all. There was hope ... hope for the future, hope that she would at least see him again. She closed her eyes, hugging her arms to her chest as it hit her ... *Henderson is alive.*

Chapter 38
WASHINGTON, DC

Edi came back to the room after only a few minutes, a cup of Starbucks in one hand, the other immediately reaching for Morningstar's zipper. "Let me make you feel better, Eddie."

Morningstar had to grit his teeth not to yell at her. Everything had gone wrong and the last thing he needed was a needy woman begging him to have sex. In spite of her long hair and luscious Arab skin, Morningstar was growing tired of her. Her dark eyes looked at him pleadingly, "Come on, Eddie. I want you."

I can't wait to get this bitch out of my life! "Not now, Edi, I've got too much to do."

Edi wouldn't take no for an answer. "Oh, come on, Eddie, just a quickie."

"No!" Morningstar shoved her against the wall, and then instantly regretted it. He still needed her. He ran his hands through his hair and sighed. He walked toward her, his grey eyes softening as he said, "Sorry, babe, things are just a bit screwed up."

Edi stared at him, her dark eyes on fire as she stripped out of her clothes, crept to the bed, and climbed under the sheets. "It is fine. Maybe later."

Morningstar stared at the floor; his hands were shaking. He walked over to the bar and poured a glass of Scotch. He drank it in one gulp. He was still shaking. He lit a cigar to cool off, but even the calming effects of the nicotine weren't enough to make him relax. Not only had Henderson killed Molinaro, but he had had the nerve to taunt Morningstar after the fact. He couldn't let him get away with it.

He sat at the desk and pulled his laptop in front of him. He typed in an address, waited, and then typed in another. Soon he was taken to a restricted site available to only a few. He clicked on a picture and stared at it, smiling as he thought of what he was about to do. He had gotten the photo an hour ago, sent by way of encrypted email from his friend in China. *Perfect timing.*

He put a hand to the screen, stroking the picture as if she was there in front of him. The hair so fair, the face so innocent, as she lay still against a snow-covered hillside. He had hoped he wouldn't need the photo, but Henderson's interference over the last hour dictated otherwise. He sneered as he wrote beneath it:

Meeting scheduled with Lili P. has been cancelled. Subject has been eliminated.

He placed the link on the same site where Henderson had left his message, and then leaned back and laughed. *That'll teach him.* Phoenix would be crippled by the news ... *he will need to come home.*

The TV was on in the corner of the room and Morningstar's attention was drawn to a newscaster from Columbia, South Carolina.

"I just received word that Homeland Security now believes the deaths from the cocaine were not part of a terrorist attack. Though they can't release details, they feel confident that a drug dealer was infected with the virus, and he, in turn, infected the addicts. They reassert that Lassa fever is highly contagious, and are urging anyone who has come in contact with one of the victims to seek medical attention at once."

Morningstar stared at the TV. He couldn't move; he could barely breathe. He picked up his empty glass and flung it at the screen, seething as both the glass and the monitor shattered to pieces. Edi pulled the sheet over her head as he stood and paced the room. "How could they be so stupid?"

He grabbed a half-filled glass of champagne and polished it off in a single gulp. He walked from the window to the desk and back again, saying over and over, "Accidental? Not an option!" He had worked too long and too hard to allow the oafs at Homeland Security to deem the deaths of the druggies a mere accident. He was about to throw another empty glass at the TV when all at once he stopped. He grinned as he walked to the desk, sat at his computer, and started typing. A website came up and he typed some more. "Edi, come here."

Edi eased the sheet from her face and looked over at him. Hesitantly, she stood, wrapped the sheet around her, and tiptoed next to him. "What do you need, baby?"

"I want your access code."

She frowned. "Again? Why?"

"For the cause, babe." He looked at her and tried to wink, though it looked more like a tic. "We need a bit more of the magic potion."

Edi sighed as she walked to her purse, pulled out her wallet, and grabbed a United Nations identification card. The card, provided to her as a UN diplomat, gave her access to hundreds of agencies throughout the world. She was about to hand it to him when she stopped. She walked behind him and looked over his shoulder at the screen. She frowned. "What are you doing, Eddie?"

"We'll need the good stuff this time, Edi. Top grade, if you catch my drift. I'll plug in your ID along with the request, and then you can call your friend in Saudi Arabia so he can go online to verify."

Edi's legs began to tremble. "Wh – why do we need 'the good stuff?' It's really dangerous, Eddie."

He spun in the chair to face her. "Don't worry, babe. It's for government research ... remember?" He winked again, this time more effectively. "You'll do it, won't you, girl ... for me?"

Edi shook her head. "I ... I don't know about this, Eddie."

He stood and pulled her next to him, allowing the sheet to fall to the floor. He began to move with her, back and forth. "Sure, you do, babe."

She leaned into him, her reluctance gone as she grabbed him and whispered in his ear, "Okay, baby, how much do you need?"

Chapter 39
RIYADH, SAUDI ARABIA

Fouad Al Rashid, the Riyadh lab coordinator, hated these requests. Nothing good ever came of them and, as he grabbed his glasses and positioned them on his hooked nose, he shook his head in disgust. He brushed back his hair and sighed. In spite of how he felt about the order, he couldn't disappoint Edi Abu. It was because of her that Rashid had access to so many of the powerful in DC

Edi had joined the movement in 1999, two years before the September 11th terror attacks in New York City. Although the Arab Freedom Coalition had not supported those attacks, they realized after the fact that the assault on America had been the needed catalyst to get things moving in the right direction in the Arab world. Only after 9-11 did the sleeping USA giant finally widen its reach in the Middle East. Rashid and his followers wanted a realignment of Middle Eastern power, and they knew the might of the West would be needed.

Edi had managed to get close to a powerful man in the Pentagon, and, though Rashid didn't know the man's name, Edi had used that access to provide much-needed intelligence to Rashid and his followers. He patted the wallet in his back pocket. Her latest communique was hidden there, and, because of details in that dispatch, Rashid had moved the coalition one step closer to the uprisings that would likely take place in the spring.

So, if Edi Abu wanted three vials of Russian V-gas mixed with Lassa fever, then Edi Abu would get three vials of Russian V-gas mixed with Lassa fever.

~ ~ ~

Soraya Gaddah had been working the night shift in the Riyadh lab for only two months, but she had learned quickly that things were happening there that probably shouldn't be. But she knew to keep her mouth shut; she needed the job. She had recently left her home in Syria and had come to Saudi Arabia in search of a better life. Her native country was becoming more restrictive; Soraya knew she would soon be forced to conform to the practices of Sharia Law, or lose her life.

But Saudi Arabia was not turning out to be much better. In spite of her background in chemistry, her role in the lab was limited. She resented Rashid with his overbearing ways and his dismissive attitude. He was no different from the men she had left behind. As soon as she could save the money, she would leave there, as well.

She was standing next to Rashid when he got the overseas phone call. It had unsettled him, she could tell. His eyes had narrowed, and he had scowled as he had rubbed his bearded chin. She and Rashid were about the same height, but she weighed twice as much as him. Thankfully, her *burqa* covered most of it. It also allowed her to spy. She could sink inside the thick dark fabric and watch him without him knowing. She saw his eyes grow dark, his lids narrow as he finished the call. She watched him put on his glasses and pull up a website. She glanced over his shoulder as he verified an access code. She saw him note it in a log book, and watched from the corner of her eye as he walked to a locked vault in back of the lab.

She busied herself at the counter, watching as Rashid opened the vault and removed three vials. She saw him carry them to a table on the opposite side of the lab and set them out of sight behind a stack of papers. He went back to the vault to lock the door. Soraya walked as calmly as she could to the table with the vials, shoved aside the papers, and read the labels. *V-gas/Lassa fever.* She frowned as she walked away. She saw Rashid return to the table. She waited until he was busy with the vials, and then walked over and checked the phone log to see if she could figure out where the call request had come from. The lab was required to monitor all incoming calls, each one electronically identified through a system similar to caller ID. She pushed a button on the phone and several numbers appeared. She scrolled through the list, looking for one that matched the timing of Rashid's trip to the vault. She caught a glimpse of Rashid; he was walking toward her. She had to hurry. She found the number and committed it to memory. Rashid was only a few steps from where she was standing. She walked away, pretending to busy herself with another task.

She could feel Rashid's eyes follow her as she walked to another part of the lab. She began to sweat. She didn't turn around, scared her guilty eyes would give her away. She reached the opposite corner of the room and immediately wrote the number on a piece of scrap paper, which she stuffed in a pocket of the burqa. *Later, when I am by myself, I will call this number and see who has requested such an order.* As she worked, she grinned. She may have just found a way out of there.

Chapter 40

OUTSIDE TRENTON, NEW JERSEY

Tuesday, January 20th, 2004

Henderson was tired, but there was no time for sleep. He had taken care of Molinaro ... now he had to make sure Maddi was safe. Morning-star was not going to let a missed opportunity get in his way.

He gave a quick wave to the trucker who had just dropped him at an off-ramp sixty miles from Trenton, New Jersey. He checked his watch. *12:50 a.m.* He had left Providence immediately after the hit on Molinaro, headed north and then west, hitchhiking until he was far away from Rhode Island. At 11:00 p.m., he had called Rozenblats from a phone booth outside Springfield, Massachusetts, and had listened as the private investigator told him once again that he hadn't found Lili but was following a lead. He had then caught a ride with a trucker who had taken him all the way to New Jersey.

As he walked down the off-ramp just south of Newton, he tried to think why Morningstar would want Maddi dead. This was the second time he had tried to kill her in less than two weeks. *Why didn't Molinaro kill her when he had the chance?* That one was simple; because Morningstar wanted it to look like 'the Phoenix' had killed her. *Then he'd have us both out of the way.* But why Maddi? What had she done? *What have you gotten yourself into, Maddi?*

The highway ramp was in the middle of nowhere; no trees or buildings to block the wind. The cold air swept through him, and he wrapped his coat tighter as he trudged down the ramp.

He pulled his stocking cap low on his forehead as he thought back to hits Morningstar had asked him to complete in the past. Never had they involved the killing of a U.S. senator. There was only one thing that would cause Morningstar to dare such an undertaking; she had somehow gotten in his way.

He reached the bottom of the ramp and looked for an all-night diner. He spotted a well-lit café and jogged to it, heartened when he saw a sign advertising free Wi-Fi. He walked in, set his pack on a table in the back, and slid in the booth. A waitress walked up; he ordered coffee and a bowl of chowder. He blew on his hands to warm them, then pulled out his laptop. He plugged it in to charge and turned it on.

The waitress brought his coffee and he nodded a thank-you, doing his best to keep the left side of his face hidden. She smiled, but he saw the look in her eyes as she caught a glimpse of the scars and the mangled jaw. She tried to hide it, but she couldn't. *They can never hide it.*

He took a sip of coffee and clicked to the website where he and Morningstar had communicated many times in the past. He wondered if the man had gotten his message. *How'd you like that, Morningstar?*

A link had been added beneath it; he looked at it and frowned. Should he open it? *Maybe it explains why Maddi has been targeted.* He clicked the link and his heart stopped. He stared at the picture on the screen. It was a little girl – Lili – with long blond curls falling in waves around her face. Her eyes were closed as she lay still in the snow. He read the message underneath, and his hands began to shake. *The bastard has done it ... he's killed her!* His eyes were burning; he enlarged the picture. Was it her? He couldn't be sure ... it looked like her, even down to the freckle over her left eye. He grabbed the table, doing his best to keep it together. Was it true? Had Morningstar killed Lili? He had to speak to Rozenblats. He looked outside for a payphone, and saw one just beyond the door.

He closed the laptop, shoved it in his bag, and carried it with him to the phonebooth. He dialed Rozenblats for the second time that night.

The private detective answered after three rings. Henderson could barely hear him over what sounded like the roar of an ocean in the distance. "Rozenblats here."

"It's me," Henderson whispered. "I was just shown a picture of Lili ... dead."

There was silence. After a minute, Rozenblats said, "I just boarded a boat. I'm chasing a rumor that she was taken to Sweden. Send me the photo." He rattled off a secure email address. "I'll see what I can find."

Henderson hung up the phone and returned to his table. He pulled out his laptop, opened it, and stared at the picture. He read the message one more time. "*...subject has been eliminated.*" He clenched his jaw. He had promised Albins he would keep Lili safe. *I have failed.* He forwarded a copy to Rozenblats.

Never had he hated Morningstar more. If the man had been standing in front of him, regardless of the consequences, Henderson would have choked him to death. He leaned back and sighed. Lili was dead. *It can't be!* After four years of killing to keep her safe, she was gone ... murdered by the very man who had forced Henderson to become an assassin. *And for what? So the bastard could kill her anyway.*

He took slow, deep breaths, holding onto the table to keep from pounding the wall with his fist. His soup arrived; he shoved it aside, struggling to breathe as he did his best to not fall apart. *Let it go, Henderson ... there's nothing you can do.* But he would never let it go ... he would never be the same. He had left a trail of murder and deceit, and it had finally ended with the death of a little girl.

He closed his eyes, wondering how he would carry on. He felt empty ... numb. He put his head in his hands, working hard just to breathe. Finally, after ten minutes or so, he raised the lukewarm coffee to his lips and, with shaking hands, forced himself to take a drink. He needed to get back to work. Maddi was in danger.

His fingers were unsteady as he typed in Maddi's Senate website. He scrolled down the page; there was nothing but routine proposals and a few legislative bills. *Lili's dead.* He frowned. *Stay focused, Henderson.* One of the proposals challenged the constitutionality of Eminent Domain. It included a list of pending lawsuits, and he read them through, flinching when he saw "Rocky's Restaurant v. the City of Providence." He shook his head. *Eminent Domain doesn't rise to the level of a high-risk hit.* He scrolled further and was about to log off when he saw a bill sponsored by Maddi and a Senator John Gray from New York. It had been proposed two weeks ago, and would require that all government arms contracts be presented to the Senate Arms Committee, and that the bids then be given to the full senate for final review. *That's it!* With that one bill, Maddi would completely undermine the operations of the Bentley Group ... *and she probably doesn't even know they exist.*

He took a final sip of coffee, leaving the soup untouched. He placed a ten-dollar bill on the table, packed up his computer, and threw his bag over his shoulder. He walked to the road and trudged up the ramp. Soon a semi slowed and pulled alongside him.

"Where ya headed, bud?"

He ran to the passenger side, climbed in, and said, "Washington, DC."

Chapter 41

WASHINGTON, DC

Maddi's mystery driver had taken her south along the coast. They had driven in silence for nearly seven hours. At one point they had stopped for gas and Maddi had quickly run into the bathroom, but that had been their only stop, and they reached the outskirts of DC just after one a.m. Maddi had done her best to stay calm, but had had little success. She had tried to nap, but every time she closed her eyes, she saw Larry hanging from the showerhead. She was having a hard time believing he was gone; he had been with her for over five years and they had gone through quite a bit in that time. She chuckled sadly, remembering his comment when she had told him she was going to a pre-school Easter pageant in Fort Wayne, Indiana. *"Senator, I'm willing to follow you into the darkest tunnels and out among the most vicious crowds, but I draw a line at wading into the untamed world of four-year-olds."*

Maddi grinned as she wiped her eyes. She would miss Larry.

And it was all her fault. Her need to find Henderson – a dead man for all intents and purposes – had placed both her and Larry in harm's way. *But only Larry died.* Another man killed ... right next to her ... while she stayed unharmed. *Why was I spared?* She had pondered the question for the past seven hours and was no closer to answering it than she had been when they left Providence.

They reached downtown DC, and she soon saw the familiar gas station a block from her house. It was clear the driver had been told her home address. She trembled, suddenly afraid. Wouldn't her house be the first place a would-be killer might look for her? She couldn't stay there; not tonight anyway. She was about to ask the driver to wait while she ran inside and grabbed a few things, when, with help from a nearby lamppost, was able to see three cars in her driveway. One of the cars bore the insignia of the DC police, while the other two were plain dark sedans. As her driver pulled to the curb, she saw officers standing next to the cars. She didn't want to get out, but she knew she had to. The driver offered to help with her bag.

"No ... no, thank you, I'll be fine." She was unsteady as she stepped out of the car. She had left her coat in the hotel room, and the cold air made her shiver. She grabbed her bag and thanked the man. "Please, send the bill to my Senate office."

She was about to hand him her card, when he said, "It's already been taken care of, Senator."

He sped off before she could ask who had paid. She watched him drive away ... one more link to Henderson vanishing into the night. Toting her bag, she walked up to an officer. "Ex – excuse me, my name is Cynthia Madison..." her voice was shaking as she added, "...I ... I live here. What seems to be the problem?"

The man took her by the arm and practically dragged her to a large, burly man standing next to one of the sedans. "Sir, I have the senator right here."

Maddi recognized the Secret Service Director, Sam Allen. "Hello, Sam."

Allen looked at Maddi. His eyes widened as he shook his head. "Do you have any idea how long we've been looking for you?" He didn't wait for an answer. "Agent Moses has been killed, Senator."

Maddi looked down. "I know."

"You know? What the hell happened, Senator?"

Maddi froze. *Think!* All that time in the car, and she hadn't even bothered to come up with a timeline of events to explain the unexplainable. She blurted out, "I ... I went to find Larry ... so we could ... go to dinner. He was–" she stopped. "I – I had to escape, and I couldn't call anyone ... because I thought they might be tracking my cell signal." She was about to cry – which she didn't want to do – so she turned away.

"How'd you get home?"

"A Town Car."

"You came all the way from Providence, Rhode Island by *car?*"

She nodded, unable to stop shaking.

"Senator, you're freezing. Let's go inside and figure out exactly what happened tonight."

They walked into the house and she dropped her bag by the door. She offered Allen a seat, which he declined, and she sat on the sofa clinging to a cushion as he stood next to her. An officer brought her a glass of water. She drank it slowly, using the time to think through what she needed to say. *They can't know about Henderson.*

Allen's eyes softened. "Senator, I hate to do this, but you gotta tell me *everything* that went on tonight."

Maddi nodded. Her hands were trembling as she took another sip of water. "First, I ... I need to know who all knows about this."

Allen frowned. "Well, there's the Secret Service, and the poor maid who found him, along with the security guard on duty at the hotel. He's the one who called us, once he found Moses' wallet. The maid had no idea who he was and, for now anyway, has agreed to keep it to herself. The guard has agreed to do the same. I spoke with the manager about six hours ago; he promised to do his best to keep it out of the news." He paused. "I doubt we'll have long, though ... it's not often a man gets killed while showering in a hotel." He sighed. "Now, tell me what happened."

Maddi told her story, starting with the flight to Rhode Island, omitting no details other than those related to the text messages. She cautiously put a hand to the phone in her pocket, hoping they wouldn't think to check it.

When she had finished, Allen frowned. "I'm still confused about one thing."

"What's that?" Maddi asked nervously.

"How on earth were you able to arrange a car to pick you up so quickly?"

Maddi took another sip of water, her mind working. "When I found Larry ... in the bathroom, I panicked. I was afraid to go to the front desk; I ... I thought the killer might be waiting for me. So, I ran out the back of the hotel ... to get help." She took another sip of water. "I saw a town car parked at the curb with a company logo on the side." She hesitated. "I don't remember what it said. Anyway, I was about to ask the driver to take me to the police, but I decided I didn't want them to know about Larry before you did. I was afraid to call you because of the cell signal, so I ... I asked him to bring me home, instead." Even as she said it, she knew the story was farfetched.

Allen narrowed his eyes. "He was willing to drive you all the way to DC from Rhode Island? Didn't you think that was a little weird?"

Maddi frowned. "Yes, but I was desperate. He offered to book me a flight, but I ... I was afraid." She took another drink. "Airline passenger lists can be traced, you know." Her hand was shaking as she set the glass on the table. "I tried to get him to stay ... when he dropped me off just now, but he drove away."

"How did you pay him?"

Think Maddi! "Cash. I paid him in cash."

Allen frowned. "That had to be expensive."

Maddi nodded. "Yes ... it was. Two-hundred-and-fifty dollars, to be exact." She took a sip of water. "I ... I didn't want anyone to be able to trace my credit card."

Allen stared at her and she squeezed the glass; she felt like she was going to pass out. He went on. "Can you tell me anything more about the car or the driver?"

Maddi frowned; she couldn't let the Secret Service find the driver; he might tell them that Henderson sent the car. "It ... it was a black town car. I barely saw the driver. He was white with dark hair; that's all I remember."

"That's it? Nothing unique about either him or the car?"

She frowned. *Come up with something, Maddi!* "Um ... like I said, the car had some sort of name written on the side."

"But you can't remember what it said?"

Maddi frowned, pretending to try. "No, I'm sorry Sam."

Allen mumbled something to an officer standing next to him. The man nodded and left the room.

Allen motioned to a tall man standing off to the side. "Senator, I'd like you to meet your new agent, Spencer Seacroft."

The agent and Maddi exchanged a nod. Seacroft was several inches taller than Larry, and thinner. His hair was brown, wavy, and cut close to his head. When he grinned, he reminded her of Andrew. Maddi tried to smile, but her lip was quivering and it was more like a grimace. "It's nice to meet you, Agent Seacroft."

"Likewise, Senator. And please, call me Spencer."

Maddi said sadly, "I'm afraid you may have gotten yourself into a bad situation here, Spencer."

He nodded. "It's what I'm trained for, Senator. We'll be fine."

Maddi smiled weakly, but it was a smile, at least. She liked Spencer Seacroft; something about him made her feel safe. *Because he looks like Andrew.* She rubbed her eyes and looked at Allen. "Sam, would it be okay if I rested a bit? I'm exhausted. I'll be glad to go over things again in the morning if you want."

Allen shook his head. "You can't stay here, Senator. Whoever killed Larry is likely after you; this is the first place he'll look."

Maddi was about to say, *"If he didn't kill me in Providence, why would he kill me here,"* when the house phone rang. She looked at Allen. He nodded and she answered it. "Hello?"

"Maddi, it's me."

Why is Andrew calling me on my land line? Then she remembered; she had turned off her cellphone. "What's up, Andrew?"

There was a pause. "Amanda's sick. She's in intensive care at St. Vincent's."

"Oh my god! The virus?"

"Yeah."

Maddi closed her eyes. "Didn't she take the antiviral?"

Another pause. "Apparently not. She thought it might hurt the baby."

Nothing more needed to be said. "Andrew, I'm coming down."

"No. I know you're busy. I just wanted you to know."

Maddi shook her head. "You wouldn't call me at two in the morning just to let me know. There's more, isn't there?"

There was silence, then, "Maddi, they want ... to take ... the baby." His voice broke. "They say her odds are a lot better if they do."

"Not another word. I'm coming, Andrew. I'll be there by morning."

"Maddi, you don't need to–"

"I'm coming!" Maddi hung up the receiver and looked at Allen. "Sam, I have a place to go where I'll be safe."

"Where's that?"

"My brother's wife is sick ... very sick, and I need to go to him."

Allen frowned. "Where is he?"

"Columbia."

Allen's eyes widened. "As in South Carolina?"

"Yes. I promised I would come down as soon as possible." Maddi's hands were shaking; she tucked them in her pockets. "It would get me away from ... here."

"I'll arrange a flight."

"No! Please ... I can't fly."

Allen frowned. "Why not?"

Maddi was trembling. "I ... I can't get in a plane when I know someone is trying to ... kill me. It puts too many people at risk. Can we drive?" She looked at her new agent. "I'm sorry, Spencer. You were likely looking forward to a quiet night."

He shook his head. "Most certainly not, Senator." His brown eyes gleamed as he added, "I've been fully briefed on you, Ma'am; 'a quiet night' was not something I had anticipated." He grinned, the resemblance to Andrew even greater. "I've been working nights for the past month. I'll be fine, Ma'am."

Maddi looked at Allen, who shook his head and sighed. "Okay, I'll allow it. But you need to leave immediately." He turned to Seacroft. "The senator's second agent, Collins, is staying in Providence to help with the investigation. I'll send George Romaros to shift you in the morning." He walked to the door and motioned to the remaining officers. "Time to go boys."

He stood at the door, waited for them leave, and then closed the door behind them. He turned to Maddi and rubbed the back of his neck. "Senator, I'm going to handle this a bit different than usual." He paused. "I normally document on our private server where every protectee is, and which agents are looking after him or her." Another pause. "Here's my question: Is there someplace you might go to get away? You know, a place to lick your wounds after something bad like this?"

Maddi frowned. Where would she go? *Nowhere ... I have nowhere I go.* She looked at him and sighed. "Home. Not here ... back in Indiana. I haven't gone home in years, but my mom's there ... it might be a place I'd go."

Allen nodded. "McCordsville, right?"

Maddi's eyes widened. "Yes, but how did you—?"

"I like to know about the people my agents are protecting." He paused. "Anyway, I'm going to say on the website that that's where you've gone."

Maddi narrowed her eyes. "You think whoever is after me has access to your private server?"

Allen sighed. "I hope not. But he managed to get past one of my best men. I don't want to assume anything at this point."

Maddi nodded. It made sense. "Okay. But won't that put my mother at risk?"

"I'll ask local law enforcement to put a car outside her house."

Maddi nodded. "Okay. I'll need to tell Hank—Dr. Clarkson, Homeland's Deputy Director. We're pretty close. But I'll be sure to tell him to keep it to himself." She hesitated. "I'm not going to tell him about Providence, though." She grabbed Allen's arm. "Sam, you can't tell anyone what happened in Providence."

Allen put his hand on hers. "I'll need to tell Hanover, Senator. As Homeland's Director, he needs to know about the murder of an agent." He paused. "But I'll specifically ask him not to share it with Clarkson." He looked at Seacroft. "You, Senator Madison, Hanover, Clarkson, and me ... we'll be the only ones who know where she is. You know what that means ... right?"

Seacroft nodded. "Yes sir. Sat phones only, GPS off, no outside communication."

Allen nodded and walked to the door. He looked at Maddi. "I hope your brother's wife is okay."

Maddi nodded. "Th ... thank you."

He walked out the door. Maddi asked Seacroft to wait while she went to the bedroom to get a few things. She glanced at a clock by the bed. It was two-thirty. Spencer could have her in Columbia by nine a.m. if he drove fast. She grabbed a coat and a change of clothes and walked out to the front room. She put on the coat and stuffed the clothes in the bag she hadn't unpacked. She was walking it to the door when she stopped and looked back at the agent. She gave him a weak smile. "Can I get you something, Spencer? A sandwich ... a thermos of coffee?"

"No thank you, Ma'am. I ate before I came. We'll stop for coffee on the way."

She nodded. They walked out and she locked the door behind her. They went to a black sedan sitting at the curb and Maddi pulled her bag in back with her as Spencer slid behind the wheel. He started the engine and looked over his shoulder. "There's more to this whole mess than you're saying, isn't there, Ma'am?"

Maddi frowned. *How does he know?* She suddenly wanted to tell him everything; the truth about Henderson, the fact that he was alive. How good it would feel to let someone else in on the secret. But she couldn't; for whatever reason, Henderson wanted to stay hidden ... she would honor his wishes, at least for now. She sighed and shook her head. "No, I'm just confused." She added, "I don't know why someone would want to kill me."

The agent frowned. "What I find interesting, Senator, is – even though you were in the room next to Moses – they didn't kill you then."

"I know … I don't get it either." She added, "I can't stand to think about it … about Larry."

He nodded and put the car in gear.

He was about to pull away when she said, "Would it be weird if I sat up there with you, Spencer?"

He looked over his shoulder and grinned. "Not at all, Ma'am."

Maddi let herself out and slid into the front seat. With her hands still shaking, she strapped on the seatbelt as Spencer pulled away from the curb. He drove downtown toward Interstate 95, which would take them the entire way to Columbia. She looked over at him. "Did … did you know Larry?"

He nodded. "I did, but not as well as I would've liked." He looked at her, his kind eyes comforting. "He was a good man, Senator … a good man, who performed his job flawlessly. There is no regret in that … only honor."

She frowned. *Dying honorably certainly isn't as good as being alive.*

As though reading her mind, he added, "It's what we're trained to do. There's a certain pride we share in being ready to die to keep someone safe, Ma'am."

She rubbed her eyes, exhausted. She hoped it was true; she hoped Larry was in a good place, feeling honorable about his death. She looked at Spencer. "Could I tell you about him? He was really funny, you know. He could always make me laugh … no matter what."

Spencer grinned. "Certainly, Senator. I'd like to hear about him."

Maddi leaned back and – starting with the day she met Larry in a police station in downtown DC – she told of the pursuits of her trusted Agent Moses as he kept her safe through the years. She talked non-stop for nearly an hour, feeling a small bit of relief as she offered what little she knew of his life. She finished by saying, "I didn't want him to go with me to Providence."

Spencer frowned. "Why not?"

Maddi wished she had kept her mouth shut. *Because I was going there to rendezvous with my dead lover, that's why.* "I don't know. It didn't seem necessary."

Spencer frowned. "Well, I'd say it's a good thing he went." He paused. "Though it didn't end well, clearly you were in danger. His death allowed you to escape unharmed." He looked at Maddi and his dark eyes cut right through her. "As I said earlier, Agent Moses died nobly. I'm certain it was an honor for him to do so."

Maddi turned away. She leaned against the seat and closed her eyes; never had she been so tired ... so tired and so utterly sad. *I'm sorry, Larry.*

But she couldn't close her eyes without seeing his body hanging in the shower. So, she stared out the window, comforted by the bright lights of Washington, DC Even though it was three a.m., people were everywhere. Why weren't they home in bed with the man or woman they loved? She thought of Amanda clinging to life in a cold, sterile hospital room with Andrew at her side. She thought of herself, exhausted and scared, running off to deal with another crisis ... but at least she had Spencer. Then she imagined Henderson ... going to the restaurant, eating alone, leaving with no one. She pulled out her phone and stared at it, knowing it was her only link to him. She turned it on.

She was startled by Seacroft's quiet voice. "Excuse me, Senator."

She glanced over and saw him frowning. "Yes?"

"If someone's looking for you, they'll likely have access to tracking equipment." He paused. "You need to turn off your phone."

Chapter 42

WASHINGTON, DC

The shipment from the Saudi lab arrived at Morningstar's house early Tuesday morning, just as the sun was starting to rise. Rashid had used a military transport plane to ship the vials, and Morningstar had stayed home that morning to receive them. The diplomatic pouch containing them was carried by a young man who obviously had no idea what he was dealing with. He jogged to the front door, rang the bell, and stood at attention, an innocent smile blanketing his boyish face.

When Morningstar opened the door, the man said eagerly, "Good morning, sir. Delivery for General Daniels?"

Morningstar signed for the shipment and practically slammed the door in the young man's face. *Stupid boy ... you handle a biologic weapon as if it's a box of chocolates.* He took the pouch and carried it to the kitchen. He set it on the table and stared at it, grinning as he thought of what he was about to do. It was big ... very big. *It will change the course of history.*

He opened the pouch and carefully removed the contents. Three vials had been shipped in sealed packaging. Morningstar removed the plastic wrap, took out the vials, and inspected each one thoroughly. He set the vials on the table and carried the packaging into the living room, where he had started a fire in the hearth. He wadded the plastic in a ball and threw it into the flames. It melted, quickly becoming nothing more than foul-smelling smoke. He threw in the pouch with the identifying label, letting it join the fate of the plastic as it vanished up the chimney. He walked back to the kitchen. He lined up the vials, grinning as he pointed to each one. "Chicago, Los Angeles, and, last but not least, Laredo, Texas."

He picked up the last vial and held it in the air. "It is you, Laredo, who will finish it ... who will make things right, at last."

Somewhere in his head he heard music ... as if an orchestra was playing. He fell into a dance, holding the vial firmly as he spun about the room. Each crescendo pushed him faster and faster, until he was spinning so fast, he thought he might fall.

Then, suddenly, he stopped. Breathless, yet with his voice bold, he said, "So it was ... that Jacob returned to Canaan ... to be reunited with brother Esau." He raised the vial in his clenched fist. "As he approached the city, an angel came to greet him." He crouched low, pulling the vial to his chest. "The angel, Esau's guardian, attacked Jacob, touching his thigh," he rubbed his leg; the leg that had been injured years ago, "... causing him to limp for the rest of his days." He raised the vial exultantly, "But Jacob wasn't beaten. He was stronger than the angel, he did not let him win!"

He gripped the vial with both hands, his eyes closed as he thought of what he was about to do. He thought of his family, the triad of traitors who knew nothing of honor. They would pay; his mother, his father, his brother ... each of them would pay penance for their weakness. *And, all the while, I'll be paving the way for the future.*

He set the vial on the table and walked to his bedroom. He pulled out a box from beneath a pile of blankets in the back of his closet. He opened it, rummaging through the contents until he found what he was looking for ... a roll of tape with the letter 'P' penciled on the outside. He grinned as he looked it over. *Your fingerprints, Phoenix.* He put the roll in his pocket and practically ran to a spare bedroom down the hall. He opened a dresser drawer and searched through the clutter until he found a metal bracelet. The word 'Diabetic' was etched in the copper. He laughed. *I always knew this would come in handy.* "Thank you, Uncle Don," he said, as he shoved the bracelet in his pocket with the tape.

He walked to a table in the hall and pulled a rolodex from the drawer. He thumbed through until he found the number for the Pentagon travel agent. He opened his phone and dialed. "Hi, Rose. Morningstar here. I need a first-class ticket to Chicago. Tomorrow morning ... early. Business at the recruiting office downtown. One way will be fine. I'll catch a ride on a military transport plane when I'm ready to leave."

He hung up and walked back to the kitchen. He stared at the three vials sitting in a row. It was time. Simeon had failed ... Abid had failed ... Molinaro had failed. But Morningstar would fix it; he would make up for all of them. He raised a triumphant fist in the air. "Let the games begin!"

Chapter 43

COLUMBIA, SOUTH CAROLINA

Maddi waited until the sun was up to call Hank. "Spencer, can I borrow your satellite phone?" He handed it to her and she dialed.

Hank answered and she could hear the sleepiness in his voice. "Hello?"

"Hank, it's Maddi."

"Whose phone are you using?"

"My agent's."

"Are you home?"

"No. Amanda's sick. She's in the ICU at St. Vincent's in Columbia. I'm on my way there now."

"Maddi, that's terrible. The virus?"

"Sounds like it. They want to take the baby."

There was silence. "How long before they have to decide?"

"I don't know." She gritted her teeth, trying not to cry. "I'm about two hours out."

"Are you *driving?*"

She sighed. There was so much he didn't know. But she couldn't tell him … not yet. "Hank, I'll fill you in later." She paused. "I'm sorry, but I have to go."

"Okay. I'll try to get down there as soon as I can."

She gritted her teeth even harder. "That would be great. By the way, you can't tell anyone where I am."

"Why?"

Maddi closed her eyes. "I'll explain later. Bye, Hank." She ended the call and handed the phone to Spencer.

They reached the outer belt of Columbia just before nine, but were slowed by a traffic jam, and didn't arrive at the hospital until well after ten. Spencer parked the car and they jumped out, practically running to the entrance. Maddi hurried to the reception desk. "We're looking for Amanda McKinney-Madison."

The receptionist stared at her computer screen. Without looking up, she said, "Room 222 – ICU. That way."

Maddi ran down the hall, with Spencer doing his best to keep up. She was about to walk into ICU when she was stopped by a stout nurse with harsh eyes who glared at her over a pair of wire-framed glasses.

"Oh, no, you don't. Can't you read that sign?"

Maddi looked at the sign. *No unauthorized admittance.* "Fine," she said. "How do I get in?"

The nurse snorted as she went to a desk and sat down in front of a computer. She typed a few keys. "Who are you wanting to see?"

"Amanda McKinney-Madison."

"And you are?"

"Cynthia Madison."

The nurse looked up from her keyboard and eyed Maddi curiously. "Cynthia Madison. You aren't that senator, are you?"

"I'm a senator, yes. Can I go in?"

The nurse rubbed her chin. "Weren't you the one involved in that explosion at a DC hotel a few years back?"

Maddi was growing impatient. "Yes, that was me. Now, can I see Amanda?"

The nurse looked back at the monitor, typed hurriedly, and then scrolled down the screen. "Some man with a daughter who died from leukemia, wasn't it?" She looked up, her rigid features suddenly relaxing into something resembling a smile. "You were actually somewhat of a hero, if I recall. You and–"

"Can I go in now?" Maddi couldn't let her say his name.

After several more key strikes, the nurse nodded. "Yes ... there's your name." She looked at Maddi. "You can go in. But your watchdog will have to stay out here with me. He can wait there." She pointed to a row of chairs by the door. "And you'll need to put on a mask and gown when you get to the isolation ward. It's in the back."

"Thank you." Maddi pushed open the doors and spotted the isolation ward. She walked through a set of double doors, trembling as she saw Amanda's name written on a board outside the first room. She looked through the window. Andrew's mask was pulled away from his face. He needed a shave, and there were dark circles under his eyes, which made him look far older than his forty-four years. She donned a mask and gown, stepped through the door, and walked to where he was sitting. "Why aren't you wearing your mask?"

Andrew looked up, his red eyes making her heart hurt. "There's no reason to. I've already been exposed, and I'm on the ribavirin. I'm not contagious." He paused. "You should take the medicine." He reached in his pocket and pulled out a bottle of pills. He opened it and handed her one. "Here." He grabbed a water from the table next to him. "Take it."

Maddi opened the water and swallowed the pill. "So … how's she doing?"

He shook his head. "Things aren't good. She's not responding to the ribavirin." She could barely hear him as he added, "...they want to take the baby."

Maddi frowned. "Does she know?"

"Yeah, I was able to talk to her a little bit about it. It didn't go well."

"I can imagine." Maddi had to fight tears. "When do you have to decide?"

"The doctor had originally said this morning, but now he's giving us forty-eight hours. If she hasn't responded by then, he says there's no other option."

Maddi sat beside him. "Andrew, Amanda is tough. I'm confident she'll pull through, along with that baby," she grinned, "...who is, after all, a Madison."

He gave a weak smile. She rested a hand on Amanda's thin arm, doing her best to block out the beeps and whirs of the machines that were keeping her alive. Maddi looked at Andrew, his empty eyes confirming the truth: if either of them – Amanda or the baby – didn't survive, it was likely her brother wouldn't either.

Chapter 44
WASHINGTON, DC

Henderson had arrived in DC at five a.m. Tuesday, and had immediately begun the hunt for Maddi. He had gone back and forth between her home and her office at the Capitol. There was no sign of her. He had tried finding her by way of her cellphone, triangulating signals between various towers. Though he had told her to keep her phone off, he knew Maddi, and he knew she might very well ignore the advice. He hadn't found her signal, and, though he desperately wanted to locate her, he was comforted by the fact that if he couldn't, then neither could Morningstar.

After several hours, he made his way back to the shed near her house. She still wasn't home.

And Lili is dead. Though Maddi's disappearance worried him, Lili's death was threatening his sanity. It had been all he could do to sneak back into the shed, check that it hadn't been trip-wired or bugged, and then lay out clothes to cushion him as he tried to get some rest. The afternoon sun had warmed the shed, and he had found a spot on the floor that had caught the light. He had laid down, draped a Mylar blanket over top of him, and closed his eyes.

But all he had seen were images of either Maddi being tortured by one of Morningstar's men, or Lili lying dead in the snow. He had been awakened by the cold. The sun had set and the temperature in the shed had dropped considerably. He snuck to a nearby convenience store, purchased a blanket and a pair of gloves, and filled a thermos with coffee. He also picked up a battery for his phone. He returned to the shed and wrapped himself in the blanket, ready to get back to work.

Using his phone as a hotspot, he opened his computer and started looking for Maddi. He went to the Senate's main webpage, wondering if perhaps there was some sort of secret congressional meeting that she might have attended which had kept her at the Capitol all day and into the night. He saw nothing, so he hacked the site. He was looking for meetings that the public wasn't supposed to know about. He found a few, but – from what he could tell – Maddi wasn't involved with any of them.

He wrapped the blanket tighter around him as he clicked to transportation websites: the major airlines, Amtrak ... even rental car companies. Nothing. He kept going, looking not only for her name, but for possible aliases, as well. Still nothing.

All the while, he held the image of Lili in the back of his mind. Her eyes closed, her hair falling in curls around her face as she lay in the snow. It was torture, and at one point he closed the laptop, unable to go on. He would miss her. He did miss her. He had missed her for the past four years.

After an hour of agony, he decided the only solution was to kill Morningstar. Lili was the sole reason he hadn't done it thus far ... *right?* Wrong. There was still his operation ... Morningstar's despotic plan to ruin the world. It would go on, regardless. He bristled. *I don't care ... I don't care what his goons choose to do once he's gone.*

He sighed; it wasn't that simple. Maddi would still be a target. *I'll make her safe ... and then I'll kill all of them.* He opened his laptop. *So, find her.*

His hands were shaking as he typed in the address for the one site that he had intentionally avoided ... the Secret Service website. He didn't want to see "deceased" written next to Larry Moses' name. He felt responsible. *I am responsible.*

He typed in the address, holding his breath as he read the statement at the top of the page. "The organization extends its deepest sympathy to friends and family of Larry Moses, who was killed in the line of duty on Monday, January 19th, 2004."

Henderson clicked to a different page. "Protectees" was written at the top, and there was a place for a login and a password. Using a device that he had used many times in the past, he hacked the site and pulled up Maddi's profile. He frowned. No agents were listed. *That can't be right.* Yes, Moses was dead, but there should have been a second agent assigned, as well as a replacement for the first.

He continued to scroll, looking for an agent, or at least a location. This, too, was different from how it was usually done. They had added an additional layer of security, and he was having a hard time getting in. *Good move, Sam Allen.*

Finally, after pulling in another spyware program – courtesy of the Pentagon – he was able to hack through the security and unmask her location. *McCordsville, Indiana.* He frowned. Maddi had never mentioned it, and, in all the time he had tracked her over the past three years, she had never gone there. She had gone to Indiana, but never McCordsville. *So ... who is she going to see?*

He wrote down the address and closed his laptop. He packed his belongings in his backpack and threw it over his shoulder. It was time to go ... to McCordsville.

Chapter 45

CHICAGO, ILLINOIS

Wednesday, January 21ˢᵗ, 2004

Morningstar arrived at Chicago O'Hare on Wednesday at 7:10 in the morning. He had used a visit to a recruiting office downtown as his reason for making the trip. The agency was involved with officer selection, and they had been pestering the Pentagon to send someone to speak to the recruits for the past several months. Morningstar had told General Daniels he was going there to arrange a lecture.

"I'll fly in early, sir. I used to live there, you know. I'd like to spend the morning downtown." Daniels had barely heard him, simply nodding his approval. Morningstar had added, *"I'll set up a time for the lecture, and then I'll use a military transport to take me to LA so I can review the new terrorism guidelines with the boys at the base."* Daniels had agreed to the plan; he always agreed with Morningstar.

He hurried through the terminal, stopping at a bathroom to paste a thick black mustache over his lip. He put on a pair of dark-framed glasses and, with his carryon over his shoulder and his briefcase in his hand, he walked outside. The bitter Chicago cold cut through him as he waited in line for a cab. When it was his turn, he jumped in back, lugging his bags onto his lap. "Holy shit, it's cold here!"

The driver laughed. "Where ya from?"

Morningstar was about to say DC, when he thought better of it. "Florida. It was nice and warm when I left."

"What part of Florida?"

Morningstar hesitated. "Uh ... Miami Beach."

The driver nodded. "Nice part of Florida. I'm from Lauderdale, myself."

Morningstar nodded, eager to change the subject. "How far to downtown?"

"It depends where you're going."

"North Sheridan Road. Sunset Institute."

The driver nodded as he looked at Morningstar in his rearview mirror. "Should be there in about twenty minutes."

Morningstar leaned back and looked out at the busy streets of downtown Chicago. He touched the diabetic bracelet on his left wrist and grinned. He reached inside his travel bag, found one of the vials – now labeled insulin – and slid it into his pocket. He chuckled nervously. Though he was eager to complete the first step of his plan, it made him uneasy to think about where he was going and who he was going to see. It had been years since he had been there, and the last time had not gone well. *"Sunset Institute ... where dreams await you."* He smirked. *More like nightmares.* He closed his eyes, remembering the smells of urine and rotten food, along with the frantic howls of unbridled lunacy. He could still feel their misery as if he had lived it ... as if he was the one who had roomed with the crazies at the Institute. Unlike most of the world, he didn't pity them ... he despised them; every single one.

"We're here, sir."

Morningstar paid the fare, grabbed his briefcase, and threw his bag over his shoulder. He slid from the car, walked a few steps, and then stopped, staring up at the building in front of him. It was an old structure, likely built in the early 1900's, and it bore the markings of its Victorian ancestry; steeply-pitched roofs, uneven facades, and multicolored eaves over each of the narrow windows. But more telling were the features that spoke of its purpose; barred windows and doors, dark curtains, and poorly-hidden barbed wire that surrounded the building like a suit of splinted armor. *Keeping out the sane.*

The sun was rising and, as it hit the structure, it cast a long shadow on the street below. The cab drove away, leaving Morningstar shivering and alone on the empty sidewalk. He pulled black leather gloves from his pocket and slid them on, trying his hardest to ignore the voice in his head. *"Come in, Edward."* He walked nervously toward the building, the long shadow his only companion as he climbed the steps to the entrance. "Welcome to Sunset" was etched in a plaque by the door. He stared at it, his entire body trembling as he thought about what lay on the other side. He reached in his pocket and gripped the vial, regaining his nerve as he remembered why he had come. He spat at the plaque, took a deep breath, and walked determinedly through the door.

Chapter 46
RIYADH, SAUDI ARABIA

Soraya Gaddah was tired. She had gotten little sleep in the past twenty-four hours, and it was catching up to her. She had gotten off work Tuesday morning and, rather than heading home, had gone to a library to research the phone number she had gotten off the machine. All she had been able to learn was that the area code was a UN exchange, which meant that it could have come from anywhere. She had spent most of the day trying to find a name to go with it, but had come up empty. She had finally called a friend who worked for the Syrian government, telling him she was conducting a routine lab audit and needed the name for verification purposes. He had been eager to help, and, within an hour, she had acquired the surname assigned to the phone number, as well as a four-digit code that would allow her to contact the caller.

She had gone home for a few hours of sleep and had returned to work that night at seven. The twelve-hour shift had been uneventful, and, at 7:00 a.m., just as she had been about to clock out, she had been asked to cover for a co-worker who had had an emergency. She had agreed, reluctantly, and had spent four more hours at the lab, doing her best to stay awake. She had been relieved to see the co-worker walk through the door at 11:35 a.m. She had finished up a few tasks and had left the lab, waving goodbye to her coworkers. Though they expected to see her back that night, she had no intention of returning.

She had gone home to her apartment, had napped for an hour, and had packed a duffel bag, which she had carried with her as she walked to the bus station. At two-thirty, Wednesday afternoon, she had boarded a bus for the hour-long ride to Al Kharj. She had chosen the city because it was far enough away that she could make a phone call without worrying if it was traced.

The bus pulled up to the terminal at Al Kharj and she stepped off, clutching the paper with the information from her friend. She walked to a phone booth, lifted the receiver, and stared at the name on the scrap of paper. *"Abu."* Next to it, were the words, *"Dial these first,"* followed by four numbers and a pound sign. With a shaking hand, she put coins in the slot, dialed the four numbers, and pushed the pound key. She then plugged in the phone number she had gotten from the lab. After four rings, she heard a click, followed by a female voice.

"You have reached Edi Abu, Saudi Arabian Consulate for the United Nations...."

Soraya hung up before the message had finished. *It is a woman!* Why would a woman want such a deadly virus? She had no idea, but it didn't matter. She now had a name and a contact number; all she needed was a plan.

Chapter 47

CHICAGO, ILLINOIS

"Shut up, you crazies! Leave me alone!" Everywhere nine-year-old Edward looked, they were staring at him. Why? What did they see? "Mama, you can't stay here!"

Morningstar fought the memories as he stood in the foyer of the institute. He could *feel* them ... the Insane Ones; their warped thoughts trying to sneak inside his head. *Stay away!* A flickering bulb from a chandelier caught his eye as he took a hesitant step toward the front desk. He breathed in and nearly choked; the smells hadn't changed. Despite the fact that over forty years had passed, odors of urine, sweat, and antiseptic filled his nose. He had to fight not to vomit. Voices were screaming in his head; he squeezed his temples to get them to stop.

"Come join us, Edward ... It's time to come home."

How did they know his name? He hadn't been there for decades. He wanted to turn around and run out the door, but he forced himself to stay. He had a job to do.

He took another hesitant step on faded tile, making sure to avoid the cracks.

"Step on a crack, you'll break your mother's back..."

He walked a few more steps to a receptionist seated behind a desk. She was old – like the institute – and a single crutch was leaning against the wall behind her. She had long grey hair, and reminded him of the old woman from Hansel and Gretel.

"Get up, you lie-abeds, we're going to the forest to fetch wood."

He stared down at her. She had the lightest eyes; a soft grey that looked as if, at any moment, it would fade into the surrounding white. She smiled, her crooked teeth offering little comfort as she said feebly, "Can I help you?"

"I—I'm looking for ... Marianna Morningstar."

The woman took a skeletal finger and sorted through a list. "Room 345, down the hall." She pointed to a sheet of paper taped to the desk. "You need to sign in."

She laid a pen in front of him. He picked it up with his gloved hand and was about to write the "E" of Edward, when he stopped himself. Instead he wrote *Mr. Phoenix,* smiling as he smoothed down his fake mustache and adjusted his glasses. He laid down the pen.

The receptionist said, "Mrs. Morningstar will likely be in the Common Room at this hour. It's down the hall and around the corner."

Morningstar trembled. He remembered the Common Room. "Thank you, ma'am." He turned and walked down a long hallway, covering his ears as voices echoed from the walls. Dark shadows seemed to follow him and he remembered what his mother had told him soon after she arrived. *"Watch out for the shadows, Edward ... they trap you ... and take you away."* He picked up his pace.

He turned the corner and stopped in front of a set of double doors. He held his breath as he opened one of the doors and looked inside. Once again, he had to fight not to vomit. Nothing had changed. It was as if time had stood still ... as if the passing years had overlooked the dismal walls of the Common Room. Tall windows along the far wall looked down on a large, open room with stained tile and cracked baseboard. Three chandeliers hung from the ceiling, their spidery arms hovering ... *like Reapers,* he thought as he rubbed the back of his neck. He cracked his knuckles and stared at oversized wall paintings ... oiled canvases filled with gaudy flowers or story-book characters. Designed to soothe, their hollowness mocked the sanity of anyone who hadn't yet lost his mind. He saw a piano in the corner, waiting in vain for skilled fingers to stroke the ivory. There were tables scattered about, covered with half-finished jigsaw puzzles or unopened board games. Plastic chairs sat around the tables and beneath the windows, most of them filled with stooped patients in various stages of mental decay. Two orderlies stood in a back corner, engrossed in a conversation that Morningstar felt certain had nothing to do with the patients in that room.

He opened the door wider; his heart began to race. He cleared his throat and loosened his collar. Still carrying his briefcase, with his travel bag draped over his shoulder, he walked in and closed the door behind him. He wiped sweat from his forehead as Hansel and Gretel's old woman whispered somewhere in the back of his mind, *"First we'll bake ... I've heated the oven, I've kneaded the dough."*

Morningstar whispered sternly, "Shut up, old woman!" A thin man with dirty gray hair was sitting cross-legged by the door, and he glared up at Morningstar, his pale eyes resembling the vacant stares of bums on Madison Avenue. Morningstar hissed at him, laughing exultantly when the man scurried off in fear. He scanned the room for his mother. Would he recognize her? It had been so long. Would she remember him? *God, I hope so. I need her to know it's me ... as I do this.*

He looked from face to face, trying to recall his mother's deep green eyes and auburn hair. She had been beautiful ... and she had been his. She had cared for him and protected him, and had even lain with him on more than one occasion. He closed his eyes, his heart full at the memory. Though others might have thought it improper, Morningstar knew better; it was love ... the simple love of a mother for her son.

Suddenly he bristled. He opened his eyes, quashing the quiver in his groin. Her departure from his life had been a betrayal; a brutal, unforgiveable infidelity. *It's all your fault, Mother ... everything is your fault.*

He took a few more steps, and then stopped. He saw her. She was sitting in a chair next to a window along the far wall. She was staring out, her eyes fixed on something beyond the trees. A blanket was draped over her shoulders. Underneath, he could see a faded nightgown with an unraveled hem, a corner of it inching up her pale thigh, exposing the edge of a diaper. Morningstar turned away, repulsed. He backed to the door and, with a shaking hand, tried to turn the knob, but it wouldn't budge.

"...she seized Hansel, threw him into a stable, and barred the door..."

He was about to scream, when he reached in his pocket and felt the solid glass of the vial. He closed his eyes and took several deep breaths as he waited for his heart to slow. *You can't leave. This needs to be done.*

He looked around for a water pitcher. A decanter and plastic cups were sitting on a tray only a few yards away. He looked at the orderlies; they had yet to notice him, absorbed in their conversation. He walked to the tray. He set down his briefcase and lifted the lid of the decanter. In one quick move, he slid the vial from his pocket, popped the top, and dumped the contents into the pitcher.

He set the empty vial on the tray and looked around. The orderlies were still caught up in their conversation, and the patients' faces were blank. No one had noticed him. Still wearing the gloves, he reached in his bag and pulled a piece of tape from the roll he had brought with the letter "P" on the side. Holding the vial with one hand, he touched two sides of it to the tape, leaving clear Phoenix fingerprints. He set the vial on the tray behind the pitcher. He looked around; no one was watching him. He poured the poisoned water into several of the cups, hoping the residents would ask for a drink. Maybe he would even offer it to them ... *when I'm done with Marianna.*

He grabbed his briefcase and picked up one of the cups. He walked to where his mother was sitting by the window. "Hello, Marianna."

He saw seventy years of wrinkles lining her face, and a pair of dull green eyes sunk in sallow skin, their luster having faded right along with her sanity. Her auburn hair was now streaked with gray, but there was no mistaking it was her. He recognized the cheeks that would blush bright red when she was anxious, and the scar over her left eye, the result of a nasty fall down the steps.

She said nothing; it was as if he hadn't spoken … as if his voice had been muzzled by the stagnant air of the Common Room.

He set his briefcase on the floor and moved closer, grimacing as he smelled soap and stale urine. "Hello, Marianna. It's been a while. How are you?"

As if in slow motion, the woman turned from the window and looked at him. She smiled, a row of yellow teeth reflecting the muted light of the chandelier.

"Hello," she muttered, her voice strained, but her green eyes suddenly alive.

Morningstar trembled. *I miss you, Mama!* Through clenched teeth he said "It's good … to see you … Mother."

The woman smiled vacantly, the brightness in her eyes fading. "What did you say your name was?"

"It's Eddie, Mom."

"Eddie?" She frowned. After a minute, she shook her head and stared out the window. She mumbled, "I don't know an Eddie."

He grabbed his stomach; it felt as if he had been punched. His jaw tightened and he began to shake. He had been spurned – again – by the only woman who had ever mattered. *Forget it, Morningstar … you've got work to do.* He looked down at the cup. His hand was shaking, and his eyes burned as he watched the clear liquid shimmer in the plastic … *like holy water waiting to cleanse the masses.* His gloved hand became steadier as he handed the cup to his mother. With a warm smile, and a cool, even tone, he said, "Here Mama, have a drink."

Chapter 48

WASHINGTON, DC

Columbia, South Carolina

Hank was sitting in his office finishing a report, trying to get it done before he hopped a flight to Columbia. Hanover had somehow learned of Amanda's illness, and had insisted that Hank leave first thing in the morning to be with Maddi and her brother. *"I'll have a plane waiting for you at Andrews,"* he had said, adding *"Don't tell anyone where you're going."*

Hank had asked what all the secrecy was about. *"Just an added precaution because of what happened in Jacksonville."* Hank had wanted to remind Hanover that Jacksonville had taken place two weeks earlier, and the secrecy had only started the day before, but had decided to say nothing. Maddi would fill him in soon enough.

He was looking forward to getting out of DC He had learned little more about either the source of the virus or its connection to West African terrorists, and he was tired of staring at the same intelligence. He checked his watch. *Time to go.*

He threw his carryon over his shoulder, and left the finished report on his secretary's desk. He walked downstairs to the street and hailed a cab. He was at Andrews Airforce Base in twenty minutes. He ran inside. The captain was waiting. He boarded the plane, set his bag in the seat beside him, and made himself comfortable for the hour-long flight. He closed his eyes hoping to nap, but all he could think about was the bioterror plot. As the plane gained altitude, he reviewed every aspect of the attack; the victims, the virus, and the man who had somehow played a role, Abid Mensah. Was he working with the West African militants? Or was he simply their pawn? And why were there so few casualties? *Why go to so much trouble to kill only a few?*

The time passed quickly and Hank was surprised when the captain announced that they were about to land. At 10:00 a.m. sharp, the wheels hit the runway. The plane came to a stop at Shaw Air Force Base. He grabbed his bag and hurried off the plane. A car was waiting. "St. Vincent's," he said as he climbed in back. The driver nodded as he left the base and traveled west on route 378. The ride took less than an hour. Hank thanked the man and stepped out of the car. He was walking into the lobby when his cellphone rang. It was Hanover.

"Hank, there's something you gotta' see. Are you near a TV?"

Hank walked up to a monitor mounted in the corner of the lobby. On the screen was a reporter wrapped in a hat and scarf, braving the wind as she stood in front of an old building. Red ambulance lights were flashing behind her, sirens blared in the background, and her voice shook as she said,

"I'm ... standing in front of a ... mental institution in downtown Chicago, where over twenty residents have suddenly fallen ill and ... died. There's no explanation. As I watch these people being carried away, I'm horrified. There's ... blood in their mouths, and the pained look in their eyes suggest they suffered terribly. We'll provide more information as it becomes available."

"Holy shit, Hanover!"

"Yeah, I know. Listen, somebody has to get to Chicago right away to look into this. I know you're down there with Maddi; I'll try to find someone else. But be ready in case

this thing gets any worse."

"Will do." Hank ended the call and walked over to the receptionist. He showed his badge. "I'm looking for Amanda McKinney-Madison."

Without checking the roster, the woman nodded and pointed down the hall to a set of double doors. "Through there ... ICU."

Hank nodded. "Thank you."

He walked to the ICU and was about to walk through the double doors when a sullen nurse stopped him. He showed her his badge and she frowned. "I suppose you're here to see Dr. McKinney-Madison?"

"I am."

She sighed as she stepped out of the way. "The isolation room ... in the back."

He walked through the doors to a ward in back marked "isolation." He entered the ward, found Amanda's room, and looked through the window. He saw Maddi sitting with a thoroughly exhausted Andrew. He put on a mask and gown, walked in, and whispered to Maddi, "How's she doing?"

Maddi stood and gave him a hug. She whispered, "Not good." She then turned to Andrew and said, "I think maybe a little better. What do you think, Andrew?"

Andrew said nothing.

Hank grabbed a chair and pulled it beside Maddi. He sat silently, holding Maddi's one hand with both of his. Her other hand clung to Andrew's, and he could feel the bond between them. Though Hank had only a vague idea what had happened when they were younger, he knew, whatever it was, it had made them fierce allies.

Minutes turned into hours. Sometime after three p.m., a doctor came in, went to Amanda's bedside, and pulled a chart from the railing. He skimmed it and said, "Has she been awake at all?"

Maddi shook her head. "No. What do you think, doctor?"

"The baby's doing great. But I fear it's at Amanda's expense."

"What about the ribavirin?"

"It appears to be keeping the infection from progressing, but it's not strong enough to destroy the virus. I'm running out of ideas."

Andrew looked at the doctor, his eyes desperate. "I just want her to wake up."

The doctor nodded. "It's her body's way of trying to keep her and the baby safe." He put a hand on Andrew's shoulder. "You're going to have to make a decision soon, I'm afraid."

"How long?"

The doctor frowned as he looked at Amanda. "She's holding her own for now, but if she doesn't turn around in the next twenty-four hours, we'll have no choice, Andrew ... we'll have to take the baby."

Chapter 49
LOS ANGELES, CALIFORNIA

It was done. The first part of the plan had been completed, and Morningstar was elated. It had gone well. But his moment of weakness as he had stared at his mother had nearly sabotaged his efforts. He couldn't let it happen again. The next two steps of the plan would require better control.

He chuckled as he thought of his mother writhing in her chair. Once he had taken care of her, he had carried cups of poisoned water to the two guards – who still weren't paying attention – and they had gulped them down without a thought. He had served several of the inmates, and then, before anyone had had time to realize what was happening, he had grabbed his briefcase and, with his travel bag over his shoulder, had left the building by way of a side door. It had sounded an alarm, but it didn't matter; the screaming had already begun. There was only one camera in the east lot, and he had made sure to stay clear of it as he had approached the barb-wire fence. Glad for his thick gloves, he had tossed over his bags, and had then climbed the fence, grabbed the bags, and sprinted away. He had been careful to keep to the alleys to avoid the closed-circuit TV that monitored the main streets. After several blocks, he had yanked off the gloves, the mustache, and the glasses, and had thrown them in a dumpster. He had then walked calmly to the corner, where he hailed a cab.

Though he would have liked to have stayed to the end, looking at Marianna's withered body had been more than he could take. The woman who had left him as a small boy had grown old and weak; he would never forgive her ... not even now, when he knew she was dead.

He had made a two-hour stop at the recruiting center in downtown Chicago to secure his alibi and had even had lunch with one of the administrators. He was now sitting on a military transport plane on his way to LA

It had been easy to justify the trip to the California army base; there were new counter-terrorism proposals that needed review, and Morningstar was the logical choice to handle the task. He had gone so far as to place himself on the schedule to meet with a Captain Jamison that afternoon. The captain, a decorated soldier who had seen action in both Iraq wars, had served under his father. *Perfect.*

The day before, Morningstar had mentioned to Josh, his technical analyst, that a threat had been issued against an unspecified U.S. military target. Under the guise of understanding how America might defend against such an attack, he had had Josh walk him through the video camera set-up for several of the bases; how they worked and how an adversary might go about disabling them.

"For example, what if a spy wanted to shut down the cameras in the LA base where I'm going tomorrow, Josh? Would it be easy?"

The young man had nodded. *"Too easy, sir. All someone would have to do is find a way to the security feed, which usually sits in a small room over the offices."*

Morningstar had feigned a frown. *"Why have we made it so easy?"*

Josh had shaken his head. *"The good guys always underestimate the bad guys."* With a quick demonstration, Josh had shown Morningstar the few steps necessary to make the video feed go to a repetitive loop, hiding all activity for up to ten minutes. Morningstar had watched in rapt silence. *That's all I'll need.*

The transport plane landed at the base at two p.m. Pacific Standard Time, which was five o'clock in DC Morningstar changed his watch to local time. He grabbed his briefcase and threw his travel bag over his shoulder as he walked to the door of the plane. He opened it, grinning as he felt the warm air against his cheeks. It was a nice contrast to the bitter cold of Chicago. He turned and informed his pilot that he wouldn't be needed until the following morning, "...and I'll want to leave early."

The affable soldier nodded. "I'll find a place to stay on the base, sir."

"Good. I'll stay the night in the officers' quarters."

Morningstar walked down the steps to a waiting sedan. A lieutenant stepped out of the car, saluted, and then helped Morningstar with his travel bag. Morningstar held onto the briefcase as he slid in back. He was driven to headquarters.

The car stopped in front of a building with "Command Post 617" written on a sign by the door. Morningstar grabbed his bags and walked inside. He went down a hallway, stopping just shy of a large room filled with soldiers busy at their desks. He turned left into the commander's office. "Good afternoon, Captain Jamison."

The young officer stood and saluted. "Good afternoon, sir."

"At ease, soldier. Are we ready to review the new counter-terrorism plans?"

"Yes sir."

Morningstar sat in a stiff chair in front of Jamison's desk and set his bags on the floor. He reached in his briefcase for a folder. As he did so, he spotted the two vials. He hid a grin as he pulled out the paperwork and laid it on the desk. "Here, Captain. Have a look."

The captain pulled the documents in front of him and skimmed through them. Morningstar took the opportunity to look around the office. There were pictures hanging on all four walls, most of them photos of prior commanders who had been in charge of the base in the past. He stared at each picture, looking for one, in particular.

He stood and paced the room, his eyes darting from portrait to portrait. He finally found what he was looking for on the wall opposite the doorway. It was a picture of an officer with a stiff beret and broad shoulders, his deep gray eyes showing pride, determination ... *and arrogance.* Morningstar read the inscription beneath the picture. *Captain Howard Morningstar, US Army, Green Beret.*

"He was a great officer, your father. He fought right alongside his men, you know." Jamison paused. "Such a tragedy when he was killed in Iraq."

Morningstar turned and stared at Jamison, saying nothing. The captain shifted uncomfortably, the brightness in his eyes quickly fading. Morningstar said, "I need a bathroom, son."

"There's an officer's lavatory over there, sir." The man pointed to a room next to Security.

Morningstar nodded. "Thank you, soldier. I'll be right back."

He walked to the bathroom, slid inside, and locked the door. If what Josh had told him was true, the security feed should be somewhere overhead. He stood on the toilet seat and removed a ceiling panel. He jumped up into a narrow crawl space and crept three-and-a-half feet to a low-ceilinged room. He saw a staircase; likely access for the security team from the room below. He looked around and found – just as Josh said he would – the device that controlled the security cameras. It looked like a large laptop. It was connected to twelve cameras and, on its screen, were twelve different views of the base. He pulled on a pair of surgical gloves and located the camera that viewed the back entrance. Using methods that Josh had taught him the day before, he adjusted a timer so it would corrupt the recording between 7:30 and 8:00 tomorrow morning. He then found the two cameras that oversaw Jamison's office, as well as two more that monitored the soldiers' work area. He set those timers to do a ten-minute repetitive loop, starting in two minutes. He checked his watch: *3:38.* The four cameras would return to normal at 3:50. *Ten minutes ... plenty of time.*

He scooted back to the opening over the bathroom and dropped onto the toilet seat. He replaced the overhead panel and stepped to the floor. He pulled off his gloves, shoved them in his pocket, and flushed the commode. He brushed off the dust from the crawl space and walked to the mirror. He grinned as he put a hand through his styled hair. He resembled his father. Both men had square jaws and deep, gray eyes. *But only I have the irresistible dimples.* He chuckled as he washed his hands, dried them, and walked out of the room.

He returned to Jamison's office and took a seat. He opened his briefcase, grabbed one of the vials, and hid it in his hand. "What do you think, Jamison?"

"It looks good, sir."

"Yes, I think they've covered about everything." He paused. "Hey son, have you got some coffee on this base?"

"Certainly sir." The officer stood and walked to a coffeemaker sitting outside his door, in the large room where the soldiers were working.

With the vial hidden in his fist, Morningstar grabbed the roll of tape from his bag and followed him. "Thank you, Captain. I can get my own coffee."

"Yes sir."

Jamison returned to his office, as Morningstar walked to the coffeemaker and poured himself a cup. He opened the top of the machine and pretended to smell the aroma, looking around to see if any of the soldiers were watching. All were hard at work. Morningstar popped the lid of the vial and dumped the contents into the carafe. He used his handkerchief to wipe it clean, and then touched it on two sides with a piece of the Phoenix fingerprint tape. He slid the roll of tape in his pocket, and hid the vial behind the coffee machine. He grabbed his cup and stepped away. He leaned into the office and said to the commander, "How 'bout we go over the material at one of these tables where the sun comes in instead of in that stuffy office?"

The officer nodded and grabbed the documents. "Yes sir." He walked out carrying the paperwork. "All ready, sir."

Morningstar grinned at the young captain ready to serve, obedient to higher authority. He knew his father had overseen many such men. He wondered if his father had beaten them, too? "Why don't you pour yourself a cup of coffee, officer?" Louder, for the others to hear, he added, "And let's give a break to these hard-working soldiers. They deserve a cup, too, don't you think, Captain?"

Chapter 50

PITTSBURG, PENNSYLVANIA

Henderson had arrived in Pittsburg just before noon, slowed by a traffic jam in Philadelphia, and a flat tire near Hershey. He had hitched a ride with a semi driver just outside DC, and had gone with him all the way to Pittsburg. In exchange for Henderson's help with the tire, the man had driven him to a cheap motel at the edge of town. *"It ain't much, but at least it gets you out of the cold."*

Henderson had been grateful. He had had little sleep and hardly anything to eat, and he took the opportunity to do both. He grabbed carryout from a nearby diner, ate it in a few bites, and then slept in a bed for the first time in weeks. By the time he awoke, it was nearly six p.m., and the sun was starting to set. He took a quick shower, and then logged onto his laptop to see if he could determine why Maddi had decided to go to McCordsville. He had figured out that she had grown up there, and that her mother still lived there. But that didn't explain why she would go back; Maddi never went home. Besides, she had nearly been killed less than a day ago ... would she really be willing to put her mother at risk?

He logged onto her senate webpage and clicked a link that took him to a site set aside for local constituents. Maybe she was planning to meet with some of her supporters, or conduct a town hall event. There was nothing scheduled, but he wasn't surprised. *She wouldn't do that ... she's trying to lay low.*

He decided to check local newspapers to see if there was an upcoming event that might explain her presence. He scrolled to the site of an Indiana paper, stunned when he saw an alert flash across the screen regarding a terror attack in downtown Chicago. He clicked the alert and was taken to a single paragraph. There were few details, and he was about to log off when he read the last two lines...

"Similar cases were identified just over a week ago at a clinic in downtown Columbia. The director of the facility, Dr. Andrew Madison, a fellow Hoosier, has been unavailable for comment."

His eyes widened. *Maddi's brother is involved in this mess!* So, where was Andrew? Had he maybe snuck home to avoid the press? Had Maddi gone home to be with her brother ... both of them needing a bit of time away from the spotlight?

Henderson pulled up the website for the Columbia clinic and hacked the personnel files, looking for something to show that Andrew had taken a leave of absence. He found nothing. He went to a different website, typed in a series of codes, and was taken to the site of a sophisticated software program that could isolate the recent activities of any given person...credit card purchases, bank withdrawals ... every transaction visible at the touch of a button, thanks to NSA technology. He typed in Andrew's name and waited as it began to sift through his financial life.

It would start with his credit cards, and then search for any bank transactions made within the last seventy-two hours. Henderson stared at the screen, watching as it sifted through data from multiple financial institutions. So far ... nothing. Andrew had made no purchases and had done no banking over the last three days. Henderson leaned back and sighed. *I guess I'll figure it out when I get to McCordsville.*

All at once there was a ping. An insurance card appeared on the screen. He looked closer. The insurance card – issued to Andrew Madison through the clinic where he worked – had been used at St. Vincent's hospital, in Columbia, South Carolina on Monday, January 19th. He frowned. *Two days ago.* Still using the software, he sifted through the hospital paperwork. Andrew had signed his name, but the info was for an employee in the clinic, Amanda McKinney-Madison. *His wife?*

Henderson rubbed his chin. He remembered a Dr. McKinney ... from the Senate healthcare hearings four years ago. She had sat with Andrew throughout those hearings, and he had brought her to the hotel the night of the explosion ... the same explosion that had more or less ruined Henderson's life. He rubbed the scars on his neck, doing his best to recall that night four years ago ... a night he had worked very hard to forget. He could see them ... laughing ... arm in arm. *Definitely his wife.*

He clicked to Admissions and hacked into the medical records department. It took less than a minute to find Amanda's name listed among the ICU patients. "Isolation" was typed on the first page of the record, next to a diagnosis of dehydration. Henderson frowned. He was no doctor, but dehydration seemed hardly serious enough to put someone in the ICU ... *especially in isolation.*

He clicked through the chart. At the top of page two, written in bold red letters, was *"Patient is three months pregnant."* His heart sank. Now he understood. Andrew's wife was pregnant, and was somehow sick enough to be in the ICU. *Does she have the virus?*

Henderson closed the laptop. Maddi wouldn't go to Indiana if her brother was in South Carolina with his sick wife. Henderson didn't know a lot about Maddi's past, but he did know the deep tie between her and her brother. She had shared it their first night together. As a matter of fact, it was one of the first things she had told him....

"I've never been to Providence."

"Really? I can't imagine why. It's such a booming metropolis."

Maddi laughed. "My brother, Andrew, has been here, though."

"What for?"

"He looked at the Medical School at Brown. Warren Alpert School of Medicine," she said proudly. She grinned. "He's really smart."

"I see. And what about you? Are you really smart?"

Maddi laughed. "Do you think I'd be in Congress if I was?" She hesitated. "I told Andrew he couldn't go to that school."

"Why?"

"He would be too far away." She frowned. "I needed him then."

Henderson widened his eyes. "Why?"

Maddi looked away. "It's not important. Let's just say ... Andrew and I have saved one another on more than one occasion...."

It was all she had said, but it was enough. They were clearly joined by something in their past ... something deeper than normal family ties. Maddi wouldn't go to Indiana; she would go to Columbia to be with Andrew and Amanda. Which meant that the Secret Service had put the info on the website to fool those who might be searching for her. *Very effective,* he thought, as he pulled on his hooded sweatshirt.

He packed up his clothes and shoved them in his bag. He closed his laptop, laid it on top of the clothes, and zipped the bag. He put on his coat, wrapped a scarf around his neck and chin, and pulled his hat low on his forehead. He threw his backpack over his shoulder and walked out of the motel room, following the road out front for about half a mile. He took an alley to an intersection, where he waved down a taxi. He climbed in back. "The bus station, please." He would take a bus as far as Clarksburg, and then hitch a ride the rest of the way. He checked his watch. *Seven-fifteen.* It would take about nine hours, which should get him to Columbia by about five a.m. He prayed it would be soon enough. If he had found Maddi, then so could Morningstar ... *and I have to get to her first.*

Chapter 51

LOS ANGELES, CALIFORNIA

Morningstar waved for a cab, chuckling as he thought of what he had just done. Immediately after poisoning the coffee and then offering it to the men, he had pretended to receive a call. He had cut short his review with the officer, telling him he had urgent business to attend to, and they would finish in the morning. He had noted the time: *three-forty-eight;* the surveillance tape had been set to resume at three-fifty. As he had walked to the door, he had looked over his shoulder and had seen every man in the office reaching for a cup of coffee. *Perfect,* he had thought, ... *no witnesses.* He had left the building and had walked to an officer's quarters on the base, where he had unmade the bed, and had left a change of clothes and toiletries to make it look as if he was staying the night. He had snuck out with his travel bag and briefcase, making sure to avoid any cameras along the way, and had walked along back alleys to the deserted corner where he now stood, waiting for a taxi.

"LAX," he said as a cab pulled up and he slid in back. The ride to the airport would take about thirty minutes. He leaned back and stretched his legs, closing his eyes as he pictured the soldiers gulping the coffee. He imagined his father watching as they grabbed their throats in unbearable pain. He envisioned blood spurting from their mouths and was overcome with a sensation beyond anything he had ever felt; it was beyond gratification ... beyond pleasure. *The joy of retribution.*

They reached the airport and the cabby pulled up to the departure lane. "We're here."

Morningstar paid the fare, grabbed his bags, and got out of the cab. He walked inside and looked for a secure place to carry out the next part of his plan. He found an empty hallway that had been abandoned as newer sections were added, and went into a bathroom at the end of the hall. He made sure it was empty, then took off his suit and tie. He had brought a blond hairpiece, a mustache, and casual clothes; he put them on. He folded his suit and set it in his bag. He put his driver's license and credit cards in a pocket in his briefcase, which he then locked, and pulled out new ID cards, which he slid in his pocket. He grabbed an ID badge from the briefcase and hung it around his neck, completing the transformation. Edward Morningstar from the Pentagon had just become John Calhoun from the Waste Management convention.

He grabbed the bags and left the bathroom, walking down several hallways until he reached the ticket counter. With a well-practiced drawl, he said, "Good afternoon, ma'am. How quickly can you get me to Laredo, Texas?"

A young woman with gold wings pinned to her chest smiled and said, "One way, sir?"

"No, I'll need a return first thing tomorrow morning."

She nodded as she typed and studied the screen. "I've got a flight leaving in forty minutes. I can have you there by 11 p.m. their time. Does that sound good?"

Morningstar smiled. "That's perfect, ma'am."

"I have two return flights. The first leaves at six in the morning their time, which is four a.m., our time. The second flight—"

"I'll take the first one, Ma'am."

"Are you sure, sir? That doesn't give you much time in Laredo."

He grinned. "It'll be enough, darlin'." He gave her his fake driver's license and credit card, and casually scanned the terminal as she checked the license and ran the card. She handed back both items and returned to her monitor. He saw a TV in a far corner, and strained to hear the announcer.

"It appears to be some sort of virus that has rapidly sickened many of the residents at this historic, century-old landmark in downtown Chicago ... "

"Here you go, Mr. Calhoun. I believe they've begun boarding." The woman handed him the ticket. He thanked her, jogged to the security check point, and fell in line. He handed the TSA agent his ticket and his driver's license, along with documentation for his remaining vial of what he claimed to be insulin. He showed the agent the diabetes bracelet on his arm and the agent waved him through. He ran to the gate, his travel bag over his shoulder, his briefcase gripped tightly in one hand.

He reached the gate just as the last travelers were boarding. He handed the agent his ticket, grinning as he walked outside to the waiting airplane. He breathed in, the evening air warm and inviting as he strode to the plane and climbed aboard. He found his seat, put his bag in the overhead compartment, and slid his briefcase under the seat in front of him, wrapping the strap around his ankle. He leaned back and closed his eyes. He would try to get some sleep; he would need it. He was about to complete the third and final leg of his journey and it would be, by far, the greatest of the three. *And the glory will be yours, God ... yours and mine ... we'll share it.*

Chapter 52
COLUMBIA, SOUTH CAROLINA

Hank was made aware of the attack at the LA military base only minutes after it occurred. It was the second such assault, and Homeland was worried there might be more. He had come out to the lobby to watch the coverage, and had spoken twice with Hanover, who had told him that he had sent every available man to either Chicago or LA *"The country is feeling like they did after 9-11, Hank."*

The media wasn't helping, fanning the fear like gasoline on a brush fire, as they showed picture after picture of the victims; blood covering their mouths, their terror-filled eyes wide open. His phone vibrated; it was Hanover. "As much as I hate to do it, Hank, I'm going to need you on this."

"I get it. We need to put a stop to this. I'll get a flight as soon as I can."

"I'm sending a plane down to Columbia right now. It'll take you straight to LA Should be there in about an hour."

Hank hung up and walked back through the double doors of the ICU. He went to Amanda's room and stared through the window at Maddi and Andrew. He didn't want to leave; he never wanted to leave Maddi.

But things had changed between them, even more than before. Maddi had changed. He had felt it the minute he had sat next to her in Amanda's hospital room. Nothing had been said; nothing needed to be. She had still been kind to him; Maddi was always kind. But she wasn't the same. And she had yet to share the reason for the secrecy regarding her presence in Columbia; he had been reluctant to push her. She was, after all, holding vigil with her brother and his dying wife and child.

So, he had let it go ... which is what he had done on so many occasions over the past year or two. He knew she loved him, but he also knew that whatever they had was gone ... or at least altered to the point where he no longer recognized it.

He threw on a gown and mask and trudged through the door. He walked the few steps to Maddi, bent over, and whispered in her ear, "I have to go."

Maddi looked up at him and nodded. "I guessed as much."

He looked at her a second longer than he might have, marking her image in his mind. The world had changed, and their relationship along with it. He knew it now; he had known it for quite some time, actually.

He gave her a quick smile and then walked out of the room. He stripped off his mask and gown, and left the unit, the hospital, and Maddi. As he walked to the waiting sedan, he tried to think when he might see her again. *Does it matter?* he thought, as he slid into the back seat. *I've lost her either way.*

Chapter 53

LAREDO, TEXAS

Morningstar's plane landed in Laredo, Texas at 11:06 p.m. He grabbed his bags, waltzed off the aircraft, and strolled to the front of the terminal. He could hear TV commentators telling of the tragedies in Chicago and LA and he grinned as he thought of what he had done. In a matter of hours, he had created panic in two vital U.S. locations, while putting to rest injustices that had burned inside him for the last forty-odd years. *And this final assault will finish it.*

He reached the front door and walked out to find a cab. As the muggy Texas air hit him, he saw a sign near the entrance which said, "Welcome to Laredo." He smirked as he thought back to the last time he had been there; the last time he had set foot on the lovely streets of Laredo...

The heat – and the teasing – made ten-year-old Eddie run even faster for home. He hated this town, even more than he had hated the last four, and he hated the kids at the Laredo Academy, too ... he wanted to get as far away from them as he could. He would go swimming; Eddie liked to swim. No one bothered him in the pool. And if they did, he could dive underwater and ignore them.

He didn't notice the boys come up behind him, only aware when he felt the sharp pain of a fist in his back. He fell to the ground and covered his face with his hands, looking up through spread fingers to see who had hit him. There were three Academy boys standing over him, laughing and spitting out curse words, as another one ran up and kicked him hard in the chest.

He tried to get up, but one of them shoved him to the ground, while another threw rocks at his head. Two of the boys then jumped on his legs and Eddie felt something give; he cried out in pain as he squeezed his eyes shut and tried not to cry.

Suddenly the hitting stopped. Eddie didn't move, afraid to open his eyes. 'Am I dead?' He could hear fists pounding fists, and grunts of anger as the fight waged on, but, for some reason, he could no longer feel them hitting him. 'I must be dead.' Finally, he found the courage to open his eyes. He was stunned to see his older brother, Timmy, trying to fight off the attackers. Though Timmy tried to be tough, he was a weak boy; he had always been weak. He was certainly no match for the gang of thugs. Timmy looked over at Eddie; his face was bloodied, his eyes pleaded for help. "Get up, Eddie! Help me!"

Eddie looked at Timmy and – though he knew he should help him – he couldn't. He felt like he was paralyzed. He finally managed to stand, but his legs were weak, his right one feeling like it might give out at any minute. He was scared and hurt and, instead of running to help Timmy, he turned the other way and limped to a nearby bus station.

He hobbled into the station and leaned against the door. There was no one in sight. He stared at the front counter, knowing he should let someone know about the fight, but he couldn't ... he was too scared. He limped to a row of chairs at the back of the lobby and knelt behind them. He hugged his knees, whispering over and over, 'Don't let anyone know you're here.' His teeth were chattering and his leg was on fire, but he couldn't ask for help; it would be like admitting he was weak.

It was late in the day and only one or two travelers straggled into the station. Eddie was glad; he welcomed the quiet. A fan hummed in the opposite corner of the room, and he let the soothing whirr comfort him as he huddled behind the chairs. He had no idea how long he stayed there, but he *saw the sun set and the moon rise. He finally fell asleep, tucked in a ball behind the chairs....*

Morningstar was suddenly jostled by a luggage cart. "Excuse me," said the man pushing the cart. Morningstar glared at him and waved for a cab, breathing in the steamy air of the south Texas night.

He waited as the taxi pulled to the curb, and then climbed in back. He looked at the dark-skinned foreigner behind the wheel, and said tersely, "The bus station."

Chapter 54
COLUMBIA, SOUTH CAROLINA

Maddi could barely keep her eyes open. She looked over at Andrew; he hadn't moved. He was still sitting at Amanda's bedside, still holding her hand, still staring at her as if she might wake up at any minute. But she wasn't waking up, and the grief was almost more than Maddi could take. She leaned over and said, "I need some air."

She left the room and tossed her mask and gown in a basket by the door. She took her coat from the rack, carrying it over her arm as she walked through the double doors of the ICU. She looked for her agent. He jumped up when she walked out.

"I need some air, Spencer."

"It's cold out there, Senator."

"I don't care. Maybe it'll wake me up."

She put on her coat and they walked out to a small garden off to the side of the hospital. She was stunned to see that it was dark. She had lost all track of time. She checked her watch. *One-thirty in the morning!* She looked at Seacroft and frowned. "Have you gotten any sleep, Spencer?"

He nodded. "Romaros shifted me twice while you were in there, Ma'am."

"You're kidding. You left and I didn't even know it!"

He grinned. "Don't worry, Ma'am. I gave him specific instructions to call me if you decided to go home."

Maddi smiled, grateful for men like Seacroft. She sat on a stone bench and pulled out her phone.

"Are you sure you want to do that, Senator?" He reached in his pocket. "Here ... use mine."

She nodded and took the satellite phone. She dialed her office intending to leave Phil a message, surprised when she heard, "Senator Madison's office, may I help you?"

"Phil, it's Maddi. What are you doing there so late?"

She could hear the relief. "My god, Maddi, it's so good to hear your voice."

"I'm sorry I haven't called, Phil. There's a lot going on."

Much quieter, he said, "I know. It's why I'm here. There was an emergency session of Congress concerning the Lassa fever attacks, and I wanted to be available in case they needed your input."

Maddi sighed. "I couldn't live without you, you know."

She heard a chuckle. "I don't know about that." He paused. "Um ... I ... I was told about Agent Moses."

Maddi closed her eyes. "It's terrible, Phil."

A pause. "Did you know there was a second murder in that same hotel?"

Maddi's heart stopped. "What do you mean ... a second murder?"

"Another guy was found ... in the elevator. I tried to call you, but you weren't answering your phone."

She could hardly breathe. She had not seen or heard any news since leaving Providence. "Do they know the identity of the guy who was murdered?"

"No, but the concierge told the police he had been hired as your driver. Did you hire someone to drive you while you were there?"

Maddi sighed with relief; it wasn't Henderson. "The Pentagon did."

"Why the Pentagon?"

Maddi began to tremble as it suddenly occurred to her that Henderson had known what was happening every step of the way. He had known she was in danger; he had told her that Molinaro wasn't her friend. *How did he know?* All at once the pieces fell into place, and she couldn't stop shaking. *Did*

Henderson kill Molinaro? She said quickly, "I'll ... I'll explain everything when I get back, Phil."

"May I ask where you are, Senator?"

Maddi hesitated. "I'm in Columbia with Andrew ... Amanda's sick."

There was a pause. "I'm so sorry to hear that, Senator. Give them my best."

Maddi sighed. "I will." She added, "...and Phil, you can't tell anyone where I am. Not anyone."

A pause. "Okay, Senator."

She shut off the phone and handed it to Seacroft.

He frowned as he slid it in his pocket. "You shouldn't have told him your location."

Maddi sighed. "I know. But your phone's secure; so is his. And he won't tell anyone."

Seacroft shook his head. "So, do you want to tell me what's going on?"

"What do you mean?"

"There was someone else murdered in Providence, and it sounds like you might know who he was, or at least how it happened."

Maddi looked at him and frowned. "Spencer, trust me when I say this. I don't know anything more than you do."

The agent said nothing.

Maddi stared at a rosebush, empty of bloom, hiding between two boxwoods. A thin film of ice had formed on the bare branches; it made her feel cold inside. Did Henderson kill Molinaro? If so, why? Had Molinaro intended to kill her? Had Molinaro killed Larry? How would Henderson have known? And, if he did kill Molinaro, how was he capable of such a thing? Was he a spy? *What happened to you since I saw you last, Henderson?*

She trembled as a blast of cold air came from nowhere. She raised her collar and pulled her coat tighter around her. She looked at the moon trying to work its way through thick gray clouds, and thought about the man she had known not so long ago: brilliant, thoughtful, invested in the world. Somehow, in a matter of years, he had become a far different man who hid in the shadows and showed himself to no one, not even her. He had protected her; he may have even *killed* for her. Who was he? What had happened to him? *What has he become?*

She had to find him, or at least let him find her, so she could understand this new man; this new Henderson. She reached in her pocket and felt for her phone. Seacroft was right; it was a beacon, capable of telling those who wanted her dead exactly where she was. *But it's also a way for Henderson to find me.* As if it was someone else's hand willing to put her and her agents in danger, she closed her eyes, touched a finger to the switch, and turned it on.

Chapter 55
LAREDO, TEXAS

he bus station in Laredo, Texas looked much like Morningstar Tremembered, though it seemed a bit smaller. As he walked to the front door, he avoided looking over his shoulder at the site where the fight with the gang of boys had taken place. He stepped inside, trembling when he saw a row of chairs in the same spot where he had hidden so long ago. *I wonder ... did they remove the stains from when I couldn't hold my piss?* He scowled at the memories, as the smell of urine came back to him....

"I can't hold it ... I can't hold it anymore." He awoke in a puddle of pee and felt ashamed. The smell made him choke. But he couldn't help it. He had been there for so long. Why had no one come for him? He had been abandoned ... again. But did he really want to be found? After all, his father would probably blame him for the fight. His father always blamed him for the fights.

The sun came up, but still Eddie didn't move from his wet, smelly spot behind the chairs.

It was another three hours before the local sheriff poked his head behind the seats and said, "I got him!"

The sheriff tried to help him up, but his legs gave out. He took him in his arms, carried him out of the station, and sat him in the back of the police cruiser. Eddie began to shake; he was scared. He knew he would seem a coward to his father. He had run from a fight, hid like a schoolgirl, and then pissed himself. Worst of all, he had left Timmy to fight the boys alone.

But Eddie was hurt; he couldn't fight when he was hurt. It was Timmy who was the fool. He was the one who had chosen to join a fight with boys who were bigger than him. He hoped his father would see it that way.

The cruiser pulled up to their house on the base, and Eddie stared out from the back of the car, trembling even more when he saw his father standing at the front door. The man looked like he did when he was about to address his soldiers; stiff, blank-faced, emotionless. But Eddie could tell that he was angry. The jaw was set; the eyes narrowed. Eddie could practically feel the man's rage. How many times had he faced that rage? 'Too many' was all he could think as he hugged the door of the cruiser, fighting hard not to piss himself again.

"Where is Timmy?" he wondered. The sheriff came around to let him out of the car and he shrunk back, begging that they take him to the hospital. "Can't you see I'm hurt?"

Finally, he was pulled from the car and he walked, limping, to his father. "Thank you, officer," his father said evenly. The officer responded, "No problem, Captain. Took us a while to find him. Probably got scared when his brother fell into the ravine." He paused. "Again, we're sorry for your loss." Eddie panicked. What ravine? What loss? His father stared straight ahead, saying nothing. The officer returned to his cruiser and pulled away from the curb. His father put his hand firmly on Eddie's shoulder and walked him inside. "Maybe it will be okay after all," Eddie thought as they walked calmly through the doorway. But, once they were inside and the door had closed, it was terrible....

A speaker overhead announced the arrival of bus seventeen, jolting Morningstar from his memories. He looked at a wall clock. *Almost midnight.* The station was empty but for a few lonely stragglers waiting for passengers from the bus. Soon the station would be filled with those passengers; Morningstar needed to hurry.

He looked up and saw a single camera in a corner of the lobby. Keeping his face turned away from the lens, he walked to a water cooler and set his bags on the floor. He opened his briefcase and grabbed the last vial, hiding it in his palm. With his back to the camera, he used his handkerchief to grab several cups from a stack by the cooler and fill them, one by one, with water. Hiding his movements, he popped the cap off the vial and dropped a small amount of liquid into each cup. He wiped the vial clean, placed the tape with Phoenix fingerprints on both sides, and then set it behind the water cooler. He heard commotion as the passengers began filing into the station. *Show time.*

Chapter 56
LOS ANGELES, CALIFORNIA

It's like a war zone, Hank thought, as he surveyed the scene. He had reached LA at eleven p.m., Pacific Standard Time, and had immediately been taken to the military base. He shuddered as he walked past the desks in the garrison. From what investigators could determine, the virus had been delivered through a large vat of coffee, and it appeared that every one of the officers had had a cup. *Which means there are no witnesses.*

And it smelled ... like death. There was no other smell like it. He recognized it instantly, a throwback from his days as Cuyahoga County coroner. He was wearing a mask, but it didn't matter. *The odor fills your nose and it doesn't leave ... not for quite a while.*

As he looked at each of the victims, he could see the bleeding from the gums, the expression on their faces leaving little doubt as to the agony they had endured. He felt for his mask to be sure it was in place.

An empty vial had been discovered behind the coffee pot, and investigators had dusted it for prints. It was then sent to a nearby lab to test the contents. Although the vial had *Insulin* written on the side, Hank felt certain it contained traces of nerve gas mixed with Lassa fever. He had just learned that a similar vial had been found near the water pitcher at the Institute in Chicago.

He walked from body to body, doing his best to examine each one without getting too close. Some had fallen to the floor, others had died sitting at their desks, pen in hand. Paramedics had arrived at the scene but had not stayed long; there was nothing they could do. The men had died almost instantly. Samples had been taken and the entire area had been dusted for prints. A surveillance tape had been recovered, but the initial inspection showed nothing unusual. It was being sent to Quantico for further review. There was little to do other than share in the horror of a nation as it watched its citizens once again under attack.

Families of the victims had been stopped outside the base, sparing them the scene that would otherwise haunt them for a lifetime. Hank had not spoken to them, knowing others were handling the delicate task of informing them of the tragedy. As he walked by bodies sprawled in chairs or lying on the floor, he tried to look past the stunned eyes and gaping mouths, to the mementos and photographs scattered on the desks; pictures of the men and their families ... happy smiles mocking the tragic end to young and hopeful lives. He tugged at his collar, struggling for air as he was suddenly unable to breathe. He ran outside and pulled off his mask, gulping in air, trying to imagine what sort of man would willfully inflict such misery on others. He wanted to kick something or shout obscenities, but he fought the urge as he took a few more breaths, replaced his mask, and reluctantly went back inside. There were no witnesses to interview; no one to offer clues. It was as if the entire base had choked and died, taking every piece of evidence along with it.

He was startled by the vibration of his cellphone. He looked down; it was Hanover. *What now?*

The Director's gruff voice sounded tired. "We've got another one, Hank. This time in Laredo, Texas."

Chapter 57
LOS ANGELES, CALIFORNIA

Thursday, January 22nd, 2004

Morningstar was on the four-a.m. flight back to Los Angeles, still disguised as John Calhoun, and the captain had just instructed the passengers to prepare for landing. While leaving the bus station, Morningstar had fielded a call from General Daniels at the Pentagon; news of the LA assault had just reached his desk.

Morningstar had pretended to be upset. *"That's terrible, sir. I'm in my room at the barracks, but I'll head up front to take a look."*

Daniels had said, *"Wait until morning. I don't want you to get sick."*

Morningstar had had to stifle a laugh as he had replied, *"Yes, sir, I'll look into it first thing in the morning."*

As the plane touched down and slowed to a halt, Morningstar grabbed his bags. He checked his watch as he fell in line behind the other passengers. *Seven-ten Pacific Time ... let's go.* They left the plane and he ran past them into the terminal. He snuck into the same bathroom he had used fourteen hours earlier and removed his disguise. He resumed his role as high-ranking Pentagon official and, as he knotted his tie in front of the mirror, he frowned at his square jaw, now covered with bearded stubble. He pulled an electric razor from his carryon and ran it over his chin and cheeks. *Much better.* He had hardly slept in twenty-four hours, but he looked and felt wide awake. *It's amazing what one can overcome when doing the Lord's work.*

He hailed a cab outside the terminal and had it drop him several blocks from the base. Using the same dark alleys he had used the day before, he ran to the base, stopping less than a block away. He checked his watch. *Seven-forty ... perfect.*

He found an isolated clump of bushes and hid his carryon where no one could see it. He then walked to a nearby mini-mart and purchased a cup of coffee. Because of the corruption of the back-entrance video tape that he had arranged the day before, there would be no way to prove he hadn't left the base sometime after 7:30 a.m.

He threw his briefcase over his shoulder and ambled to the gate, having timed it so the guard would have just begun his eight-a.m. shift. The guard would assume that Morningstar had gone for a morning stroll prior to him coming on duty.

As Morningstar approached the gate, the soldier saluted. "Good morning, sir. I would have been glad to get you coffee, sir."

Morningstar frowned. "I needed to stretch my legs, son ... after learning what happened yesterday." The man glanced at the briefcase. Morningstar added, "And, as you can imagine, there are reports to write." The soldier nodded and opened the gate. Morningstar walked to the corner barracks where he was to have spent the night and stepped inside. He threw the covers back from the bed and then ran the shower, dampening a towel and leaving it hanging in the bathroom. He grabbed the items he had left the night before, stuffed them in his briefcase, and turned to leave. At the last minute, he pulled a well-worn manual from inside his briefcase, and walked back and put it on a table by the bed, marking a spot two-thirds of the way through. It would look as if he had left it behind. He strolled the quarter mile to the front office, looking on with others as the FBI and Homeland carried out their analysis of the scene.

"I just heard about the tragedy from General Daniels," he said to a lieutenant standing next to him.

The man's eyes widened. "Mr. Morningstar! We thought you left, sir."

"No, son, I decided to stay the night and get some reading done. I made myself at home in the officers' barracks. I was hoping to go over more of our terror readiness program this morning." He shook his head. "It doesn't look like that's going to happen."

The soldier shook his head sadly. "No sir."

"So, what do we know so far?"

"It's some sort of poison, sir. Homeland Security's been working it since last night. FBI was pulled in a few hours ago."

Morningstar shook his head and frowned, having to turn away to hide his grin. He slipped away and walked out the gate. He stole to the row of bushes where he had hidden his carryon. He grabbed it and threw it over his shoulder, and then walked the block-and-a-half to his plane. He had nearly reached the aircraft when he was stopped by an FBI agent, who flashed his badge and said sternly, "Are you Ed Morningstar?"

Morningstar tightened his jaw. "Yes, I am. Can I help you?"

"Sir, we understand you were in the base office yesterday afternoon, just prior to the deadly attack."

Morningstar tensed. "Yes. I've been on the base for the past sixteen hours."

"Did you happen to see anything amiss? Something out of place ... someone here who didn't seem to belong?"

Morningstar relaxed, pretending to ponder the question. "Well, now that you mention it, I saw a man hanging around outside when I first arrived."

The officer wrote on a small pad. "Can you tell us anything about him?"

Morningstar had to work to keep from grinning. "I was surprised by his presence; he didn't fit in. He was dressed in civilian clothes, and was tall, maybe about six-four. I didn't get a good look at him; he had on a ball cap and it hid his eyes." He paused. "I think he had blonde hair. He was wearing a torn jacket and the collar was pulled high around his neck." Morningstar pretended to think some more, then sighed and shook his head. "I'm sorry, agent, but I can't think of anything else."

The officer was still writing. "You've been very helpful. Thank you, sir."

Morningstar nodded. "Will that be all, then? I really need to get back to DC"

The officer straightened. "Absolutely, sir. We'll call if we have questions."

Morningstar reached in his pocket and pulled out one of his cards. He handed it to the agent, who nodded and smiled his appreciation. "Thank-you sir."

"Not at all." Morningstar chuckled as he walked to the aircraft. His pilot was waiting outside. The man jumped to attention.

"At ease, soldier. Are we ready to get out of here?"

"Yes sir. You're lucky, sir. Those men were killed soon after you left the office."

Morningstar nodded, trying hard not to laugh in the officer's face. He climbed the steps and took a seat. The pilot followed him onto the plane and walked into the cockpit. Morningstar dropped his bags in the seat beside him and buckled his seatbelt. He leaned back, hoping to get some much-needed sleep. He closed his eyes as he felt the plane lift into the air. He replayed the events of the last twenty-four hours over and over, the feel of it like nothing he had ever experienced. He had either truly or symbolically taken the lives of every one of his family members, and had done it with uncommon flair. First, at the institute where his mother resided, then at the office where his father had held command, and finally, in the bus station in Laredo, Texas, where his brother had turned him into a cripple. In the time span of a single day, he had managed to crucify every unpleasant reminder of the painful, pathetic life he had been handed. All that remained was the fantastic world he had created, where he was master over the minions; a father to his sons. Edward Morningstar – *Jacob* – was free at last.

Chapter 58

COLUMBIA, SOUTH CAROLINA

Hank was exhausted. He had traveled from Columbia to LA, made a quick stop in Laredo, and was now on his way back to Columbia. He had managed to get a few hours of sleep on the plane and, though he would have liked to have gone to the hospital to be with Maddi, he couldn't. Abid was scheduled to return to the clinic that afternoon. It was a long shot, but Hank needed to be there if he showed.

Hank's agent, Tom, was traveling with him, and they landed in Columbia just before noon. Hanover had arranged for a car to pick them up and they were immediately driven to the clinic. They got out of the car and, as they walked to the front door, Hank glanced over at the temporary isolation quarters. He shook his head and frowned. *The new America.* He walked into the clinic and approached the desk. He smiled at the receptionist. "Hello Lisa, it's good to see you again."

"She nodded." You too, Dr. Clarkson."

"I wish the circumstances were different."

"Me too."

"Could you tell me what time Abid Mensah is scheduled to come in today?"

Lisa checked her schedule. "One-thirty."

He nodded. "Tom and I are going for lunch. Can I get you something?"

"No thank you."

Hank and Tom left the clinic, found a café about a block away, and walked in. Hank bought a paper. They sat at the counter and ordered coffee and a sandwich. The waitress filled their cups, and Hank sipped his coffee as he read about the attacks. He looked at Tom and frowned. "I wonder why these last attacks were so different."

Tom shook his head. "Notice there's no cocaine this time around."

Hank nodded. Tom was right. So, what had been the significance of the cocaine? And why had there been two waves of attacks, the second so much worse than the first? How did the West African militants fit in? Were they behind all four attacks? He sighed. He hoped Abid could answer at least a few of his questions. *If he even shows.*

He laid the paper on the counter as the waitress brought their meals. He took a few bites of his sandwich, and then shoved it aside. He waited for Tom to finish, and then stood and put on his jacket. He paid the bill, and they walked back to the clinic. The air was cool, but the sun was shining ... an uplifting afternoon. *How misleading.* He checked his watch. *One o'clock.* Abid was due in thirty minutes.

They went inside and Hank walked up to Lisa. "Any sign of him?"

"Not yet, Doctor."

The two men took a seat in the reception area. Tom thumbed through a magazine, while Hank watched Lisa as she answered the phone and greeted patients. In spite of a ready smile, he could see the strain of the past ten days in her eyes. He frowned. *It doesn't just affect those who get sick.*

At one-twenty-five, Tom set his magazine on a table and both men stared at the entrance, hoping to see Abid Mensah walk through the door. Hank recalled Amanda's description: *"Early thirties, olive-skinned, about five-six, and chubby."*

A mother walked in with three children, followed by an old man with a walker. A minute later, two young girls sauntered in laughing glibly at some private joke. Several more patients came in, none of them Abid, and, at two o'clock, the men had all but given up. Hank stood, stretched his arms, and walked to the reception desk. "Doesn't look like he's going to make it."

Lisa looked up and sighed. "No, Doctor, it doesn't."

Just then the door opened and a dirty, overweight man wearing ratty clothes stumbled into the waiting area.

Lisa said, "Or maybe he will." She came around the desk to help him. She took one arm while Hank took the other. The poor man could barely walk, and they practically carried him to a treatment room. Hank couldn't help but notice the smell; the man clearly hadn't bathed or changed his clothes for days. Hank held his breath as he helped him onto the treatment table, careful not to get too close. Lisa found them masks and gloves, and left to get Abid's chart. They slid on the gloves and masks, and Tom stood by the table keeping Abid steady, while Hank went to the sink and filled a paper cup with water. He handed the cup to Abid, who finished it in one gulp.

Hank refilled the cup, handed it to him, and then sat on a stool next to the table. "Is your name Abid Mensah?"

The man stared at him through dull, tired eyes. His skin was grey and his lips were dry and cracked.

"I said, are you Abid Mensah?"

The man took a drink, choked on the water, and nodded. "Yes."

"Can I take your jacket?"

Abid pulled off the dirty coat and handed it to Hank, who did his best to ignore the smell as he folded it and laid it at the end of the table. He helped Abid lay back, cushioning his head with the jacket. Abid grimaced, and Hank searched his mouth for signs of bleeding. He saw nothing; no blood, no swelling of the gums. He grabbed a tongue depressor from a nearby shelf and looked closer. There was no blood anywhere. "Were you able to get the prescription filled?"

Abid looked at him curiously.

Hank said, "The medication. Did you get it?"

Abid shook his head. He lifted a trembling hand to the pocket of his shirt and pulled out a crumpled piece of paper. Hank looked at it and frowned. It was the ribavirin prescription. He said to Abid, "Why didn't you fill this?"

Abid stared at the ceiling, saying nothing.

A Medical Assistant entered the room and took Abid's vitals. His blood pressure was low, but his pulse was strong and regular. *Why is he okay?* Hank looked at the MA and said, "Could you please have Dr. Settles come in?"

A minute later, Lorraine walked into the room. Hank looked at her and shook his head. "It's the damnedest thing, Lorraine. Other than dehydration, Abid is doing okay."

She walked over to Abid lying on the table. "Did he take the antiviral?"

"No."

Lorraine's eyes widened. She did a quick exam, looking in his mouth, listening to his chest, pressing on his abdomen. She turned to Hank. "He is definitely dehydrated, but, you're right. He no longer shows any symptoms of the virus." She paused. "But he's dry as hell. We need to get him to a hospital. I'll take care of it."

She left and Hank looked at Abid. "What can you tell me about the cocaine?"

Abid's eyes widened and he made an effort to speak, but – though his lips were moving – there was no sound. Hank lifted Abid's head, helped him take another sip of water, and asked again. "Abid, I need to know about the cocaine and its connection to this virus."

Abid's eyes flashed. "Where is Kofi?"

Hank frowned. "Who is Kofi?"

"He come with me ... to America. He sick?"

"He's likely dead, Abid ... from the same thing that should be killing you."

Abid looked at Hank, his wide eyes suddenly angry. "Simeon. He did it. He did something to shirts, I know it."

Hank frowned. "Who's Simeon?"

Abid tried to lift his head. Hank helped him and gave him another drink of water. Abid whispered, "He works for–" he stopped and looked at Hank suspiciously. "You ... you tricked me." He laid back and closed his eyes.

Hank felt his pulse. Weak, but steady. *Why isn't he dead?*

Hank suddenly bolted from the room. He ripped off his mask and gloves as he reached the reception desk. "Is an ambulance on the way for Abid Mensah?"

"Yes, Doctor."

"Make sure they take him to the same hospital as Dr. McKinney."

Lisa nodded. "St. Vincent's ... it's where we've sent all the cases."

Hank pulled out his phone and dialed.

Hanover answered on the first ring. "Hey Hank, any luck with Abid?"

"Yes, that's why I'm calling. He's here and he's doing okay. Dehydrated, but otherwise, okay. No bleeding from the gums, nothing."

"Great! The medication must be working after all."

"That's just it. He didn't fill the prescription."

There was a pause. "Why is he okay?"

"My question exactly. Which makes me think he has antibodies to this virus." He paused. "I'm thinking those antibodies could help Amanda and the others." He paused. "Oh yeah, and Hanover?"

"Yeah?"

"He blamed this on someone named Simeon. Do we have a Simeon on our watch list?"

"I'll check it out."

They ended the call and Hank ran back to the room. The medics had arrived and were carrying Abid to the ambulance.

Hank motioned to Tom. "Let's go."

They climbed in back with Abid, and Hank contacted the hospital. He spoke to the doctor taking care of Amanda, and told him that Abid had beaten the virus without medication. "Maybe his antibodies could help Amanda."

Though Hank heard doubt in the doctor's reply, the man agreed to at least test Abid's blood to see if it was compatible.

They arrived at the hospital's emergency entrance in less than fifteen minutes. The medics wheeled Abid inside, and

Hank and Tom ran to the ICU. The nurse sergeant was standing watch.

"They've moved her," she said, and pointed down the hall. "She's in a room across from the OB department."

That's not good. They ran to the new location and Tom took a seat outside, while Hank put on a mask and gown and walked into the room. He could feel the despair. Even the monitors seemed to echo the ominous beat of a death march.

He walked over to Maddi and mouthed, "How is she?" Maddi shook her head sadly. He sat down beside her. No one said a word.

The doctor came in several minutes later. He saw the new visitor and shook his head. "Andrew, I think maybe we should limit how many–"

Andrew looked up. "No one's leaving."

The doctor nodded as he looked at Andrew with the knowing eyes of someone who had seen far too many cases end badly. He walked to the bed and thumbed through the chart. "Have you noticed any change?"

"No," Andrew said flatly.

The doctor double-checked the IVs, repositioned one of the monitors, and leaned over and put his stethoscope to Amanda's chest. He pulled it away and looked at Andrew, his eyes sad, his voice somber. "We'll need to make a decision soon. Her blood pressure continues to drop, and her pulse has become irregular."

Andrew said nothing.

Hank spoke up. "What about the transfusion?"

Andrew and Maddi both turned and stared at him.

"Can it be done?" he asked.

The doctor shook his head. "We're waiting to see if he's a match, but, even if he is, it's doubtful it would be effective in time to save her."

The doctor left the room. Andrew looked at Hank, his tired eyes confused. "What the hell are you talking about, Hank?"

"I wanted to know if it was an option before I said anything."

"If what was an option?"

"One of the patients with the virus didn't take the ribavirin, but he's fine. Other than severe dehydration, he seems okay. No bleeding from the gums, no headaches, nothing. We're thinking he must have developed antibodies to Lassa fever. We're hoping those antibodies could save Amanda."

Andrew stared at him; Maddi turned away. Hank knew it was a long shot. Not only were there challenges to matching the blood, but there was the factor of time; the virus had likely seized every part of Amanda's body. It would take nothing short of a miracle for it to work. As Hank looked at Andrew, with his sagging shoulders and his dark, hollow eyes, he thought, *So, now we pray for a miracle.*

Chapter 59

WASHINGTON, DC

The Bentley Group was holding an unscheduled meeting, called once again by Morningstar. He had gotten back to town at four in the afternoon and had insisted they meet immediately. He had told the members he had critical information concerning the Phoenix. *"Trust me ... this is a meeting you won't want to miss."*

Morningstar went straight from Andrews to the Morgan building. He was the last to arrive, his limp hardly noticeable as he strutted into the dimly-lit room and took a seat. He pulled his briefcase to his lap and thumbed through papers, not waiting for Chief to start the meeting, instead saying evenly, "I think Phoenix is behind the terror attacks."

The men in the room looked at him in stunned surprise. Chief frowned and said, "What makes you think that?"

Morningstar laid several documents on the table. "These are reports of his locations over the past week. He was spotted in Providence, and was then seen in Chicago, Los Angeles, and finally, Laredo, Texas."

Chief frowned. "Why didn't one of your men bring him in?"

Because he wasn't really at those places, you dumbass. Morningstar had to fight to hide a sneer. "As I think you're aware, sir ... the guy's a highly trained assassin." He paused. "He will have to come in willingly."

Chief shook his head. "So why the hell would he pull off these terror attacks?"

"I told you at our last meeting ... the guy's lost it." Morningstar leaned forward. "We need to take him out."

Chief bristled. "I thought you were the one who said we shouldn't 'eliminate' him, but should use him to our advantage."

"I did say that. I think we can do both."

Chief scowled. "Get to the point, Morningstar."

"At the scene of each terror attack, a vial was left. The authorities are trying to keep their existence a secret, but I have it on good authority they were there. They've been checked for prints. Guess whose prints will most likely be on the vials?"

Chief frowned. "Phoenix? I thought that explosion – or whatever it was that nearly killed your boy – had pretty much destroyed his fingerprints."

"It destroyed the ones he had. I gave him new ones. Untraceable ones. So, the authorities have fingerprints of somebody, they just don't know who. But the prints will show up in the system because of his previous assassinations."

"How does that help us, if they can't identify him?" Chief paused. "No one knows about him but us, right?"

"Right." Morningstar frowned. "Well, not quite. As I said at the last meeting, the CIA has utilized his services a time or two. But they have no idea what he's capable of, or what's he's done ... for us."

"They *used* him? I thought you said you buried him in their bureaucracy."

Morningstar grinned. "I did. But I figured we might need cover someday; someone holding the bag on this guy instead of us. So, I had him do a hit or two for the agency. But don't worry; it has always gone through me." He laughed. "I'm the pimp to the Phoenix whore." He looked around the room; no one was laughing.

Chief said, "How are we going to let the country know it was Phoenix?"

Morningstar smirked. "I'm going to tell them."

"How will you do that?"

"I'll issue another alert, only this time I'll mention that he was last seen in Laredo, Texas, outside the bus terminal. I'm sure some brilliant investigator will put two and two together."

Chief frowned. "How does it help us to have Phoenix blamed for these attacks?"

"Once he's been targeted by the entire nation, we'll be all he's got. He'll need us just to stay alive. He'll be forced to come in."

Chief scowled. "Then what?"

Morningstar leaned back in his chair. "We kill him. But first, we do what we were going to do originally. We have him ... take care of Madison." He put the papers in his briefcase and stood from the table, preparing to leave.

Chief screamed. "Sit down, Morningstar! I have not ended this meeting!"

Morningstar sat, barely hiding a scowl.

Chief looked at him, annoyed. "How will he do that?"

Morningstar sneered. "Don't worry about it, Chief. The less you know, the better."

Chief fumed. "I thought you were going to take care of Madison in Providence?"

For the first time since the meeting started, Morningstar felt uneasy. Providence had been a total failure and he didn't like to think about it. "That won't happen again."

Chief smirked. "Why won't it happen again?"

Morningstar glared at the man with the bloated cheeks and the wild gray hair. "Because this time, I'll oversee the entire operation myself."

Chief stood to leave. "I thought you oversaw it last time." He stared down at Morningstar. "She's pushing ahead with that legislation, you know."

Morningstar frowned. "I know."

"So, make sure it's done right this time." Chief walked to the elevator, the others trailing after him. Morningstar stayed where he was. He needed to think. *God, I hate that man.* But Chief was right. Madison had to die. And once again, Henderson, the Phoenix, would have to be the one to do the killing.

Chapter 60
CAIRO, EGYPT

Soraya did her best to stretch her legs on the crowded bus. She was sitting next to a Yemen man who was thankfully small and kept to himself. He had been with her since Nuweiba, and, now that they were less than an hour from Cairo, it looked as if he might go all the way. She had packed all she owned in a duffel bag that was shoved under her seat. She wouldn't be back; she was leaving the Middle East for good.

She had been on the bus for over six hours, and that was after a twenty-hour bus ride from Al Kharj in Saudi Arabia to the ferry in Aqaba. An hour on the ferry had put her in Nuweiba, which is where she had boarded the bus she was now on. *Over a day of travel ... for a phone call.*

But it wasn't just any phone call. The call to Edi Abu was likely the most important call she would ever make. She had originally intended to use the same phone booth as the day before, but the more she thought about it, the more she decided it wasn't safe. Calls to UN consulates were likely monitored; it would be better to use a different location ... somewhere far away.

She had done her best to sleep, but, other than short naps, she hadn't had much luck. It was catching up to her. She yawned and rubbed her eyes, checking her watch as she stretched her arms. *Eleven o'clock ... I will be in Cairo soon. Then I can sleep.*

She reached the city just after 11:30 p.m., found a cab, and asked the driver to find her lodgings. He dropped her at a guesthouse at the south end of town, *Hotel Oda*. She paid him, walked inside, and went to the front desk. "I need a room."

The clerk stared at her, likely curious about a woman in a burqa traveling alone so late at night. She opened her bag and pulled out 1,000 Saudi Riyals … the equivalent of about 270 U.S. dollars. It was nearly all she had, but what did she care? *Soon I will have much more.*

The clerk's eyes widened and, with only a moment's hesitation, he handed her a key. "Room 213."

She gave him the money and took the key. As she walked to the stairwell, she heard a newscast coming from a TV in a corner of the lobby.

"There is more terror in America. There have been three more attacks with the same deadly virus that hit the East Coast over the past ten days. Many have died, and authorities are scrambling to find those responsible."

She watched, stunned as the scenes played out on the screen. *Three more attacks. Three vials.* She knew about those vials. She knew who was likely behind the attacks. Perhaps she should have told somebody … maybe tried to stop it. She turned away from the TV and smirked. *What do I care what happens to a bunch of greedy Americans?* She climbed the stairs and walked down the hall to her room. She had a phone call to make.

Chapter 61
WASHINGTON, DC

Morningstar left the Morgan Building, and had a cab drop him three blocks from the secret warehouse south of town. He needed to hide his roll of fingerprints somewhere besides his house. *One can never be too careful,* he thought as he locked the door behind him.

He walked a few blocks, waved down a cab, and had it drop him half a mile from the Pentagon. He hurried into the building and down the hall to his office. He hung up his coat, went to his desk, and turned on his computer. He typed in his security code and began a search for Senator Madison. *Time to die, bitch.* He would have one of his sons kill her, and plant evidence to suggest that Henderson was the culprit. Should be easy ... right? *After all, I just tied him to a terrorist attack with little more than a spool of tape.*

Then again, he had tried the same scheme in Providence, and it had not gone well. But he knew why: he had waited too long. Henderson had had too much time to uncover the plot against the senator, and then disrupt it. *This time, I won't put off the hit.* But first, he needed to find her.

He found nothing on the computer; no posts on her senate page, no indication as to where she was or might be headed. He picked up his desk phone and dialed her office. "This is Ed Morningstar at the Pentagon. I need to speak with the senator."

"I'm sorry, Mr. Morningstar, but she's out of the office indefinitely."

"I don't think you understand, son. It's critical that I find her."

A pause. "I'm ... I'm sorry, sir. But that is all I can tell you at this time."

Morningstar had to grit his teeth not to yell at the man. "Thank you."

Prick. He leaned back and crossed his legs. *Where are you, bitch?* Normally, he could use NSA software to track her phone, but he'd been trying since Providence and had had no luck. She must have turned off her phone after the attack. *Smart lady.*

He leaned forward and stared at his computer. He would give it one more try. He logged onto the NSA site, put in her number, and was amazed when he saw a signal pinging from her cellphone. It had started just after two a.m. and was coming from South Carolina. With a bit of effort, he was able to isolate it to Columbia, and finally to St. Vincent's hospital. *Why is she there?* It didn't matter. He had found her.

He rubbed his chin, trying to think which son to send to South Carolina to handle the task. *Reuben?* No, though he was likely in nearby Charleston, he wasn't equipped for such a task. He could kill poachers, but a sitting U.S. Senator? *No way.*

Simeon was on his way back from Providence; he wouldn't get to DC until morning. There was no way he could get to South Carolina in time. Molinaro – *Levi* – was dead, and Judah was far too vital for this type of work. Dan, Gad, and Zebulun were overseas, and Naphtali had gone missing. Issachar had not yet been replaced and Joseph was still on the run. He flinched. *Looks like it's you, Asher.* Asher wasn't his best, but he certainly wasn't his worst. Morningstar grabbed his cellphone and dialed.

"Yes Father?"

"It's time, my son. You've been waiting for a chance to prove yourself, and the time has come. You need to go to South Carolina ... tonight. I'll have a plane waiting at Andrews." He paused. "I'll put the details on the website. I want it taken care of by morning." He added, "Stop by the warehouse. There's a blonde wig and makeup in the locker. Grab them. You'll see a spool of tape on the top shelf. Take it, too. You'll use it at the scene. You know how to do that, right?"

"Yes, Father ... of course I do."

"Good. Go." Morningstar ended the call.

He leaned back, grinning as he put his hands behind his head. By tomorrow morning, Madison would be dead, and Henderson would be wanted, not only for her murder, but for the senseless slaughter of sixty-plus Americans. The poor man would have no choice; he would need to come home. And Morningstar would be waiting. Though he had told the Bentley Group that he wanted the man dead, he could never kill Joseph. In spite of his betrayal, Morningstar would welcome him with open arms. Why? *Because Joseph is a masterpiece.*

He kicked his feet on the desk, thinking back to when he first became aware of Martin Henderson. It was during the healthcare debate four years ago. Morningstar had read a Times article about the dashing man from Boston who walked the corridors of power with uncommon ease. *"America's Future?"* the article had been titled. Morningstar had watched him – for months – and it had taken little time to see that Henderson would be an asset to the Bentley Group. Unlike the others, he wasn't a politician, and he had never been in the U.S. military. He would bring an outsider's perspective, along with much-needed respectability. The best part; he was willing to work with about anybody. But, convincing Chief, without giving away the well-known magnate's identity, had been another story ...

"I think this guy is perfect."

Chief scoffed. "What guy ... and perfect for what?"

"For our group. For those tasks that require the delicate hand of a true pragmatist. A man who makes his decisions not on idealism, but on expediency."

Chief frowned. "What the hell are you talking about, Morningstar?"

"I've been watching him. He waltzes in and out of DC like he owns it; he aligns himself with the most immoral man in

the Senate, yet associates with one of the more respected Senators in the chamber. The guy's a chameleon."

"Who is he?"

"I'd prefer not to say."

"Why?"

"Because if he declines, it's best you never know." Morningstar paused. "I'm still working on a way to persuade him. I'm sure something will come along..."

And something did. By the grace of God, the hotel explosion occurred three nights later. And, because Morningstar's men had been surveilling Henderson, within minutes they were able to pull him from the rubble. They had brought him to a safe house outside DC, and a medic on Morningstar's payroll had stabilized him. He had then been flown to a private hospital in Russia, where he could recover without anyone knowing he had survived. He had been near death; broken, bitter ... he was perfect. But not for the role Morningstar had originally intended; the esteemed Martin Henderson was dead. The man in the Novosibirsk hospital room had become so much more; he was the ideal weapon ... dead to everyone ... and hollow, inside and out.

Morningstar reached in his briefcase for the fake documents 'proving' that Henderson's locations had coincided with the Lassa fever attacks. Could he do it? Could he create a scenario where the world would think that the rogue agent, Phoenix, had terrorized a nation, and had then killed the adored Senator Madison in a fit of rage? *I can ... and I will.* He chuckled as he stared at the documents. *Phoenix will be wanted, the Group will think I've had him killed, and then my son ... my beloved Joseph ... will be my own secret weapon.*

Chapter 62

COLUMBIA, SOUTH CAROLINA

Henderson was watching Amanda's hospital room. He had gotten to Columbia around six a.m. and had found an abandoned warehouse a block from St. Vincent's. He had spent an hour or two getting it ready and had spent the last ten hours sitting on a box in front of a second-story window. Using a high-powered lens, he had kept an eye on those in the room, especially Maddi. More times than he could count, he had seen her tuck her hair behind one ear and yawn as she fought sleep. He had watched her look at her brother, and then at the woman lying in the bed. He had ached with her, knowing what it was to hurt for people you love. How he longed to sit next to her, put his arm around her, and tell her everything would be okay. He imagined her leaning into him, smiling sadly as she hugged him, comforted by his words.

The illusion had been shattered when, about three hours ago, Hank had walked into the room, and Henderson had been forced to see the look Maddi gave him – the shared glance between a man and a woman as they endured unspeakable heartache ... together.

He had then tried to turn his focus to Andrew, but it was even harder to watch him. Red eyes with dark circles underneath, he looked like he hadn't slept in days.

Henderson laid the lens on the floor and backed away from the window. He leaned against the wall, closing his eyes as he tried to imagine what might have happened if there had never been an explosion; if he and Maddi had had the chance to build a life together. Would they have gotten married? A big ceremony with long dresses, tailored tuxes, and people spilling out of the aisles of St. Joseph Cathedral in downtown Boston? Maybe be like his parents, Walter and Dora, who oversaw the City on the Hill like a revered duke and duchess?

He flinched. He knew better. His father hid a secret. And, though Henderson didn't know all the details, he was well aware of his father's betrayal ... his rejection of the sacred vow requiring a man to love only his wife ... forever.

The fading sunlight found its way through the window, highlighting the scars on his forearm. He pulled down his sleeve.

He crept back to the window, sat on the box, and resumed his watch. Nothing had changed. Maddi was still at the bedside, clinging to Andrew with one hand, holding onto Hank with the other. He saw Hank reach over and pull her close and, as she laid her head on his shoulder, Henderson stiffened. This was his life. He would have to get by with nothing more than memories of one perfect weekend and thoughts of what might have been. And he would have to live with the fact that, each time he saved her, it was someone else she ran to. As if he was handing her to Hank, saying, *"Here she is. I love her, I'll keep her safe, but she's yours."*

Chapter 63
WASHINGTON, DC

Cairo, Egypt

Though it was nearly midnight, Morningstar had not left the Pentagon. He had too much work to do. Not only was he about to implicate Henderson in the terror attacks that had claimed over sixty lives across the nation, but he also had to make sure that Henderson was blamed for Madison's upcoming murder.

His cellphone rang; he checked caller ID. "Yes Asher?"

"I've got a problem."

Morningstar frowned. "What sort of problem?"

"One of the men with our target is a government agent; he'll have a gun."

Morningstar sighed. "So, figure out a way to get him out of there."

There was a pause. "Okay. I'll have it done by daybreak."

"Good. And make sure to place blame appropriately."

"I will, Father."

"Call me when it's done."

Morningstar ended the call. *Is Asher up to it?* He sighed. *Of course, he is … he's former CIA; he can handle a simple hit in a hospital room.*

Morningstar leaned back and kicked his feet on the desk. Asher would come through … *he'll be too afraid not to.* Which meant, by morning, Madison would be dead and Henderson would be wanted for her murder. *Along with the murders of Americans in Chicago, LA, and Laredo.* He laughed. *And to think ... Daddy wanted me to waste my talents in the Green Berets.*

The phone rang again; he checked the ID. It was Edi. She had called several times and he had let the calls go to voicemail. Couldn't she see that the country was in an uproar? He wondered if she realized her role in the week's events. *You supplied the poison, Laertes, which has allowed me to kill Hamlet.*

He ignored the call and got back to work. He had just completed the memo that would unequivocally seal the fate of his beloved Phoenix.

"Recently spotted in South Carolina, and known to have stalked the senator in the past, there is little doubt that the rogue agent, Phoenix, is behind the tragic murder of Senator Cynthia Madison from Indiana."

The memo was simply awaiting his release ... *once I know the bitch is dead.*

He had written another memo which implied that Phoenix had worked with West African militants during the tribal wars of the late nineties. He had hidden it in the archives. Once Phoenix was noted to have been in Chicago, LA, and Laredo at about the same time as the attacks, it would surely be uncovered. Then it would be a small leap to tie him to the terror attacks. America would be forced to declare war not only on West Africa, but on Henderson.

His phone rang. Edi again. *Why do you keep calling me, foolish girl?* He answered with a terse, "Hello!"

She was breathless. "Eddie, it is terrible. A woman called; she threatened me. She says she knows what I did."

Morningstar frowned. "What do you mean, she knows what you did? What did you do?"

"That's just it, I don't know!"

Morningstar sighed. "Then don't worry. It's nothing."

"I think it is something. She mentioned Saudi Arabia and the lab."

Morningstar tensed. "The lab?"

"Yes. She said she knows what I did and she will tell the world unless I pay her lots of money."

Morningstar looked around furtively. "Edi, we shouldn't discuss this over the phone. I'll meet you at the hotel in twenty minutes."

"Okay, I will go there now."

Morningstar ended the call and shut down his computer. He threw on his coat, grabbed his briefcase, and left the building. The cold air took his breath away and he popped his collar as he hurried past the cars at the curb, walked two more blocks, and then hailed a cab. He climbed in back, and the driver said, "Where to?"

Morningstar looked out the window, raising his hand to hide his face. "The Starlight Hotel."

~ ~ ~

Though it had taken most of the night, Soraya had finally gotten up the courage to call the number scribbled on the paper. A woman had answered, and the minute Soraya had told her why she was calling, she had known she had the right person; Edi Abu had been scared to death. Soraya had threatened her, telling her she would notify the authorities if Edi didn't pay her one million dollars, American. Edi's voice had trembled. She had said she was in the U.S., and the banks had closed for the day. She would need to wait for them to open the following morning, Friday. Soraya had given her until nine a.m., Eastern Standard Time.

"I will call you then. You get me the money, or I tell the world."

Soraya had then tried to sleep, but had failed miserably as she lay awake making plans for the money. And now, as darkness gave way to daylight, she looked at a clock by the bed and grinned. *Almost seven a.m. ... midnight in the U.S. Only nine more hours.* She stood and opened the curtains, and then walked to a chair in the corner of the room. She sat and grabbed a Mansion Global magazine. As she thumbed through pages of elaborate estates, she grinned. One-million dollars, American. With that kind of money, she would be able to leave the Arab world behind. *I will build myself a paradise ... where men will be subservient to me.*

Chapter 64

WASHINGTON, DC

The driver pulled the cab in front of a small yet tasteful hotel buried in a quiet section of DC "Here you go, sir."

Morningstar said nothing as he paid the fare, stepped out of the car, and walked into a back door of the hotel. It had been chosen specifically for its low profile. Though there was a camera in the lobby, there were none in the hallways or the back exit; he could come and go as he pleased. He didn't go to the front desk; he didn't have to. He knew exactly which room to go to. His collar hid his face as he walked to the elevator and pushed the button for the third floor. He stepped off, walked to suite 311, and knocked three times.

Edi greeted him, but not how she normally did. Instead of a nightgown and a glass of champagne, she wore street clothes and eyes filled with terror. "Eddie, I'm scared."

Morningstar stepped into the room and closed the door behind him. "Tell me everything the caller said."

Edi repeated the conversation. The fact that the woman had called Edi's number meant she knew something. But could she prove it? Couldn't anybody say that so-and-so bought vials of a virus? Without proof it would be a difficult case to make. He tried to reassure her, but she wouldn't let it go. With her voice shaking, she said, "I ... I think we should go to the police."

"The police? What the hell are you talking about, Edi?"

"I don't have a million dollars. I will never have that much money. The woman will be angry and then she will tell the world. They will hang us, Eddie."

Edi had become hysterical. Morningstar couldn't calm her down. Finally, he pulled a bottle of champagne from the mini bar, poured two glasses, and handed her one. She drank it down quickly and he poured some more, all the while rubbing her back and whispering, "It's alright, baby ... it's gonna be okay." All at once, he ripped off her blouse and pulled back her hair. She cried out and he put his mouth over hers. She fought him but then gave in, falling against the couch as he did his best to make her forget, at least for a while, the woman on the phone.

When they had finished, he poured more champagne and rubbed her thigh. "Tell me again when you're supposed to get back to her."

"She gave me until the banks open ... 9:00 a.m. She said she will call and give me instructions on wiring the money at that time. If I don't get the money, she said she will call the authorities and tell them what I've done."

Morningstar shook his head. "Edi, all she has is your phone number. Anyone can rattle off a phone number."

Edi was shaking. "She ... she said there's a record of the call ... at the lab. Normally no one would look, but if she directs their attention, they ... they will be forced to check it out."

Morningstar frowned. Was it true? He had no way of knowing, but, somehow, he had to take care of the situation before it got out of hand. He looked at Edi sitting next to him, her legs draped over his lap, her eyes frightened, yet trusting as they looked to him for guidance. How could he keep her from falling apart and ruining everything he had worked so hard to build? *No one knows about us; no one knows we're lovers.* He rested his hand on her thigh. Even if the phone call was traced to Edi, it didn't mean it would implicate him. *Unless Edi gives me up.*

He watched her as she trembled like a frightened bird, and imagined her under interrogation in a military prison. *She would fall to pieces ... and tell them everything.* He knew what he had to do.

"Edi, do you have any idea where she was calling from?"

"No. Except that she was overseas. The call had to go through an exchange."

"Okay," he checked his watch, "...it's one a.m.; we've got plenty of time. I'll get the necessary equipment and come back in the morning. We'll hook up your phone and wait for her call. You'll need to keep her on the line long enough for us to get a trace, do you understand?"

Edi nodded.

"Good. I want you to stay here for the night, and when the sun comes up, I want you to call in sick. No one knows you're here, right?"

"No one."

"I'll be back in the morning with the equipment. We'll nail this bitch, baby; you don't need to worry about a thing."

Morningstar stood, put on his clothes, and looked down at Edi lying helpless on the couch. Should he take her again? *A last roll in the hay before I take my leave?* He decided against it; he had a lot to do before morning. He buttoned his shirt, threw on his coat and walked to the door. He looked back at her and grinned. "See ya, babe."

He left the room and snuck out of the hotel through a back door that led to an alley. He ran several blocks and hailed a cab. He had the driver drop him two blocks from the Pentagon, and then walked briskly to his office, thinking the entire time about how to handle the situation with Edi. He would need to involve two of his sons...one in America, one overseas. *A perfect job for Simeon and Gad.*

Chapter 65

COLUMBIA, SOUTH CAROLINA

Friday, January 23rd, 2004

"There's a call for you, Dr. Clarkson."

Hank was sitting with Maddi and Andrew in Amanda's hospital room, where he had been almost non-stop since Thursday afternoon. He frowned. "For me?" He pulled out his phone and looked for a missed call. There was nothing. Who would call him on a hospital landline instead of his cellphone? "Who is it?"

"The caller wouldn't say." The nurse paused. "He says it's urgent, however."

Hank squeezed Maddi's hand and left the room. He pulled off his mask and rubbed his chin; what he wouldn't give for a shave and a nap. He followed the nurse to a phone located at the far end of the unit.

"Line two, Doctor."

Hank picked up the phone. "This is Dr. Clarkson."

"Dr. Hank Clarkson ... from Strongsville, Ohio?"

Hank frowned. "Who is this?"

The voice was low and even. "I'm sorry to tell you, sir, that your ex-wife has been critically wounded in an accident."

Hank stared at the phone. *Jenny.* Though he and Jenny had been divorced for over fifteen years, they were still close, and the thought of her clinging to life halfway across the country was unbearable. "What ... what happened?"

There was a pause. "Um ... I don't know the details. I'm just an orderly who was asked to make the call."

Hank's hands were shaking. He had to go to her. He hated to leave Maddi, but he couldn't let Jenny be alone if she was badly wounded. "Which hospital?"

"Strongsville General."

"Okay. I'll get there as soon as I can."

Hank hung up the phone. Should he go back and tell Maddi? No ... he needed to go. *I'll call Maddi from the road.* He ran out of the ICU and was about to leave the hospital when he stopped. *Wait a minute. How did that orderly know where I was?* Hanover was the only person who knew. *And Hanover would've called me himself.*

Hank turned and sprinted back to the unit.

Maddi scooted closer to Amanda's bed, curious about Hank's phone call. *Why not call his cell?* She dismissed it as she looked down at her brother's wife. The color had returned to Amanda's cheeks, and her eyes were bright. *Welcome back, Amanda.*

It felt like a miracle. Amanda had received a transfusion from the man named Abid, and it had helped immensely. Against all odds, she had regained consciousness, and had even said a few words. Her blood pressure was still low, but her heart rate had slowed and her breathing had returned to normal. The baby was doing well and, though it was too soon to say, things were definitely looking up.

The mood in the room had changed, as well. Bits of laughter had replaced the grief that had filled the air; the talk was of happy memories rather than hushed comments about sickness and death. Even Andrew had allowed himself a chuckle as they brought up when he met Amanda at a malpractice forum in Indiana.

"I knew then, Andrew, you were a goner." Maddi said as she hugged him.

He nodded, his tired eyes gleaming for the first time in days.

It was early morning and the sun was just starting to rise, though it was hard to tell from the dark clouds that blanketed the sky. Maddi took Amanda's hand. "And remember the first time Hank and I came down for a surprise visit?"

There was a weak giggle, as Amanda said, "And ... we ... weren't even here."

Andrew squeezed Amanda's hand. "Yeah, we were on our way to D.C ... to surprise you guys."

No one noticed the orderly who walked into the room, more or less invisible as he went about his work.

Maddi said, "Hank and I went back and forth for over an hour on whether we should try to find you or just leave a note and fly home."

The orderly slid next to Maddi. A flash of lightning lit up the room, startling her as she saw him move awkwardly close. His face was hidden behind a surgical mask, his forehead covered by stringy blonde bangs. All she could see were dark eyes over the mask. She frowned. "What are you doing?"

The man refused to look at her. There was another lightning flash; Maddi saw him reach in the pocket of his scrubs. She caught the sheen of a pistol. "Gun!" she yelled, as he aimed it at her forehead. She turned to run.

Andrew grabbed Amanda from the bed, and then used his foot to shove the bed at the orderly. "Go, Maddi!" he said as he ran into the bathroom with Amanda.

The impact of the bed threw the orderly off balance. There was a gunshot, followed by the sound of breaking glass. Maddi braced for a bullet. She felt nothing. She looked over and saw the orderly on the floor, blood spurting from his arm. He was still holding the gun; it was aimed at her chest. She ran for the door.

She heard another gunshot, and was stunned to feel strong arms pull her to the floor. There was a third shot, followed by more breaking glass. She looked over her shoulder. The orderly was still on the floor; this time he wasn't moving. She saw Hank lying next to her, his eyes closed, his jaw clenched. "Hank ... are you ... OK?"

He muttered, "I'm ... fine."

Andrew ran out from the bathroom just as Seacroft burst into the room. Seacroft shouted, "Window, Andrew ... shooter out there!"

Andrew dropped to the floor. "Get Maddi; I'll check the orderly."

Seacroft ran to Maddi. "You okay?"

"Yes, but Hank's been shot!"

Seacroft pulled her to the side of the bed away from the window. "I'll take care of Clarkson, but I need to get you out of here."

She grabbed the rail of the bed. "I'm not leaving until Hank's safe."

Seacroft stared at her. "You have got to be−" He sighed. "Stay put!"

He ran to Hank, grabbed him under his arms, and dragged him next to her behind the bed. He yelled for Andrew. "I need help with Clarkson."

Andrew had checked the orderly's pulse and was running back to the bathroom. "I'll check on Amanda, then I'll come back for him."

Seacroft frowned. "No ... go in with her and stay. I'll send officers."

"What about Hank?"

"He's fine. Go!"

Andrew crawled to the bathroom.

Seacroft turned to Maddi. "You first, then I'll get Clarkson."

"No. Hank saved my life; he goes first."

Seacroft stared at Maddi. He sighed as he grabbed Hank under his arms. He dragged him to the hallway, and then crawled back for Maddi. "Keep low," he said, making sure to stay between her and the window as he led her to the hall. He yelled to a group of officers with shields, "Two civvies in the bathroom! Shooter outside!"

Maddi ran to Hank, who was leaning against the wall. There were spatters of blood on his hospital gown, with a thick circle of red over the right arm. She ripped off the gown, and helped him with his jacket. Blood was pouring from his arm. She tore off a piece of the gown and wrapped it above the gunshot to act as a tourniquet.

She saw an officer run from the room, followed by Andrew, who was carrying Amanda. A second officer was behind him, his shield between him and the window. "This way," the first officer said as he led Andrew down the hall away from them.

Maddi looked at Seacroft. "Where are they taking them?"

"To a secure room."

Hank tried to stand but fell against the wall. Seacroft grabbed him by his good arm. "You're gonna need more than that tourniquet, Dr. Clarkson. Let's go."

Maddi took Hank's other arm, and Seacroft led them to an office at the front of the hospital. The room had only two chairs, a desk, and an artificial plant in the corner. Seacroft helped Hank to one of the chairs. "Stay put while I find a doctor."

Seacroft left and Hank pulled his cellphone from his pocket. He dialed, and Maddi was surprised when he said his ex-wife's name.

"Jenny … you okay?" He sighed. "So, no accident?" He paused. "Thank god." Another pause. "No, I'll call you later." He slid the phone in his pocket.

Maddi put her hand on his arm. "Is everything okay?"

He narrowed his eyes. "I was set up. I'm just glad I came back when I did."

Maddi hugged him. "Me too."

A young man in scrubs wheeled a tray into the room. "Dr. Clarkson, my name's Doctor Avery. I came up from ER to check your arm." He handed Hank a bottle of water. He moved the tourniquet, numbed the arm, and probed for a bullet. After a minute, he nodded. "No bullet. It's a through-and-through."

He stitched up the arm, and was wrapping it with a bandage when Seacroft walked in. "Feeling better, Dr. Clarkson?"

Hank had finished the water. "I'm fine. I need to get back to that room."

Seacroft shook his head. "I can't allow it."

Hank bristled. "I'm the Deputy Director of Homeland Security, and–"

Seacroft raised his hand. "Fine. Let's go."

Maddi said, "I'm coming, too."

Seacroft shook his head. "No. It's not safe"

"Spencer, I'm coming."

He sighed. "Okay, but you're staying in the hall. Got it?"

"Got it."

Accompanied by two hospital guards, they followed Seacroft down the hall to the same room where Hank had just been shot. Seacroft told Maddi to wait outside. He and Hank bent low and crept into the room. Maddi stood at the door. She counted six investigators, each one either kneeling or standing at the far wall, clear of the window. She saw an agent talking to a forensics officer; she leaned in and listened.

"...slowed by a bullet to the shoulder, then killed with a shot to the head." A pause. "I don't think the guy outside was aiming for the senator; it looks like he was after the attacker." He added, "Definitely the work of a professional."

Maddi looked at the window, barely able to see two holes where bullets had pierced the glass. "...*the work of a professional.*"

In spite of Seacroft's orders, she knelt down and was about to crawl into the room, when Seacroft saw her. "Stay out, Senator! I told you it's not safe."

But I know that it is. She stood at the door. "Who was it, Seacroft? Who shot the orderly?"

He stepped out to the hall. "I don't know. I was hoping you could tell me."

Maddi frowned. "I have no idea."

He stared at her and said evenly, "I think maybe you do."

Hank had just come through the door. He looked at Seacroft, then at Maddi. "Everything okay?"

Seacroft said nothing and walked into the room. Over his shoulder, he said, "Senator, if you think of anything that might help us figure out who shot this guy–"

"Spencer, I have no idea who shot him."

Seacroft kept walking.

Hank looked at Maddi and put his hand on her shoulder. "My god, Maddi, you're shaking." He hugged her. "Are you okay?"

Maddi could feel her entire body trembling. It was the third time in a matter of weeks that someone had tried to kill her. "I'm … I'm okay. How about you?"

"I'm fine. What was Seacroft talking about?"

"What do you mean?"

Hank stepped back. "Do you know who killed that man, Maddi?"

Maddi looked away. "No."

Hank forced her to look at him. "Is there something you're not telling me?"

She turned and walked down the hall; he followed her. Though she wasn't sure who had fired the shot, she had a good idea. It felt wrong to keep it from Hank. She couldn't tell him about Henderson, but she had to tell him something. She turned to him and whispered, "I need to talk to you … alone." With her hand on her forehead, she walked up to a guard. "Excuse me, Officer, I'm not feeling well."

"Let me get you a doctor."

"No, that's not it. I think I just need some air."

He frowned.

"If I could just go outside for a few minutes."

He shook his head. "There's no way, Ma'am. It's dangerous … and it's cold."

She looked at him with pleading eyes. "Please … I just need some air."

He sighed. "Wait here. I'll see what I can do." He walked up to an officer. Maddi overheard him say, "Is it still raining?"

"No, it stopped."

"See if the Secret Service guy is okay with us walking the Senator out to the courtyard for some air." He paused. "Let him know she isn't feeling well."

They waited. Soon the guard walked back to where they were standing and nodded. "He's setting up a perimeter. It should only take a minute."

Seconds later, Seacroft walked up and handed each of them a blanket. "You'll need these."

Maddi smiled. "Thanks Spencer."

Two officers led the way, while Seacroft and the security guard fell in beside Maddi and Hank. Wrapping the blankets over their shoulders, they walked down a hall and out the door to a small courtyard surrounded by trees.

The rain had stopped, the occasional roll of thunder the only evidence that a storm had come through. It wasn't as cold as the day before, and the sunlight through the clouds made it feel like spring. Someone – likely Seacroft – had been thought-ful enough to place a tarp on a wooden bench. Maddi and Hank sat on the tarp.

She looked at Hank and sighed. *Just say it, Maddi.* "Some-one tried to ... kill me ... in Providence."

Hank frowned. "What?"

"Someone tried to–"

"I heard you." He stared at her. "That explains it."

"Explains what?"

"All the secrecy." His eyes flashed. "So, when did you plan on telling me?"

She looked at him, defiant. "When Amanda was no longer dying."

He stared at her, his eyes a mixture of anger and relief as he reached for her hand. "I'm ... I'm sorry, Maddi. Tell me what happened."

Maddi told him about Providence, leaving out any refer-ence to Henderson. "And then I received a text telling me to leave."

"From who?"

"Does it matter?"

"Of course, it matters!"

Maddi looked away. She said softly, "I don't know who."

She could feel Hank staring at her. Could he tell it was a lie? After a long pause, he said, "So why did you believe it?"

She shook her head "I don't know, I just did ... and thank god." She turned to face him. "Someone was looking out for me, I guess."

Hank turned away. When he finally looked at her, she could see the hurt in his eyes. "So why would someone want to kill you, Maddi? That's three times now."

"I don't know." She grinned. "I do have a way of pissing people off."

He stared at her, finally giving in to a laugh. "Yes, you do."

She laid her head on his shoulder. There were sirens every-where as various agencies arrived at the scene. Through the trees, Maddi could see a stretcher with a black body-bag being carried to a van. *Good riddance,* she thought, as she heard the doors close. She huddled closer to Hank, thinking about his questions: Who was trying to kill her, and who was keeping her safe? She had no idea how to answer the first question, but she was certain of the answer to the second.

~ ~ ~

It had been easy. Without hesitation, Henderson had shot the would-be assassin in the arm, hoping to keep him alive for interrogation. Henderson needed to somehow compel the in-vestigators to start looking at Morningstar; he knew the guy would give him up if pushed. But, when the man aimed at Maddi's chest, Henderson had had no choice; he had killed the man with a single shot to the head.

He was now hiding in the trees, well beyond the perimeter set up by her Secret Service agent, watching with a high-pow-ered lens as Hank wiped tears from Maddi's eyes. He flinched as he saw her lay her head on his shoulder. His heart ached as he realized he couldn't rush in and claim his rightful place by her side, having saved her once again from certain death. But he couldn't ... he was too far away.

He lowered the binoculars and shoved them in his pack. He took a final look, and then backed out of the trees, knowing, in every sense of the word ... he would always be too far away.

Chapter 66

WASHINGTON, DC

Cairo, Egypt

At eight-thirty a.m., Morningstar and Simeon walked up to room 311 of the Starlight Hotel. Morningstar knocked three times. There was no answer. He knocked again. "Shit!" He didn't have his key. He looked at Simeon and nodded. Simeon had been a munitions expert in the first Iraq war; he pulled out a pack of C4 and made quick work of the lock. They walked in and found Edi passed out on the couch. The bottle of champagne was gone, and there was another one opened, only a third of the way full. Morningstar kicked the foot of the couch. "Get up, Edi."

She didn't move.

He nudged her. "Get up." Still nothing. He pulled her from the couch and dragged her to the shower. He turned on cold water, slid off her clothes, and sat her under the icy spray. She cried when it hit her face, but Morningstar held her there. "You need to be at your best, *sweetie.*" After several minutes, he turned off the water, lifted her out, and dried her off. He wrapped her in a robe as he checked the time. *8:50.* The call was expected soon. They needed to get ready.

He walked her out to the living room and sat her on the sofa. He made coffee and forced her to drink it. Simeon was setting up the equipment to trace the call. By 9:00 everything was ready, and Edi was, for the most part, sober. They waited.

"Remember, Edi, you have something she wants, so don't go easy. Make her guarantee your number will disappear. Make her talk. I've prepared a few things for you to say." He handed her a page of typed notes as he sat beside her.

Edi took the paper and nodded. They waited, saying nothing as the morning sunlight streamed through the draped window. Edi's phone rang and she jumped.

"Calm down!" said Morningstar. They waited for Simeon to give them the signal. He nodded and Edi answered her phone. It was on speaker so Morningstar could hear both sides of the conversation.

"Hel ... hello?" Edi's voice was shaky.

"Have you got the money?" The voice was female, Middle Eastern.

"Y ... yeah, but I need assurance," Edi looked down at the paper, "...assurance you won't be calling in a month for more."

There was a brief silence. "You have my word."

Morningstar shook his head. Edi said, "That's not good enough. Your ... your word means nothing to me. You're a blackmailer and a thief."

"Yes, but you're a cold-blooded killer."

Edi started to tremble. Morningstar knew she was about to cry. He leaned over, patted her leg, and nodded reassuringly. She continued, still reading from Morningstar's script. "You have no way of proving that I'm the one who made that call."

"You're right, but if I go to the authorities and give them this number, they will trace it to you. And something tells me, if they investigate, they will not like what they find."

Morningstar looked at Simeon to see if he had had enough time. He shook his head. Morningstar motioned for Edi to continue. She looked down at the paper.

"I ... I need a guarantee that this will be the end of it. I have the million dollars, but you need to convince me I will never hear from you again."

There was a pause. "I don't know how I can convince you."

Just then Simeon motioned to Morningstar. He had the location of the caller. He scribbled it on a piece of paper and held it up. *Cairo, Egypt. Hotel Oda.*

Morningstar nodded. He motioned for Edi to keep going, patting her gently on her leg as he stood and walked into the next room. He closed the door and pulled out his phone. He dialed and waited as he heard it connect through an overseas exchange.

"Yes Father?"

"Gad, I have a job for you. Where are you?"

"The Suez Canal."

"Perfect." Morningstar told him the location he had gotten from Simeon, and ended the call with, "Take her out, son."

He walked out to the living room just in time to hear Edi say, "Okay, I will get you your million, but I will need at least an hour to arrange the transfer. Give me your bank's information."

The woman gave her routing and account numbers and ended the call.

Morningstar looked at her and grinned. "It's all taken care of, baby. There's nothing more to worry about."

Edi smiled, relieved. She stood and, ignoring Simeon's presence, allowed the robe to fall open. She caressed her body as she strutted toward Morningstar. He was so tempted to take her ... *one last time.* But he couldn't; he had too much to do. He nodded at Simeon, who slid next to her and – in a single motion – took a garrote from his pocket, placed the thin wire around her neck, and pulled. She struggled, her arms flailing as the robe fell away and her dark eyes pleaded for mercy. Morningstar shook his head and sighed; he would miss his exotic sex partner. With a final gasp, she fell to the floor ... naked, the robe lying next to her, blood trickling from her nose.

"Clean it up, Simeon. She was never here, I was never here. Got it?"

Simeon nodded. Morningstar left the room, walked downstairs and out the back door. He stayed in the shadows as he skulked through alleys for nearly half a mile and then hailed a cab. Again, he had the driver drop him several blocks from the Pentagon. As he walked the final hundred yards to his office, he grinned at how well he had handled the mess made by his weak whore, Edi Abu. He would miss her; she was good in bed. He sighed. *Ah yes ... but so many of them are.*

~ ~ ~

Soraya hung up the receiver. *I am free at last!* The call had gone better than she thought it would. Within hours she would be a millionaire. It was nearly four p.m. in Cairo, and Edi Abu had said it would take at least an hour to make the transfer. The Cairo banks would be closed. But, first thing in the morning, she would go to the bank, get her money, and then leave Egypt and the Middle East for good.

She laughed aloud as she reached over and turned on a lamp. With so much cash, she would never have to answer to a man again. She stripped off her burqa and lay on the bed naked, basking in her newfound independence. Though nothing had changed, everything had changed.

She put a hand to her large belly and rubbed it as she made plans. She thought of the town where she would live and the house she would buy. *No one will ever tell me ever again how to dress or what to say.* Maybe she would even lose weight so she could wear the sexy clothes she saw in the magazines. The hours passed as she lay on the bed and imagined the life she would have, free of men, and free of the constraints of Sharia Law. *I will be in charge ... of my body and myself.*

There was a knock at the door. Soraya frowned as she stood and wrapped the burqa loosely around her. *No one knows I am here.* She opened the door and leaned her head into the hallway. She never saw the shot coming. The burqa fell away as she dropped to the floor, her naked body sprawled in the doorway with a bullet between her eyes. There was no commotion, no noise. The assassin left as quietly as he had come. As nightfall descended on Cairo, in a second-floor room of the Hotel Oda, Soraya Gaddah was dead.

Chapter 67
WASHINGTON, DC

The first call came two hours after Morningstar had returned to the Pentagon.

"It's Gad, sir. It's done."

"Good work, my son." He hung up. The extortionist in Cairo, whoever she was, was dead. Gad, his overseas son, had done his job well. Now Morningstar just needed to get the call from his other son, Asher, whom he had sent to kill Madison. He checked his watch. *Almost noon ... I should've heard from him by now.*

He was staring at his laptop when an alert appeared on the screen.

There was an attempt on Senator Cynthia Madison's life earlier today. The would-be assassin was gunned down by an unknown assailant. The senator is unharmed. Another party was injured in the assault but is recovering with a flesh wound to his arm.

"Shit!" Morningstar kicked the desk, forgetting that he was across the hall from the nosy civilian clerk, Cecile. She glared at him over a long, narrow nose. He forced a grin as he shook his finger, pretending he had slammed it in his desk drawer. She rolled her eyes and went back to her work.

"*...gunned down by an unknown assailant.*" He stared at the news release. *Damn you, Henderson!* The man had disrupted his plans ... again. He would be forced to send only one of his memos ... the one that tied Henderson to the West African militants. The authorities would still hunt him down for the terror attacks, but not for Madison's murder. *And now, because of your insolence, I won't be there to save you.*

What did he care if Henderson was captured? *Let the CIA have him!* It no longer mattered that he was the favored son ... that Morningstar valued him like no other; it was done ... *he* was done. He slammed his fist on the desk. Henderson had defied him; he had betrayed the very man who had created him ... the man who had saved him from the brink of death. *I made you, you son-of-a-bitch!*

The more he thought about it, the madder he became. He stood and paced the floor, ignoring the stares of the haughty Cecile. He would let the authorities find Henderson, and then laugh as they put him through the rigors of a military trial. Would it be enough? *No ... I need to put an end to that bastard myself!*

He returned to his desk, seething as he stared at his laptop screen. *"...would-be assassin ... gunned down ... by an unknown assailant."* He slammed it shut, and then stood and put on his coat. He had to find Henderson ... and then he had to kill him.

Chapter 68

WASHINGTON, DC

Sunday, January 25th, 2004

Maddi sighed as she stared at the paperwork on her desk. She had been in her office since 6:00 a.m. and was tired of looking at it. The only good thing; it had distracted her from the attacks on her life ... from her fear that whoever had tried to kill her – three times now – would likely try again.

"Spencer, could you come in here, please?"

Seacroft had swapped shifts and was now covering Maddi during the day. Though he had insisted it was a formality, Maddi knew he had personally made the request. She was glad. Seacroft had become more than an agent; he was a comfort in her very uncomfortable life. He stepped into the room. "Yes Ma'am?"

"I thought we could go out for lunch."

"That sounds good, Ma'am."

Maddi smiled. "We'll leave in about ten minutes."

He nodded and returned to his post outside the door. She sighed as she spun her chair to the window. The sun was once again hidden by clouds, casting everything in shades of gray. It seemed appropriate. It had been two days since the attack on her life ... two days since she had once again been targeted by an unknown assailant. She had returned to DC Friday evening, and, after a reasonable night's sleep – helped along by a sedative – she had awakened early and had come straight to her office. She had spent nearly every waking minute there, not going home until bedtime, coming back soon after she woke up.

The identity of the man who had tried to kill her remained a mystery. According to one of the FBI agents, they had found nothing to identify him ... no ID, no dental records. Even his fingerprints were of no help; they had been shaved off and scarred over. It was if he had never existed, and it unnerved her. Though she wanted to think that the threat to her life had ended with his death, she knew it hadn't. After all, Molinaro had been killed in Providence and she had been targeted only days later.

She had been informed that a roll of tape with the letter "P" on the side had been found in the man's pocket. Investigators had no idea what it meant. The tape had been taken to Quantico. The FBI promised to let Maddi know if anything came of it.

Reporters had bombarded her Senate office, but – between Phil and Seacroft – they had been kept away for the most part. She was glad; the last thing she wanted was to talk to the press about threats on her life. *To put into print how scared I am.*

She leaned forward and grabbed the stack of documents. She would try to get through another page or two before she left for lunch. A TV in the corner of the room was tuned to a 24-hour cable news network, the anchor jumping back and forth between the terrorist attacks and the attempted murder of a U.S. Senator. Maddi was half-listening, wading through paperwork, when all at once she stopped.

"...We have just received word that vials recovered at the scenes of the last three attacks originated from the Middle East. There are rumors that a West African group has claimed responsibility, and that they may have had help from someone within the U.S. military."

Maddi turned up the volume.

"An anonymous source within the Pentagon has informed us that the suspect is a rogue agent. He says the man has been on the run for about a month, and that he's a highly skilled assassin. The source offered the following description: Six-foot-

four, 210 pounds, blonde hair, blue eyes, with scars on his face and hands."

Maddi began to shake. The documents fell to the floor. *No.* It was impossible. Whatever had happened to Henderson, there was no way he had become a rogue agent capable of poisoning innocent Americans. *Six-foot-four, blonde hair, blue eyes ... with scars.* The newscaster moved on to the next story, but Maddi was no longer listening as she sat staring at the screen.

She grabbed the controller and shut off the TV. She laid her head on the desk. Four years without a word, and Henderson had finally reached out to her. *Why now?* She frowned as she recalled the announcer's words, *"...the man has been on the run for about a month."* She balled her hands into fists. *No ... it can't be true!*

She wanted to cry but fought the urge; a few quick sobs were all she would allow. She rubbed her eyes as she stood and walked to the window. She stared out at the grey sky and the faded yellow bushes and wished she could leave ... disappear to a place where flowers never faded, and bombs didn't kill people ... or change them into monsters. What if it was true? What if Henderson had somehow survived the hotel blast, only to become a mass murderer? *It can't be.*

Maddi wanted to throw open the window and feel the cold against her cheeks, but she couldn't; it was nailed shut.

She flinched; she thought she saw something in one of the windows on the other side

of the knoll. Likely just a shadow as noon approached. But what if it wasn't? What if it was Henderson ... watching her; keeping her safe.

She whispered, "Are you out there?" She imagined him looking after her, protecting her, ready to save her ... again. He had saved her twice now ... maybe even three times. How could that same man kill innocent people in Chicago, LA, and Texas? She shook her head. There was little she was sure of anymore, but one thing was certain: Henderson couldn't have done it ... he was too good of a man.

She continued to stare at the window across the courtyard. She frowned. Had she seen a blind open and close? *Is it him ... watching me?* In spite of her efforts to stop them, tears came from nowhere, burning her eyes, staining her cheeks. She brushed them away as she tightened her jaw and gazed across the weather-beaten knoll. *No matter what it takes, Henderson ... how long or what the cost to my career, my future, or even my life ... I will find a way to see you again.*

Chapter 69

WASHINGTON, DC

Morningstar had barely slept. He knew Madison had returned to DC, which meant that Henderson had come back, as well. That was how it worked; wherever Madison was, Henderson wasn't far away. Morningstar had spent the last two days looking for him, first online, and then on the streets of DC He had found no trace.

He ran a hand through his hair as he climbed the steps to the Morgan Building. It was noon, and the Bentley Group was holding another emergency meeting. Once again, Morningstar would be the last to arrive.

He took the elevator to the top floor, far less confident as he limped into the room. He sat down without a word. In spite of forcing himself to shave and change his suit, his grey eyes were bloodshot and his cheeks were drawn.

Chief looked at him and frowned. "You look like shit, Morningstar."

Morningstar glared at him.

Chief chuckled. "Well. what happened?"

Morningstar was finding it more and more difficult to hide his contempt for the man. "What do you mean?"

"I'm assuming the *failed* attempt on Madison's life was your doing?"

"We don't kill people, remember?"

Chief grinned. "I see. You promised us you were going to 'take care of her.'"

Morningstar said nothing as he stared at the table.

Chief sighed. "So, now what? Do you know where Phoenix is?"

Morningstar looked at Chief, his eyes narrowed as he hissed, "I do."

"So … where is he?"

"Wherever Madison is."

"And where's Madison?"

"Here … in DC."

"I'm assuming you have a plan?"

Morningstar forced a grin. "Of course, I do." He stared at the faces around the table, hating every one of them. "Phoenix has been 'outed' as a rogue agent, and his fingerprints will soon be linked to the Lassa fever terror attacks. Madison will be … dealt with. They'll both go down … I'll do it myself this time."

Chief snorted. "Didn't you say that the last time?"

Morningstar bristled. "Yes, but this time I'll leave nothing to chance."

"Whatever you say, Morningstar." He paused. "I have to congratulate you on the increased arms sales. Silverton is cranking out the weapons, and we're cranking in the bucks. Good job. Now, just get Madison out of the way before she figures out what's going on."

Morningstar sneered. "Trust me, nothing will please me more."

Chapter 70

WASHINGTON, DC

Henderson was exhausted, but there had been little time to sleep. Though Maddi was alive, she was still a target, and he wasn't willing to let her out of his sight. He had found a place where he could watch her through the window of her Senate office; a private room in a building a half-mile from the Capitol which he had managed to get to without being spotted. The room, likely a filing area before the days of computers, was no longer used. He had been left alone ... at least so far.

Dusty blinds were pulled nearly to the sill, and he had inserted an eyepiece underneath, which had allowed him to see Maddi as she worked. He had spent the last two days either there or in the shed near her house, watching her. He felt certain Morningstar was looking for him, so, he kept on his cap and scarf, with his collar pulled to his chin, especially when coming and going. Fortunately, Maddi arrived at her office before dawn and returned home well after nightfall. He at least had the advantage of darkness.

He had thought many times about contacting her. Sending her another email or even writing a letter. But he couldn't; he couldn't put her in any more danger than she already was. And he couldn't risk exposing himself. If he was captured, there would be no one to keep her safe from Morningstar.

So, he watched her ... nearly every second of every day. Starting from the moment she had gotten back to DC Friday night, he had kept an eye on her. And today, just like yesterday, she sat glued to her desk, staring at paperwork, periodically combing her hands through her hair as she shoved aside papers in frustration. Every now and then she would stand, stretch, and walk to the window. Those were the moments he liked best. It was as if she was looking at him. She would lean against the glass and stare out at the garden, her eyes glancing at the old building across the knoll. She would stop at the window where he was hiding. His heart would race, his breaths quicken; he'd pretend they were communicating. Maybe they were ... maybe on some separate plane in the universe, they were making love in the ether.

He laughed. *You're losing it, Henderson.* He stared through the lens, suddenly angry. Was this it? Was this his life? Watching Maddi as she went about her day? So far it had been painless; she had done nothing more than go to work, come home, eat a quiet meal, and then embrace the quilt that had once been his. After that, she would go to her bedroom and stare out the window before her agent would make her close the drapes and disappear. In his mind, he would go to bed with her. He would lie next to her and hold her as she slowly fell asleep. He would sleep, but only for a few hours, afraid she might leave the house without him. And, for now anyway, he was content with it; he was content with loving her through the lens. But what would he do if she found someone else? Or if she and Hank picked up where they had left off and he was forced to watch them make love in front of the fire? What then?

He bristled as he threw the lens to the floor. He couldn't do it. He had to figure out a way to keep her safe ... without having to watch her every move.

He pulled a flash drive from his backpack and held it in his hand. *Maybe this is the answer.* It contained footage from an obscure army website that monitored isolated feeds from around the country. The software could be calibrated to detect the unique features of any one person. Months ago, Henderson had programmed it to keep an eye on Morningstar. Whenever his face was detected on any camera around the country, the computer would record the footage. And yesterday, Henderson had hit pay dirt. The video feed was from four days ago, and would hopefully serve as a guarantee that Maddi would never be harmed again ... at least not by Morningstar.

He shoved the flash drive in his pocket and picked up the lens. Maddi was still at her desk and he watched as she laid her head on her arms. She was shaking. He tightened the lens. Was she crying? She stood and walked to the window. He could see her perfectly; yes, she was crying. His own eyes burned as he watched her look at the building where he was hiding ... *as though she's staring right at me.*

Suddenly he stood and lifted the blinds. He threw open the window, the cold air cutting through him as he pulled off his cap and felt the wind blow back his hair. He could see her. Without the lens it was difficult, but he could see her shadow at the window. He was about to jump out and run to her, when he saw his image reflected in a nearby window. He slammed down the window, shut the blinds, and pulled on his hat. *How could I have risked letting her see me?* He tossed the lens in his backpack, left the room, and ran out a back door into a park. He followed a path to the Metrorail, like he had done for the past two days, finally aware that he needed to disappear ... forever. He could never let Maddi see him; not the way he looked now.

He hopped on the tram and found a seat in back. He put his face to the glass, watching as the buildings and trees raced past. Though his eyes were dry, he was crying; endless tears that came from the deepest part of him. He could watch Maddi forever, but he could never have her ... not as long as he wore the face of a monster.

He reached in his backpack and pulled out a wrinkled piece of paper. He smoothed it on his lap. It was a release he had printed from an online Russian newspaper, only days ago.

"Dr. Boris Vitayev announces revolutionary surgery."

He read it through for the hundredth time and then folded it and returned it to his pack. He had pondered it for days, half-frightened to consider another surgery doomed to fail. But he knew Dr. Vitayev, and he knew Russia ... *like the back of my scar-ridden hand.* He had spent quite a bit of time there ... six months, to be exact, and had undergone eight surgeries already. *And every one of them was a failure.* He frowned as he rubbed a hand over his cheek. He couldn't do it; not again.

Then he thought of Maddi ... and how she would react if she ever saw his face.

He closed his eyes. He would make the trip; he had to. He didn't know what the 'revolutionary surgery' consisted of ... only that it promised to change him. He had to try. No matter the outcome, he could no longer live with the face he now wore.

He looked out the window as he sunk lower in his seat, doing his best to hide from anyone and everyone. Maybe it could work. Maybe, like the phoenix for which he was named, he could rise from the ashes ... *one more time.*

As the train disappeared into a tunnel, Henderson pulled off his cap, more at home in the darkness than the light. He ran a hand through his hair and touched his jaw, feeling its jagged edges as if for the first time. Again, he thought of Maddi – beautiful Maddi – and, as a single tear fell over bitter scars, he whispered, "For you, Maddi ... I'll try one last time ... for you."

Epilogue

Tuesday, January 27th, 2004

Morningstar brushed back his hair as he stared at his computer. The sunlight was fading; he could barely see the keyboard. He reached to turn on a lamp, shoving aside stacks of files on his desk. He was in his office at the Pentagon, where he had been for the past two days; ever since he had made his promise to the men of the Bentley Group. *"They'll both go down ... I'll do it myself this time."*

He was exhausted. He had tried to nap on a sofa in the office, but his need to find Henderson had made sleep nearly impossible. In the last few minutes, however, he had come up with a plan. *What if I bomb the Capital?* Madison would be killed, Morningstar would make sure that Henderson was blamed, and he and his sons would be in the clear. *Meanwhile, Washington, DC would be paralyzed.*

He laughed. "A perfect job for Pocks."

He leaned back and put his hands behind his head. It was late in the day; there were few in the darkened hallway outside his office. The annoying Cecile was there, however, and he scowled at her across the hall. She had been assigned to watch for the first sign of a renewed bioterrorist attack. *You're wasting your time, honey ... I decide when and where this nation is attacked.* He smirked and she returned the gesture with a condescending glare. It was enough to make him want to kill her. He hissed and then looked back at his screen. His cell phone rang. "Yes?"

"I just learned that Abid is being transported from St. Vincent's to a DC prison late tonight."

Morningstar frowned. "We can't have that, Simeon. He won't hold up under interrogation."

"Don't worry, Father. I know what to do."

"Take care of it, son." Morningstar ended the call. Abid – Reuben – would soon be an afterthought. Though the African had done his job well, he had become a liability. Simeon would kill him and then erase his existence.

But that left Morningstar with a deficiency of sons. Asher and Levi were dead, Reuben soon would be, and Naphtali had gone missing. Joseph had gone into hiding, and, with Benjamin not yet chosen, that left him with only half of the twelve. He would need to address it. *But not until I've taken care of Henderson and the bitch.*

There was a soft ring from the computer. He leaned forward, staring at a link on a website that he and Henderson had used in the past. His hands began to shake and he hesitated, afraid to open it. He clicked the link. It took him to a secure site with another link embedded in a paragraph written in barely-legible font. He clicked it and a new site appeared. The screen was bare except for seven blanks. Below the blanks were written the words

Who am I?

Morningstar stared at the writing as the music from "Jeopardy" began to play. With a shaking hand, he typed the letter P. He paused, then typed the letters H, O, E, N, I, and X. Suddenly the screen was filled with footage. It was a bathroom. A man was changing his clothes. It was Morningstar at the airport in Los Angeles, putting on the clothes he would wear to Laredo.

"You son of a bitch!" he yelled as he pounded his fist on the table. He stared at the monitor, oblivious to the stunned Cecile who was gawking at him from across the hall. He pulled the screen closer, seeing the hairpiece and mustache. He watched as the camera caught his face perfectly in its lens. The clip ended and the music stopped. Words scrolled across the screen:

SHE DIES ... YOU'RE DONE

===

About the Author

Dr. Jill Vosler is a family physician whose medical studies took her abroad to the University of Edinburgh in Scotland and on to extensive travel throughout the UK and Europe. Her love for these places has flavored her novels, along with the many years spent as a deputy coroner under the guidance of her father, who was the county coroner well into his eighties. She has a keen interest in politics and a passion for music, but most enjoys traveling the world with her husband, John, and their son and daughter.

NewAtlantianLibrary.com or AbsolutelyAmazingEbooks.com or AA-eBooks.com

Thank you for reading. Please review this book. Reviews help others find Absolutely Amazing eBooks and inspire us to keep providing these marvelous tales.

If you would like to be put on our email list to receive updates on new releases, contests, and promotions, please go to AbsolutelyAmazingEbooks.com and sign up.

For sales, editorial information, subsidiary rights information
or a catalog, please write or phone or e-mail

AbsolutelyAmazingEbooks
Manhanset House
Shelter Island Hts., New York 11965, US
Tel: 212-427-7139
www.AbsolutelyAmazingEbooks.com
bricktower@aol.com
www.IngramContent.com

For sales in the UK and Europe please contact our distributor,
Gazelle Book Services
White Cross Mills
Lancaster, LA1 4XS, UK
Tel: (01524) 68765 Fax: (01524) 63232
email: jacky@gazellebooks.co.uk